the
Little Village
Bakery

ALSO BY TILLY TENNANT

the Little Village Bakery

TILLY TENNANT

bookouture

Published by Bookouture

An imprint of StoryFire Ltd.
23 Sussex Road, Ickenham, UB10 8PN
United Kingdom

www.bookouture.com

5 7 9 10 8 6 4

ISBN: 978-0-75154-857-0
eBook ISBN: 978-1-78781-015-1

For my mum, who taught me that anything is possible.

Chapter One

On the hottest day of the year so far, the sprinklers on the green of the tiny village of Honeybourne made miniature rainbows in the shimmering air. Jasmine Green's triplets, Rebecca, Rachel and Reuben, squealed as they raced backwards and forwards through the water, while Jasmine folded the last of the bunting from her stall of homemade crafts and furnishings.

'It's been a fabulous day for it,' she commented cheerily to the vicar as he wandered over.

'Certainly has,' he agreed, looking round at the other stalls lined up around the perimeter of the green, their owners also packing away. 'I love the fête, the one day of the summer when the whole village comes together to have fun.'

'The children have certainly enjoyed it this year.' She looked fondly over at her offspring, now soaked through but grinning all over their faces.

'Some of the adults have had a good time too,' he replied, angling his head to where Jasmine's husband, Rich, was sitting on a deckchair looking distinctly sunburnt despite his dark hair and complexion, grinning drunkenly and staring into space.

She blew a ringlet the colour of candyfloss from her damp forehead and giggled. 'I told him to be careful with Frank Stephenson's scrumpy.'

'Who's got scrumpy?' Rich asked, now squinting up at them.

'No more for you today,' Jasmine scolded, but only half-heartedly. He pouted like a little boy and she smiled indulgently. 'If you can manage to walk in a straight line, how about you gather the kids up and help me get this stock back to the van?' She folded her arms. 'I suppose I'm driving home too as you've lost the ability to coordinate your limbs properly?'

He pushed himself up from the chair and made a move to take her into his arms. 'Who can't coordinate his limbs? You wait till later, my gorgeous little hippy chick,' he said, wrapping her in his strong embrace. 'I'll show you how to coordinate limbs.'

'*Richard Green*, the vicar is standing right there!' Jasmine giggled.

'Don't mind me,' the vicar said amiably, 'I'll just peruse the lovely items you have left on your stall here. Honestly, this metalwork is quite spectacular.' He picked up a pendant and turned it over in his fingers. 'You have lots of special things here, Mrs Green, but in the main a remarkable talent for making unusual jewellery.'

'Take something home for Mrs Vicar,' Rich said with a grin. 'Pretty trinkets always work on the missus.'

'Not when the missus has made them herself, they don't,' Jasmine said with a mock scowl.

'Fair point.' Rich hiccupped. He was a good foot taller than Jasmine and she had to stretch up to kiss him.

'Go and get your children, there's a good boy,' she laughed.

He let go of her and staggered off. But when Jasmine looked up again, he was chasing the children through the sprinklers, making monster noises as he went, sending them scattering and squealing with delight. Some of the other villagers had joined in with their children. Jasmine stopped her packing for a moment and watched them all play their elaborate game.

'You know, Vicar,' she said in a voice full of lazy contentment, 'I really don't think there is a happier place to live on Earth than here.'

In her kitchen, a hundred miles to the north of where Jasmine Green was ushering her reluctant family into a van, Millicent Hopkin – Millie to the handful of people who dared get close enough – was sobbing. It felt like she did little else these days, though she was always careful to save it for when she was alone. Some would take great satisfaction in her pain. She probably deserved it, but that still didn't give anyone the right to victimise her.

The car had been the last straw. She'd spent the last three hours trying to scrub away the vile words. Whoever wrote the old rhyme about sticks and stones was wrong. The smashed windows, the faeces shoved through her letterbox, the mysterious taxis and pizza deliveries in the early hours that she had ended up having to pay for when they insisted she'd ordered them – she'd borne it all with a quiet fortitude. But the words... Words had magic, they had power – the power to heal, to hurt, to make things happen, and the ones she'd failed to remove from her car, even though she'd rubbed and rubbed until her hands were raw, had hurt her as much as any stick or stone could. She'd had enough.

Drying her tears, she tried to concentrate on the task in front of her. The only constant in her life now was her creativity, and baking was the one creative thing she could still do that brought pleasure to others. Although these days she didn't know who she could share this one with when the people she had once called friends had all turned against her. She had tried to be a good person, to set things right, but in the end it had meant nothing. Turning her attention to the mixing bowl in front of her, she added ingredients to the mix – cinnamon and nutmeg, vanilla, a pound of dried fruit, a sprinkle of heartsease, her unintentional tears – and thought about how she needed a new start, somewhere far away where people didn't know her. Somewhere people wouldn't judge her or hurt her or blame her for everything that had gone before.

She focused on the thought, on the photo of a tumbledown old building on a property website that had captured her imagination, four walls in an adorably named village that might just be the new start she'd been searching for. She closed her eyes, pictured the bakery – *her* bakery – and tried to imagine the sweet smells, the bright colours of the cakes, the chatter of customers, opening the shutters on every new day and welcoming it in; she tried to remember what happiness felt like, how it was to want to live. She longed for it with every fibre of her being. In less than a week, if the universe was finally smiling on her, maybe she would find out.

When the mix was done, she poured it into a tin and whispered a last wish before she put it into the oven. She needed a new start. Perhaps the cake would make it so.

'Who's that?' Rich nudged Jasmine as he watched a woman stagger into the old bakery under the weight of a huge box she had just pulled from the back of a van bearing the name 'Countrywide Vehicle Hire'. She was slim and looked to be in her late twenties to early thirties, with sleek black hair cut into a cute bob and a feline beauty that made you want to stare.

At least, it was making Rich stare.

'Perhaps,' Jasmine replied, giving her husband a wry smile, 'you might want to roll your tongue in and ask her if she needs any help…'

'I could,' he said, 'but I don't want to make you jealous.'

'I think I'll survive,' she replied, raising her eyes heavenward as he walked backwards across the deserted road, grinning at her all the while.

'Hello!' Rich whipped himself back round and called to the woman as she emerged from the shop door, wiping a hand across her brow. 'Are you moving in?'

The woman looked at him. There was something wary in her eyes and he faltered for a moment. 'I'm Rich,' he said, collecting himself and sticking out a friendly hand.

The woman took it in a loose grip and shook. 'Millicent…'

'You're taking over the bakery?' he asked, nodding at the building. Before Millicent could reply, Jasmine had joined them, slipping an arm through her husband's. 'Oh, this is my wife, Jasmine.'

Millicent's smile for Jasmine was warmer. 'Pleased to meet you,' she said.

'And you… Millicent did you say?'

'Call me Millie. Millicent makes me sound like someone's great-aunt.'

'Are you doing all this alone?' Jasmine asked, glancing at the open doors of the van.

'Sadly, yes.'

'We'd be happy to help. Rich and I have a couple of hours to spare before we go to get the terrors from school.'

'Terrors?' Millie asked.

Rich grinned. 'Otherwise known as the Green children. They're probably not as bad as people tell us, but the teachers have all been given standard-issue canisters of tear gas and riot gear, just in case.'

Jasmine elbowed him in the ribs with a giggle.

'Help would be most welcome, in that case,' Millie said, relaxing into a smile. 'When I started to pack all this stuff, it didn't look like much. It's not until you're on your twentieth box with no sign of stopping that you realise just how much you own.'

'We found that when we moved from our tiny cottage into where we live now. You wouldn't believe what you can fit into a one-bedroom house.' Jasmine pushed a stray curl back from her forehead. 'And we still have boxes in the loft that we've never unpacked, even years later.'

'Just goes to show how much we needed the stuff,' Rich grinned.

'Or how lazy you are,' Jasmine replied with a smirk.

'Hey, I have a highly demanding job!'

'Don't listen to a word he says,' Jasmine said to Millie in a loud stage whisper. 'He sits on his backside all day tinkering in a home recording studio and he calls that work.'

'You're a musician?' Millie asked, looking at Rich with obvious awe.

'Some might argue that point,' he laughed, 'but that's how I make my living.'

'So… you're taking on the old bakery?' Jasmine asked.

'It's going to take a lot of work, I know,' Millie said, resting her hands on her hips as she turned her gaze to the building. 'But I hope to get it back to its former glory and trading again.'

'The village could certainly do with it,' Jasmine said. 'It used to be a lovely place to meet people and stop for something yummy. We have the supermarket about five miles away, and a general store that sells allsorts, but it's not the same as a proper cake shop.'

'Where did you say you'd moved from?' Rich asked, shoving his hands into his pockets with an amiable smile.

'I didn't.' Millie's expression suddenly darkened. Rich threw an uncertain glance at Jasmine, but the moment quickly passed.

'Ignore him,' Jasmine said. 'No concept of social boundaries – size elevens straight in every time.'

'Well,' Rich said with a self-conscious laugh. 'I suppose you could tell us where you want these boxes and we'll crack on.'

'I can always get the kids myself if we don't finish here,' Jasmine told Rich. 'And you could carry on moving Millie's stuff.'

'I can't ask you to drop everything and carry my boxes all afternoon,' Millie said, looking mortified by the idea. 'I'm sure you must have plans.'

'Nothing that can't wait,' Jasmine said with a smile. 'And as we both work for ourselves, the bosses are pretty lenient about time off.'

'You write music too?'

'God no! I have a craft business. I make jewellery and homey knick-knacks.'

'Is that one of your pieces?' Millie glanced appreciatively at a burnished silver pendant hanging around Jasmine's neck.

'Oh yes,' Jasmine said, running a hand over the piece to remind herself which one it was.

'It's beautiful.' Millie stepped forward and took it gently in her fingers. She looked up at Jasmine with a bright smile. 'You know this is a Celtic symbol?'

'Is it?' Jasmine laughed. 'I got it out of a book.'

'Yes, a very apt one too, in your case. It's the symbol for inspiration and creativity.'

'Wow. You seem to know a lot about it,' Rich said.

Millie shrugged and let the pendant go, the darkness crossing her features again. 'A little. I read a lot of mythology.' She turned to Jasmine again, the storm clearing from her eyes as quickly as it had come. 'Your hair looks amazing too. I noticed as soon as I saw you across the road.'

'It's kind of hard to miss, I suppose.' Jasmine twisted a pink ringlet self-consciously. Her hair was pinned up, an explosion of sugary curls piled on her head, the odd corkscrew escaping to frame her face.

'I wish I was brave enough to colour my hair like that.'

'Why would you do that? Yours is glorious as it is.'

'But sometimes you just feel like you need a huge change, do something completely different… you know what I mean?'

Their conversation was interrupted by Rich clearing his throat. 'I suppose we really should get these boxes in.'

'You're right,' said Millie. 'The van will have to go back soon.'

'In that case we're at your service.' Rich saluted. 'So tell us where you want everything.'

'She seems nice,' Jasmine commented as she shook salad from a bag onto five plates. The sun was still intense outside the open window despite it being early evening, the scent of newly cut grass drifting into the kitchen over the smell of roasted chicken. Jasmine was bare-foot, and had discarded her long summer dress for a pair of denim cut-offs and a lightweight smock top embroidered with Indian designs. Jasmine had never been self-conscious about her curves, and that confidence in her own body seemed to shine from her, making her all the more attractive, despite the little extra padding here and there.

'Who?' Rich licked his fingers.

'Hey,' Jasmine frowned. 'What have I told you about that when you're carving? Lick your fingers after, not during.'

'Sorry, Miss,' Rich said with a pout. 'I forgot.'

'You're a disgusting pig.'

Rich sidled over and hooked an arm around Jasmine's waist, pulling her close. 'I know; that's why you married me...'

Jasmine slapped him playfully on the arm. 'Not now! We have three starving children in there,' she angled her head at the door to the conservatory where their triplets were playing with an enormous box of Lego. 'Your naughtiness is the reason *why* we have three starving children in there.'

'It takes two to be naughty, Miss.'

'Quite. Which is why you can keep your chicken-lickin' hands to yourself and go and make some drinks for the kids before you tempt me into making more trouble.'

Rich grinned and kissed her lightly on the nose. 'Don't think I won't try again later.'

'You can try, but it doesn't mean you'll succeed.'

'Don't worry,' Rich said as he padded over to the fridge, 'come nine o'clock I'll be too knackered to do anything more than snore.'

'Hmm, it must be so tiring pushing buttons on a Yamaha keyboard all day.'

'Hey, it's emotionally draining!' Rich put three plastic beakers out onto the worktop. 'Besides, I have been moving boxes as well.'

'I think you'll find we moved most of the boxes.' Jasmine paused. 'Perhaps we should have invited her for dinner. I bet she doesn't have anywhere to cook yet.'

'Who?'

'Millie.'

Rich waved his hand vaguely. 'I'm sure she can get a takeaway and sit on her floor. It's what everyone else does on their first night in a new place.'

'Yes, but everyone else isn't alone in a tumbledown old bakery for their first night in a village where everyone is a stranger.'

'Don't you think it would be a tad over-friendly?'

'Inviting her for dinner?'

'It's a bit forward – we only met her today.'

'That's never stopped you before.'

Rich stopped pouring juice and looked up at Jasmine. 'I know… there's something about her… I don't know… something I don't quite trust.'

'Really?' Jasmine rifled in a drawer for cutlery. 'I thought she seemed lovely. It's not like you to form negative opinions so quickly.'

'She seemed evasive.'

'You were being too nosey, that's why.'

'It's my natural friendliness and easy-going charm that you're confusing with nosiness there.'

'Have you ever thought that some people might be immune to your easy-going charm?'

'What!' Rich grinned. 'How could you say that? It worked on you.'

Jasmine raised her eyebrows. 'I think we established a long time ago that I'm not like other people.'

'That's true, my sweetness.' Rich bounded across the kitchen and caught her in his arms again. 'And that's why I love you.'

Jasmine giggled as she kissed him. 'Nutter.'

Millie sneezed as she brushed a cobweb away from her hair and gazed around the dreary room. She felt sticky all over from the damp heat blowing through the open window. The sun was beginning to sink now, but the evening was still sultry. No wash-down in the cracked old sink that served as her luxury bathroom yet though, at least not until she had cleaned it, turfed out the huge spider (any creature that big should be paying council tax) and got the water back on. When she had seen the old bakery for sale online, it had seemed like the perfect move for her, but now she didn't feel so sure. Her judgement wasn't always sound, at least, not lately. Perhaps she should have come to view the place before she bought it… She looked around the bare walls and cracked ceiling – had the tarot cards got it wrong? This certainly didn't look like the place for a successful new start. And she hadn't even dared to look at the ovens that she'd need in order to make a living yet. She let out a huge sigh.

'I'm here now,' she announced to the empty room, 'so I suppose I'll just have to make the best of it.'

Idly, with the toe of her ballet pump, she traced a circle in the dust of the old tiled floor and then stepped into it. Was Honeybourne somewhere she could be safe? She glanced at the pile of boxes lined up against the wall. She might not be able to locate all the things she needed to settle down for the night, lost as they were in the bottom of various unopened boxes, but she could locate the nearest supermarket, as she had passed it in the van that morning. A bottle of wine with a sandwich felt like a good idea. Grabbing her keys, she headed for the door.

Just as she was locking up, a deep voice hailed her. 'Evening.'

Millie looked up to see a man, somewhere in his mid-twenties, dressed casually in a pair of loose jeans and grey T-shirt, smiling down at her. He looked familiar, although she couldn't say why – something in his smile and the natural, fearless warmth of his gaze.

'I didn't mean to make you jump,' he said apologetically. 'I noticed your van outside earlier and wondered if someone had moved in. I was going to knock, but you beat me to it by coming out. I live just over there, you see…' He pointed across the green, past a small duck pond. Millie followed his finger to a tiny stone cottage.

'The little white place?' she asked.

'That's the one.'

'Just you?'

'Oh yes. It's so small I struggle to fit a broom in there with me, let alone other human beings.'

Millie smiled politely but offered no reply.

'I suppose I should let you get on then…' the man added awkwardly, clearly sensing Millie's reluctance to engage in any meaningful conversation.

'I'm sorry, I'm very tired and I really need to get some food before I pass out.'

'The supermarket's miles away. There's a convenience store a bit closer. Or I could bring you something over to see you through until morning? It'd be no trouble.'

'I'd rather get my own, if you don't mind.'

'Of course…' He hesitated. 'Or you could come over… for a welcome drink and a sandwich. I mean, I can't promise cordon bleu but—'

Millie stopped him with a hand in the air. 'Really, it's very kind but I've got so much to do here still…'

'Right, sure. Well, if you need anything, I'm just over there. Don't worry about disturbing me, just knock any time.'

'Thanks. I will.'

He gave her a little nod of the head that was almost like an old-fashioned bow. 'Don't forget now.'

'I won't.'

Without another word, Millie pocketed the bakery keys and walked to the rental van she was still using, sensing the man's eyes on her back as she went.

Men. Millie had had quite enough emotional trauma with men to last her a lifetime. Attractive though Mr White Cottage was (and there was no denying that his floppy sandy hair, soft hazel eyes and athletic physique were all very desirable attributes), it was best to steer well clear. Some said that she had brought the misfortune upon herself, but a great deal of heartsease had been employed in mending her last broken heart, and she still wasn't sure it was fixed completely. That wasn't a place she wanted to go again.

Chapter Two

'Dylan phoned, by the way, when you were in the bath last night.' Rich popped his head around the doorway of the workshop the following morning. The day promised to be as hot as the previous one, and already, just after nine, the sun blazed in through the tiny windows of the outhouse.

'Did he say what he wanted?' Jasmine asked, looking up from the delicate metal rose she was shaping.

'Not really. I told him you'd phone him back.'

'Honestly, he lives three yards away,' Jasmine muttered as she bent back to her work. 'He could just come round.'

Rich grinned. 'That would consume far too much energy.'

'I know. If that boy took life at a slower pace, he'd be going backwards.'

'You love him really.'

'To bits. It's just that he's infuriating.'

'You'd better call him though.' Rich's voice trailed off as he went back into the main house. 'I don't want him thinking I didn't tell you. And you'd better have a word about *the thing* as well…'

'What thing?' Jasmine called back. She knew what thing, of course, but she was inexplicably irritated by the fact that Rich had brought it up. They'd had a whole hour of discussion over *the thing* only the night before. Her family wasn't perfect, but there was no need for him to keep rubbing it in. His wasn't so bloody perfect either. She knew she had to and she fully intended to speak to Dylan about *the thing* in her own time, without being nagged. Not that it would do any good.

When Rich failed to reply, she picked up a tiny pair of pliers, twisting a sliver of metal on her rose with a practised and precise motion. Leaning back, she examined it from a distance for a moment before bending her head back to twist at a second section. She worked for a few moments more, delicately moving bits of the sculpture here and there, until she was satisfied with the way it looked.

'Right, Mr Lazy Bum,' she said, putting the piece to one side and checking her watch, 'let's go and see what you want this time.'

Jasmine knocked at the door of the tiny cottage. The sun burned the back of her bare neck as she waited in the doorway, the lazy drone of bees and the perfume of the honeysuckle reaching her from the sprawling climber that wound up the side of the house. If someone wanted an image of the perfect British summer's day, Jasmine was pretty sure it would look like this. It seemed like a good day to be out visiting, despite all the work that was piling up in her outhouse at home. Perhaps it would be better to tackle it later anyway, when the kids had gone to bed and it was cooler; there had to be some perks to being your own boss.

When she had waited for a few minutes and nobody answered the door, Jasmine knocked again, more forcefully this time. Knowing Dylan, he'd been on some all-night gaming bender and was still in bed, or worse, he might have a random girl in there. It was none of her business, of course, but the idea of that irked her. What gave him the right to live like that? Why couldn't he grow up and take some responsibility for his life, like the rest of the population had to, instead of behaving like a lazy adolescent? He was her brother, and she loved him dearly, but that didn't mean she wasn't angry with him from time to time. She had to be honest, though, and wonder whether it was the not working that bothered her, or the fact that he could easily afford not to work after inheriting his half of their parents' estate. He was choosing to live like some sad playboy whereas she and Rich had ploughed her half into their respective businesses and now had nothing to show for it apart from long hours to pay the mortgage and keep the kids in shoes.

A familiar voice interrupted her musings and she turned to see Dylan coming up the path from behind her.

'Bloody hell, is your bed on fire this morning?' Jasmine called, shielding her eyes from the glare of the sun as she watched him approach.

Dylan grinned. 'If you must know, I was doing my charitable deed for the day.'

'Now I know there's something wrong with the world. What was this? Ade ran out of beer? Julian needed the number of a good dealer?'

Dylan's grin turned to a frown. 'Alright, enough of that…' he said, glancing around warily, despite the fact that the nearest house was too far away for anyone to hear their conversation. 'I was across the road with Millie.'

'That was quick work, even for you; she only moved in yesterday.'

'It's not like that,' Dylan said as he rifled in his pocket for a key. 'Are you coming in or have you just come to pass judgement on my social life?'

'A bit of both. Rich said you phoned. And I wanted to ask you round for dinner.'

'We have phones and emails and allsorts, you know, to save your legs.' Dylan opened the door and Jasmine followed him into the cool, slate-tiled hallway.

'I'll go then if you're going to be like that.'

'Don't take it so personally. I just meant that you're taking time out of your work schedule just to see me.'

'Well…'

'I know. You promised Mum one day when you were having a deep and meaningful conversation that you'd always look out for me. It's funny how she never had any of those conversations with me.'

Jasmine frowned as they went into the kitchen and she noted the dishes piled up in the sink, a bluebottle doing lazy circuits of the top-most pot. There was a faintly worrying smell too, like meat that was just going off. Jasmine tried not to think about it and hoped it was coming from Dylan's bin and not from his larder. By now, she knew better than to lecture him about his domestic affairs; he never listened and she always ended up sounding like a grade-A nag, something that went against her whole nature. Dylan, seemingly oblivious to Jasmine's discomfort, headed for the fridge.

'Want something cold?' he asked as he yanked it open.

'What have you got?'

'You want beer?'

'Dylan, it's the middle of the day…'

Dylan pulled his head from the fridge and grinned at his sister.

'Very funny,' Jasmine sighed. 'So what *have* you got?'

'Cola, cola, or cola.'

'Nothing else?'

'Um… flat cola…'

'You know I don't drink that crap.'

'I didn't know you were coming. And Threshers were clean out of wheatgrass-with-added-hippy-essence juice.'

'Don't you at least shop with the idea that you might get visitors, and that maybe you should have something for them when they call?' Jasmine flopped down at the table and folded her arms. 'A simple glass of orange juice would have sufficed.'

'Cool kids don't shop.'

Jasmine tried to frown, but after a second or two, couldn't help a small smile. Despite how frustrating he could be, there was something infectious about Dylan's personality. Infuriatingly, he *was* cool; there was no other word for him. Everything he did, everything he said, was effortlessly charming and impressive. 'So what were you doing across the way with Millie?' she asked, changing the subject as Dylan sat opposite her and cracked open a Coke can.

'Oh, this and that.'

'Meaning?'

'I was helping her move some boxes.'

'You were actually helping someone do manual work?'

'I'm not completely useless, you know.'

'You are completely lazy, however.'

Dylan laughed. 'You underestimate the power of an attractive woman, sis.'

Jasmine rolled her eyes. 'I wondered when that would come into the equation. I don't think you'll get anywhere there. She seems far too mature and level-headed to fall for your corny chat-up lines.'

'You can't blame me for trying though.' Dylan peered over the top of his can as he sipped his drink.

'I wish you wouldn't. Don't you ever get bored of chasing conquests?'

'I'm just looking for the right woman.'

'Yeah. That's why the only women in this village not on your radar are me and old Ruth Evans.'

'That's harsh.'

Jasmine paused. 'Ok. Let me put it this way – have you been shagging Amy Parsons?'

'What?'

'Amy Parsons. Pretty... blonde... a bit gullible...'

'That's charming. I thought you liked her.'

'I do, but she must be gullible if she fell for one of your chat-up lines.'

He leaned back in his seat and folded his arms. 'Go on then. Who's been blabbing?'

'Nobody. Her son, Jake, is in the same class as the triplets, or had you forgotten that? Kids talk; they share all sorts of secrets. Jake told Reuben that you went round to their house on Saturday night. He said he woke up because he heard a noise and went out on the landing to see you there with his mum. He said you were laughing and wrestling. Amy told him to go back to sleep and then he heard you and Amy laughing some more and jumping up and down on the bed...' Jasmine raised her eyebrows. 'Did you have fun jumping on the bed with Amy? How do you think I feel when Reuben comes home and tells me things like that – my child hearing that sort of thing about his uncle? Not only that but he told Rich too.'

'Reuben doesn't know what it means,' Dylan retorted, but Jasmine wondered if she detected the faintest blush. There was something immensely satisfying about it. It made her want to push the conversation; perhaps the only way to make him see what a mess he was making of his life was to shame him into it.

'Now he doesn't but one day he will. One day he'll work it all out. What kind of role model is that?'

'He's got his dad for a role model. That's not my job…'

Jasmine frowned.

'Ok, look… I was drinking in the pub and she just happened to come in. We got chatting, she got a bit tipsy and then I walked her home. She asked me to go in and before I knew it…' He shrugged. 'I didn't mean for things to get out of hand.'

'Hmm. I'm sure that makes it ok then. I wonder who else Jake has told his little story to. I wonder if his dad, who's working away in Düsseldorf, will get a phone call to hear the story of his mum and Dylan Smith jumping up and down on the bed in the middle of the night.'

'I'll have a word with Amy when I see her—'

'That's not the point! You can't keep covering your tracks and hoping you'll stay bulletproof! You have no responsibilities, and seemingly no conscience. Amy, God love her for the idiot she is, has everything to lose and you should have a bit more consideration for that.'

'Hey! It takes two to tango, sis. I didn't make her come down to the pub and get drunk and ask me back to her house.'

'It only takes one to walk away, though.'

Dylan let out a sigh. He was silent for a moment as he stared out of the window. 'Ok, ok… I know you're right and I'm a total shit.'

'Why do it then? If you know you're a shit, then why do you keep doing it?'

He leaned forward on the table. 'God knows. I wish I did, Jas. It's like there's someone else in my head, telling me to do it, even when I know I shouldn't.'

'Whoever that person is, they need a good slap. I love you, Dylan, but I'm tired of defending you. Everyone in this village knows what you are, and they tar us with the same brush.'

'Nobody thinks that about you. Everyone loves you and Rich, you're like Honeybourne's own Posh and Becks. You're just being paranoid.'

'Am I? Can't you, just once, show a bit of self-restraint?'

'Maybe I don't want to...' He winced at the look she gave him. 'You're right. I don't know what it is. I get in the zone and then it's like... I can't help myself. Sometimes I feel so lonely and it's company, you know?'

There was a bit of Jasmine that could understand that. She had Rich and the children, but Dylan had no one, not really, and she couldn't imagine what life must have been like for him when their parents were killed. But he couldn't keep hiding behind his grief. They had both lost their parents, as had many others before them, and they didn't all go off the rails. If the endless casual sex was a symptom of something deeper, then he needed to face that and deal with it.

'Why don't you go and get that counselling we've talked about?' Jasmine asked gently.

Dylan shook his head. 'It's bollocks.'

'You won't know until you try.'

'You tried. Are you any different for it?'

'I'm not shagging everything that moves.'

'You have Rich. You've always had someone, even... well, never mind.'

'Maybe you should try actually dating a woman, one you intend to stay with, and then you might have someone too.'

'I want to. I want to get to know the new girl, she seems nice.'

'Millie? She does seem nice but I don't know if that's wise. You'll end up shagging her and leaving her like all the others.'

'I might not. Anyway, how do you know that isn't what she wants?'

Jasmine's forehead creased into a deep frown.

'Kidding!' Dylan laughed. 'Honest! Anyway, how come you know all about her? She's only been in the village two minutes.'

'Rich and I saw her pull up yesterday and we helped her move her stuff into the bakery.'

'Well, she seems nice, and she's fit as…' He stopped as Jasmine frowned again. 'She's gorgeous and she doesn't know me yet.'

'Well, you'd better hope she doesn't strike up a conversation with Amy Parsons any time soon.'

Dylan's gaze wandered to his phone lying on the table. Jasmine groaned as she interpreted the look. 'Jesus, Dylan! Please tell me Amy hasn't been texting to see you again!'

He shrugged.

'Don't you dare!' she squeaked. 'She's married, or have you forgotten that detail, *again*?'

'I wasn't going to; I'm not that stupid.'

'Stupid enough to go there in the first place. This isn't London; people talk and news travels fast here.'

'I know, I know, you said that before… You're right. I'm sorry. Is that what you want me to say?'

'I want you to stop dicking around.'

'I will. I'm going to get it together, I promise.'

'So you're going to leave Millie alone?'

Dylan stared at her. 'I thought you wanted me to date properly. Why do I have to leave her alone now?'

'Because I like her and I like you and I don't think I could cope with the awkwardness.'

Dylan waved a dismissive hand as he reached for his drink. 'It'll be fine.'

'I mean it,' Jasmine said, suddenly serious. 'It's a disaster waiting to happen.'

Dylan put his can down and ran a hand through his hair. 'How can you possibly know that?'

'Please, Dylan. Just don't.'

Dylan grimaced. 'You're not Mum. And even Mum wouldn't have told me who to go out with.'

'I'm not telling you who to go out with; I'm just telling you that it will end badly.'

Dylan took a swig of his Coke and winked at Jasmine, the old cockiness returning as if to prove her point. 'We'll see.'

An hour later Jasmine headed back out into the sunshine, quite undecided what sort of mood she was in. Conversations with Dylan often made her feel like that – a strange mixture of disapproval and envy at the way he seemed to sail through life without a care for what it may throw his way. She knew he was vulnerable and lonely, but he presented himself as emotionally bulletproof with an uncanny ability to look on the bright side of life. It was oddly attractive, as his long string of discarded girlfriends could testify. Their mother had often expressed a wish for him to settle down with a nice girl, and Jasmine understood that more than ever as she watched him grow older in his self-imposed emotional bubble. She often wondered how she would feel watching Reuben grow into a man like Dylan, and the idea saddened her in a way she couldn't put into words.

'Hey, Jasmine!'

Jasmine looked up from her reverie to see Millie waving from across the square. She was dressed in old jeans and an oversized denim shirt, her sleeves rolled up to reveal dirty forearms and her hair scraped into a floral headscarf. Even in her scruffs, she looked dainty and radiant in a way that was almost unreal.

'Hey to you too,' Jasmine called back, crossing the road to meet her. Given that Millie had been the subject of a difficult conversation only an hour before, Jasmine felt a strange mix of emotions at seeing her. The woman had made quite an impression on Jasmine the previous day, and she couldn't help the broad smile that spread across her face, but that nagging voice at the back of her mind tempered it. Knowing Dylan as she did, he wouldn't be easily persuaded to give up on Millie now that he had targeted her, and God only knew what sort of trouble might be in store for all of them. Jasmine smoothed her features as the two women met outside the bakery.

'I never really thanked you properly for all your help yesterday,' Millie said warmly. She seemed a good deal more relaxed than she had when Jasmine and Rich had left her the previous evening.

'It was nothing,' Jasmine smiled. 'Rich loves a damsel in distress; you wouldn't have been able to keep him away if you'd tried.'

'And what's your excuse?'

'I have to make sure he doesn't drop anything.'

Millie laughed. 'You did a cracking job then.'

'How's it going in there?' Jasmine angled her head at the open door of the building, where an unsteady tower of boxes was just visible amongst a floor full of assorted clutter.

'Oh, it's still got about fifteen years' worth of dust in every room, the ovens are coated in enough grease and grime to waterproof a Viking longship and I've had to get an eviction order for the larger spiders… but I think it's ok.'

'Did you sleep here last night?' Jasmine asked with a grimace.

'Well… the man from over the road – who, incidentally, has the worst chat-up lines I've ever heard – offered me his bed, but I thought I'd take my chances with the mice over here.'

'Dylan?' Jasmine asked more sharply than she'd meant to.

Millie paled. 'He lives in the white cottage… Oh God, you know him? I mean… he said he'd sleep on the sofa… I didn't mean anything when I said he was…'

Jasmine inwardly chided herself. She'd overreacted, as she knew she would. Dylan was a grown man and she had to keep reminding herself of that. She shrugged apologetically. 'He's my brother. I can't say which side of the family gave him the silver tongue, but it certainly didn't pass to me.'

'He helped me move a few things this morning. He's very nice. I didn't mean to say anything bad. I didn't know he was your brother, but even if I had…'

Jasmine put up a hand to stop her. 'Don't worry. I know exactly what he's like.'

Millie glanced back to her open door and then back at Jasmine, and an awkward silence descended on them.

'I'll let you get on,' Jasmine said.

Millie chewed on her lip. Then she nodded. 'I probably should make a start on those grotty ovens.'

'If you need anything,' Jasmine said as she turned to leave, 'me and Rich live in the last barn conversion at the edge of the village. You can't miss us,' she smiled, 'we're the ones with the huge metal sculpture of Poseidon in the front garden.'

* * *

Millie turned back from the stark sunshine into the dim gloom of the bakery. Damn it, why did she always say the wrong thing? Now she'd upset Jasmine, the first woman she had met in the village, who she had instantly warmed to; someone she felt could be a kindred spirit. If she was going to make a new life here in Honeybourne and leave her troubled past once and for all, a friend like Jasmine could be just what she needed.

With a sigh of resignation, she turned her attention to the interior of her new home. What she needed right now, she mused as she surveyed the mess of the main shop and calculated how much work there still was to do, was some serious, full-on Mary Poppins magic. But sadly, life didn't work like that. So she would have to roll her sleeves up and shift things with her hands like everyone else. And after the terrible night's sleep she'd had, maybe the best place to start would be the bedroom after all. She could have the ovens and kitchen clean and neat, but it would be pointless if she was too tired to run the business. More than ever she was beginning to wish that she'd waited, looked for a partner to take the business on with her. It was a huge enterprise, much bigger than the celebration cakes that she had made to order from her small, homely kitchen up in the midlands. She must have been an idiot to think she could run this alone. She didn't even really know how to keep her books in order, let alone all the other things she'd need to do – public liability insurance, food hygiene, advertising, business banking and a list of sundries as long as her arm. Her cosy idea of making cakes in a rural idyll was crumbling around her already, like the rafters above her head which were crumbling away from centuries of being gnawed by woodworm.

Her thoughts were interrupted by a rap at the doorframe. Millie span round to see Jasmine's brother grinning at the open door.

'Sorry, me again. I just had to get rid of my sister before I could pop back over.'

'As I told you earlier, kind as your offer is, I can manage to clean and unpack and you really don't need to bother yourself.'

'Uh-huh.' Dylan stepped over the dusty threshold and folded his arms as he leaned against the doorway, backlit by the bright sun. 'That might be true, but I'm rattling around over the way doing nothing. Imagine how guilty I'll feel knowing that I'm on my backside with a can of Stella while you're lugging huge boxes around all alone.'

'I didn't realise Jasmine was your sister,' Millie replied, steering the conversation away. Much as she needed help, she wasn't sure that she wanted it from Dylan. Somehow, his easy charm and confidence scared her.

'Jas?' He turned his face in profile and stroked his jaw. 'Could you not see the striking family resemblance?'

'I can now.'

He grinned. 'I suppose it's the pink hair that threw you. And the curls. And the nose piercing. Maybe the breasts too,' he added with mock thoughtfulness. 'As I don't have any of those, I can see why people are confused at first.'

Millie couldn't help but smile. 'I can see it now. She's prettier than you though.'

'Damn that woman!' Dylan clicked his fingers. 'No wonder Rich Green wouldn't marry me.'

Millie crossed her arms and surveyed him. 'You never stop the act, do you?'

'Nobody would laugh if I did. And what else is there in life but laughter?'

Millie crossed over to a box and peered inside. 'I'd offer you a cup of tea, but I have no idea which box contains the kettle and no electricity to boil it with.'

'Then let me make one for you.'

'No, I—'

'Don't worry, you won't have to come into my house.' He pretended to shudder.

'Actually, definitely don't come to my house. I'll bring you a cup over. How does that sound?'

Millie paused for a moment, frowning. Then she smiled slightly. 'That does sound nice.'

'Right.' Dylan turned to leave, but then stopped and turned back. 'I hope you're not too thirsty though, because I have to go to the shop first. I'm clean out of milk… and tea… and possibly sterile crockery too.'

And with that, he bounded out of the door and into the bright street outside, leaving Millie to shake her head in wonderment.

Millie was elbow deep in a box of cleaning products as Dylan walked back in half an hour later with two mugs.

'As promised,' he grinned.

'Oh, that's so sweet of you.' Millie wiped her hands on a cloth hanging from her belt and wandered over to the counter.

'I bet you're gasping, aren't you?'

'Actually, Miss Evans who lives a few doors up came by and said hello. She offered to make me a drink so… I've already had one,' Millie replied sheepishly. She couldn't help but laugh as Dylan's face fell, it looked so pitiful.

'I could manage another one,' she added.

He handed her a mug. 'I might have known old Ruth Evans would have sniffed you out. I'm surprised she wasn't round here yesterday, she doesn't miss a thing that goes on in the village.'

'Apparently she was particularly troubled by her irritable bowel yesterday and was…' Millie grimaced, '*a slave to her toilet seat.*'

Dylan laughed and plonked himself on an old wooden bench in the bay window as Millie leaned on the shop counter. 'That's Ruth,' he said. 'She doesn't miss a trick but she also thinks that everyone else wants to know her business, no matter how grim it is. You should have heard her go on about her hysterectomy. I was only nine when she had it done; the words I learned that week scarred me for life, I can tell you. I'm as interested in the female reproductive system as the next man, but I don't need *that* much anatomical detail.'

Millie couldn't help but giggle, despite being aware that she was giving out the wrong signals by doing it. There was no doubting that Dylan, with his lithe figure and twinkling eyes full of mischief, had a magnetism that was hard to ignore. Her gaze fell on the contours of his chest, showing in subtle relief through the fabric of his loose T-shirt. Where his sister was all comfortable womanly curves and soft edges, Dylan was taut and angular, not a spare inch of fat to be seen. Even his jawline looked as though it had been hewn from stone, like some classical statue. Millie shook herself as she became aware of her sudden silence and Dylan regarding her with a quizzical expression.

'Sorry, thinking about all the stuff I have to do here,' Millie explained. 'I'm beginning to wonder if I'll have to hire some help.'

'You weren't seriously thinking of tackling the building work yourself?' Dylan spluttered.

'What does that mean?' Millie replied with sudden coldness. 'I'm a woman so I can't do DIY?'

'No, no, of course not.' Dylan held his hand up in a gesture of surrender. 'But I wouldn't tackle all this myself.' He glanced up at the wooden beams above them. 'It looks like a huge amount of structural work.'

'You think?' Millie asked, a note of anxiety creeping into her bravado.

'Didn't your survey pick it all up?'

'Well… I didn't have a survey…'

'You needed one for the mortgage, right?'

Millie bit her lip. 'I didn't need one because I paid cash from the sale of my house.'

Dylan shook his head slightly. 'You still should have got a survey done.'

Millie paused. Now probably wasn't the time to tell Dylan that she'd simply had a *good feeling* that the shop would be ok, and that she was on the run from the miserable life she was so desperate to leave behind. 'It was a lot of money that I thought would be better used setting up the business.'

'That's all very well, but you can't run a business if your premises are falling down.'

'I know that,' Millie snapped. She wasn't stupid, so why were Dylan's observations making her feel that way?

Dylan studied her for a moment, unperturbed by her outburst. 'I have some mates who might be able to help. They're cheap as chips and will do a decent job.'

'But I don't even know what needs doing.'

'Why don't I call them? They can come and take a look, list what needs to be done, and then at least you'll know. It's a start, right?'

Millie nodded uncertainly. She had come to Honeybourne with the intention of starting afresh, with no obligations and no ties to anyone but herself, and already she was running up moral debts and favours that would need to be returned, or at the very least acknowledged. But then she looked around at the state of the old bakery – her new home – and had to admit that she was going to need help, whether she liked it or not.

'Ok, that would be good, thanks.'

'I'll phone them when I've finished my brew.'

Millie took a sip of her drink. 'They are proper builders, aren't they?'

Dylan frowned. 'What do you take me for?'

'Sorry, it's just… This is my whole life, right here in this falling-down building. I have nothing else.'

'Don't be so sure about that,' Dylan winked. 'You have me.'

Chapter Three

'Rebecca says Mr Johns is looking for volunteers to help with the school trip next week.' Rich looked over his paper the next morning as Jasmine buttered some toast and handed it to Reuben, the only child still at the table finishing breakfast. He was always the last one ready for school, simply because his appetite was so much bigger than that of his sisters.

'Oh yeah, that's right.' Reuben nodded before cramming a triangle of toast into his mouth.

'I remember last time I volunteered,' Jasmine said. 'Somebody was sick all over me on the back seats of the coach…' She gave a meaningful glance towards Reuben, who blushed.

'Sorry, Mum.'

'Come on, Jazzy, you can't be too hard on him. I was travel sick all the time when I was eight.'

'It's obviously you I have to blame then, for my ruined Monsoon dress,' Jasmine observed as she turned a pretend frown onto her husband. 'I had to make an awful lot of lanterns to get the money for that.'

'When I'm rich and famous, I'll buy you a whole shop-full of Monsoon dresses,' Rich grinned in return.

'You've been saying that for fifteen years.'

'Never say never, my sweetness. This time next year we could be millionaires.' Rich shook his paper and began to read again.

'Please, Mum,' Reuben said. 'The other kids love it when you help out.'

'Really?'

Reuben nodded vigorously. 'You're the coolest mum in the village.'

Jasmine laughed as she put the lid on the butter. 'Thank you, my gorgeous boy, but that's not saying much. After all, it's a very small village.' She ruffled his hair as he folded the last of his toast into his mouth and swallowed hard.

'Now, go and get changed before we're late again and Mr Johns gives *me* detention.'

Reuben grabbed a spare slice of toast from Jasmine's abandoned portion and scampered obediently away.

'It's scorching again.' Jasmine turned her eyes to the kitchen window, where the sun bounced off the stark white frame and a bee tapped at the glass a few times before bumbling off to find some flowers.

Rich looked up from his paper and followed her gaze. 'I know. I would pick the hottest week of the year to go and sit in some stuffy bloody office. On a normal day I could be lounging around in the garden humming to myself.'

'It's only today. You need to nail this deal that Ollie's worked so hard to set up.'

'Of course, and I intend to. It's practically in the bag anyway; they really like what they've heard already. Today is about formalities, and then tomorrow I'll have a lovely contract for a film score about a romance set in nineteenth-century Greece, with English village rain for inspiration.'

'I doubt it's going to be raining any time soon. Doug at the pub says the long-range forecast is more of the same. Besides, I'm sure a man of your creative power can easily overcome a little obstacle like rain, if Doug turns out to be wrong.' Jasmine balanced a pile of plates and cups as she made her way to the sink and plopped them into a bowl of soapy water. Rich followed her across the room and folded his arms around her waist from behind, nuzzling into her neck, while she tried to wash up.

'Rich, I need to get these finished quickly, I'm not even dressed yet and you can't take the kids in today.'

'I know,' he said lazily, his breath hot in her ear. Tucking his hand into her pyjama bottoms, he lightly worked his way down to her crotch as he kissed her neck. 'But this won't take long…'

Jasmine gasped, a slow smile spreading across her face, heat spreading through her loins as he stroked her.

'The kids…' she said, gently pulling his hand out and then turning to flick him with suds.

Rich grinned. 'Alright. But don't think I won't get you later.'

She kissed him, her insides fizzing with anticipation. 'If you can catch me, you can have me.'

'Oh, I'll catch you alright…' Rich pumped his arms like a body-builder as he walked away laughing.

'You're a bad man, Richard Green,' she called after him.

'What's Daddy done now?' Rebecca appeared at the back door.

Jasmine frowned. 'What were you doing in the garden? You're meant to be upstairs getting ready for school.'

'I am ready. I went out to feed Clarice.'

'The rabbit could have waited till I fed the chickens. Right now I need you to sort yourself out.'

Rebecca gave her mum a quick, meaningful glance up and down. 'You still have your pyjamas on.'

'Well, I wouldn't have if other people would let me get on. Now go and make sure Rachel and Reuben are dressed, would you, there's a good girl.'

Rebecca wandered obediently off. Jasmine watched her go. Although the children were triplets, they weren't completely alike. Rebecca was slightly taller than the other two, and had also been the biggest when they were born. She was darker than the others and her hair had a natural curl to it. Rachel and Reuben looked more like twins, with Rebecca the older sister, both of them with sandy hair the shade of Jasmine's own natural colour, but straighter like Rich's, and darker eyes than Rebecca's brownish-green. With no medical intervention, Jasmine had conceived the three of them completely naturally and had made quite a splash locally when the news got out. Rich had been so proud, they had joked about his *mighty sperm* for months down at the Dog and Hare. They certainly had got a ready-made family. It had been hard work at first, but, as Jasmine had often commented with a laugh, they would never have to potty train again after this batch. A year earlier, Kate Stephens had given birth to twins and when the local paper got wind of the story, the village was dubbed 'the most fertile village in Hampshire' in an evening headline.

Jasmine shook herself and returned to washing up the breakfast dishes. Often, Rich took the kids to school so that she could get an early start working, but today she was already behind schedule and the school run was going to make that worse still.

* * *

After the morning greetings and a few exchanged bits of gossip in the playground, the bell rang for the start of the school day and Jasmine was kissing the triplets goodbye. Just as she had watched them go in through the doors, a man in his late twenties rushed out, making his way towards her with a broad smile.

'Morning, Spencer! Or should I say *Mr Johns* while we're at school?'

'Hey, Jas,' Spencer grinned. 'Did the kids mention anything to you about helping out on the school trip?'

'They said something about it this morning…'

'And?'

Jasmine chewed her lip as he waited earnestly for her reply, his huge blue eyes fixed on her under long black lashes.

'I am kind of busy in the workshop at the moment. Summer is when most of the craft fairs and fêtes are.'

'We're really stuck, Jas. How about I call one Saturday and help you out in the workshop to make up for it?'

'*Spencer Johns*, I saw what sort of stuff you produced in art at school. There is no way I'm letting you loose in my workshop. I'd trust Dylan first, and that's saying something!'

Spencer laughed. 'How is Dylan these days?'

'The same old Dylan.'

Spencer's smile seemed a little sad to Jasmine. It pained her to see that things lurking in their past might still be fresh in his mind. 'I hardly see him lately,' he mused. 'I suppose he's got more interesting friends to spend time with.'

'Hmm, there was a time when he idolised you. Remember when he used to follow you all over the village showing you his Top Trumps cards?'

Spencer laughed. 'I do. I suppose it was the older kid thing, not because I was remotely cool. Funny how the tables turn, though, isn't it?'

'What do you mean?'

'Well, now I'm never able to get an audience with *His Grand Coolness*, and he obviously thinks I'm a huge nerd for going into primary school teaching.'

'Why don't you ask Dylan to help on the trip? He's hardly got anything else to do.'

'Dylan? I'd have to stuff cotton wool into the ears of all the kids.'

'I'm sure he could behave for an hour or so. Go on, why don't you ask him? He was saying only yesterday how he wanted to turn over a new leaf and become an upstanding member of the community or something. Please ask him. For me? I hate to see you two still at odds.'

A shadow crossed Spencer's features. The banter had gone, and he was tense, brooding. The hairs on Jasmine's neck prickled and she couldn't quite say why, but the sight of him like that worried her.

'I really don't think he'd want to help me out,' Spencer insisted.

'What is it with you two? You've been back in Honeybourne for a year and you still can't just move on? Has something else happened? Has he said anything, because if he has—'

Spencer held his hand up to stop her. 'Nothing happened. I guess he's got his other friends now and I'm not really the sort of person he wants to hang out with anymore.'

'I had hoped we could put all that stuff behind us,' Jasmine said.

'I think we have. It's just that things can't be the same as they were. You understand that, surely?'

'But *we're* ok, right?' Jasmine asked uncertainly. 'I mean, I know we haven't really talked about it much since you got back but…'

'Of course we are.'

Jasmine held him in a measured gaze. He'd left Honeybourne, travelled the world and trained to be a teacher before he'd finally returned. That was enough time to sort his head out, wasn't it? But sometimes she had a nagging feeling that he was still hiding an awful lot of pain.

'So, what do you think about next week?' Spencer pressed, appearing to rally himself to brightness again.

'Next week?'

'The trip…'

'Oh, Spencer—'

'Please, Jas. It'll be a laugh for me if you come, and the kids love you, and you'll be doing me such a massive favour.'

Jasmine let out a huge sigh. 'Alright then.'

'Thanks so much, you're a star.' Spencer made a move to hug her, and then seemed to check himself as he glanced at the windows of the school building. Instead, he gave her an awkward smile.

'Sucker is more like,' Jasmine smiled back.

'You said it.' He started towards the building; the caretaker was waiting for him to come in so he could lock the main door.

'Oh…' Spencer spun around and called to Jasmine as she turned to leave. 'If Rich can come and help out, even better.'

'You know how to push it, don't you?' Jasmine shouted in return.

Spencer simply grinned as he disappeared into the building.

Jasmine wasn't really sure why she had felt the need to take the detour that led her past the old bakery as she walked home from school, but she was suddenly gripped by an urge to see if Millie was ok. When she got to the open door, she could hear voices. She peered in to see Millie vigorously scrubbing at the counter with a cloth, her jaw clenched and teeth gritted. She was clearly out of breath and struggling to be civil; Ruth Evans was sitting on the bench in the bay window, watching Millie work and sipping tea, looking for all the world as though she was at an afternoon luncheon at the WI.

'So I told the doctor,' Ruth was saying, 'I told him that if there was any more vaginal discharge, I would be suing him for medical negligence. I mean, that sort of thing can ruin your life. Not to mention how much laundry it makes…'

Jasmine popped her head in. Millie stopped mid-scrub and looked up.

'Not interrupting anything, am I?' Jasmine asked, with a wry smile at Millie and a barely perceptible nod of the head in Ruth's direction.

'Not at all!' Millie squeaked with such eagerness that Jasmine wondered whether she would leap over the counter and kiss her. 'The more the merrier! Tea?' she added in a voice that was definitely laced with more than a touch of hysteria.

'I'd love a quick one,' Jasmine said.

'Oh Ruth, you know that I don't have electricity yet. Would you be an angel and get Jasmine a tea from your house?'

'Oh hello, Jasmine,' Ruth said as she gripped the windowsill and pushed herself up on her arthritic legs. 'Did that water infection clear up?'

'I didn't have a water infection.'

'Didn't you? I could have sworn it was you.'

'Not me.' Jasmine shook her head.

'Oh…' Ruth looked thoughtful for a moment. 'How's your mum?' she finally asked brightly.

'Ruth...' Jasmine said gently, 'Mum and Dad died, remember? It was quite a while ago too.'

'Oh gracious, so they did. Lovely woman, your mother. Always had time for a chat.' She looked at Jasmine, her frown suddenly clearing. 'Tea?'

'Tea would be fabulous, Ruth.'

Ruth shuffled out past Jasmine with an amiable smile.

'Oh dear God, thank you for rescuing me,' Millie said as soon as Ruth was out of earshot.

'Not at all. I've heard every one of those stories enough times to write them verbatim. You develop an uncanny knack of letting them wash over you after a while. And you learn how to handle her. You'll get there one day.'

'I hope that day comes quickly,' Millie frowned. 'Because I'm in serious pain here.'

'She means well.'

'She's perfectly lovely,' Millie agreed. 'It's just that I'm not so keen to hear about her vaginal discharge.'

'Yes,' Jasmine agreed, 'perhaps she ought to know you for a whole week before she shares that sort of intimate detail.'

Both women giggled. Jasmine took Ruth's seat in the window. 'How's it going here?'

'Cleaning is about all I can do right now,' Millie said, dropping her cloth into the bucket and wiping a hand across her brow. 'There's lots of repair work to be done, but first I need to get rid of the dirt so that I can actually see what needs repairing.'

Jasmine gave the place a sweeping glance with raised eyebrows. 'You want to be careful, the dirt might be the only thing holding the place together.'

'I know,' Millie smiled.

'Please don't be offended,' Jasmine began slowly, 'but I've been thinking about your situation. Are you planning to run this place entirely alone?'

'Yes, why not?' Millie replied somewhat defensively. 'I have run a business before.'

'It's not that,' Jasmine elaborated, 'it's just that it's a big place and it seems there's an awful lot of building for you to be covering alone every day. When you're baking, for example, who's going to be in the shop?'

'I'll bake everything in the morning before I open.'

Jasmine blew out a thoughtful breath. 'That sounds like a long day,' she observed.

'Long days are just what I need at the moment,' Millie replied briskly, hauling the bucket of dirty water off the counter. She made her way to the street outside and sloshed the contents down the storm drain before returning and plonking the bucket back down.

'Ignore me,' Jasmine said, sensing the tension in the air. 'I should learn to mind my own business.'

Millie leaned on the counter and her expression softened. 'I'm sorry. Ignore *me*, I know you meant well. It's just that I seem to be getting reminders from a lot of people these last couple of days that I haven't thought this venture through very well.'

'Oh?'

'Your brother asked me about the building work yesterday. Call me stupid, but I sort of assumed that a lick of paint and some nice gingham bunting at the window would make the place good as new.' She glanced up at the dusty beams. 'I might be a bit wide of the mark there.'

Jasmine gave her a sympathetic smile. 'I wouldn't listen too much to Dylan. He's hardly an expert. Maybe it's not as bad as you fear?'

Millie shook her head. 'I'm afraid he might be right.'

'That'll be a first.'

Ruth Evans returned with a tray. On it were three delicate bone china cups, filled with strong tea, and a pot of sugar. Millie and Jasmine shared a conspiratorial smile.

'Staying for a while?' Jasmine asked as Ruth tottered over to the counter and set the tray down.

'Ooh, thank you, don't mind if I do,' Ruth replied as she took her cup and sat herself down next to Jasmine, who raised her eyebrows slightly at Millie.

Millie took a cup and handed it to Jasmine. 'It seems a bit hot to be drinking tea in a stuffy old bakery,' she said. 'We ought to be in a lovely pub somewhere with ice-cold drinks.'

'Tea cools you down,' Ruth said serenely. She took a sip of hers and made a smacking sound with her lips.

'Hmm,' Jasmine replied noncommittally. 'So…' She turned to Millie. 'Do you have a schedule to work to for the bakery?'

'You mean to get up and running?'

Jasmine nodded.

'I had one.' Millie sighed. 'But I think that's gone out of the window. I had no idea of how much work I'd need to do before I could open.' She peered over the rim of her cup at Jasmine. 'I suppose you think that's a bit idiotic?'

'It's your first business venture?'

'This big, yes. I made occasion cakes to order from home before, just me and my little bitty oven. Nothing on this scale.'

'Then you can't be expected to make the right decision every time,' Jasmine said. 'I've made enough cocks-ups since I started the craft business. It's a wonder I didn't go bankrupt in the first couple of months. Things are just getting on an even keel now and I'm only just starting to feel confident in my business decisions.'

'You have a craft business?' Ruth put in.

Millie and Jasmine turned to her in some surprise, as though they had forgotten she was there.

'I've been doing it for years,' Jasmine smiled. 'I thought you knew.'

'I thought you were a barmaid at the Dog and Hare,' Ruth said with a confused frown.

'That was before I got married.'

'Well,' Ruth mumbled, 'I don't go in there, do I?'

Jasmine smiled patiently at her. 'This is a lovely cup of tea, Ruth.'

'Yes, that's another one I owe you,' Millie put in.

'Oh, don't worry, dearie, I don't mind at all.'

Jasmine drained her cup and placed it carefully back on the tray. 'I really should be getting some work done, otherwise I *won't* have a craft business.'

'Thanks for calling,' Millie smiled.

Jasmine turned to go but then stopped at the door. 'Tell me to mind my own business, but if you need to chat about anything business related – not that I'm any expert, of course – I'd be happy to. Why don't you call one day this week while the kids are at school?'

Millie paused, but then smiled slowly. 'That sounds nice, I might just do that.'

'Great, let me know.'

'I'd better get cracking too…' Millie said, eyeing a pile of boxes stacked in a dusty corner. 'Erm, Ruth…'

'Oh, don't mind me,' Ruth said cheerfully. 'You get on and I'll sit quiet as a mouse and drink my tea here in this corner.'

Millie gave a helpless glance in Jasmine's direction, who simply left them with a huge grin.

'Your dad is here!' Jasmine scooped up wax crayons and shreds of paper from the dining table. 'Let's hope he's got good news, eh?'

'I've had all my things crossed all day,' Reuben said. Rebecca and Rachel nodded solemnly in agreement.

Jasmine looked up to see Rich in the kitchen doorway.

'How did it go?' she asked. They had agreed that whatever happened, Rich wouldn't tell her on the phone, but wait until he got home so they could discuss it face to face. All day she had kept herself busy and promised herself that she would stay calm when he arrived home. But this job was a huge opportunity for him – for them all – and she was finding it hard to contain herself.

He gave a huge sigh. 'Well,' he began, 'I might need some help drinking this…' He produced a bottle from behind his back.

Jasmine flew across the room and flung her arms around his neck. 'Is that champagne?' she squealed.

'I know it's not good for bodies that are temples and all that, but we could let loose tonight to celebrate?'

'Oh sod the detox!' She kissed him. 'You clever boy!'

'I like to think so,' he grinned.

The curtains billowed in the gentle breeze that whispered through the open bedroom window. Jasmine lay naked across Rich's damp chest, her legs tangled with his.

'I think you've been practising,' he said with a lazy grin. He stroked her hair back from her face and kissed her gently.

'You're not the only one who can be clever,' Jasmine murmured back.

'Gorgeous, funny, sexy as hell… What did I ever do to deserve you? I must have been very good in a previous life. In fact, I must have been a monk or something.'

Jasmine giggled. 'I have no idea, but keep talking. I'm enjoying the compliments too much for you to stop now.'

'Hmm, maybe I *should* stop; you'll be getting ideas that you can do better than me.'

'Never.' She kissed his chest. 'Besides, I'm not going to throw all those years of living with a pauper away just as he's about to get stinking filthy rich.'

'I wouldn't say rich, exactly. It's only one film score.'

'But there will be more, once people hear how amazing you are.'

'You think?'

'Of course I do. And then you'll be loaded.'

'Oh, I see, you only want me for my non-existent money now.'

'Hopefully, it won't be non-existent for much longer.' Jasmine was silent for a moment as Rich traced a gentle finger back and forth across her shoulder. 'Just imagine…' she began slowly, 'actually having some spare cash. I know we have this house and our businesses and stuff, and we're a lot better off than some, but to have that little bit spare to be more spontaneous in life…' She sighed softly. 'Wouldn't it be lovely?'

Rich laughed and began to sing. '*All I want is a room somewhere, far away from the cold night air, with one enormous chair…*'

'Ha ha.' Jasmine nudged him playfully. 'You're *soo* funny.'

Chapter Four

An hour after Dylan's builder friend had left the old bakery, having muttered and tutted his way around the building and then handed Millie a sheet of paper with very large numbers written on it, Millie sat in Dylan's kitchen with a beer. Usually, she wasn't one for beer, and certainly not in the kitchen of a man she was trying desperately not to be attracted to, but the day had been particularly stressful. Drunkenness and dangerously attractive men were the least of her worries. Dylan's kitchen was spotless – an equally rare occurrence for him – but he seemed to be under the illusion that his day was about to get a whole lot luckier. The fact that he had also cleaned his bedroom and changed the sheets corroborated this.

'What are you going to do?' Dylan asked as he cracked open his own beer.

Millie sighed. 'I have no idea. But I certainly can't raise that sort of cash any time soon. And every week the bakery stays closed and I can't earn eats into the small amount of start-up cash I do have. At this rate I'll have a spanking new building but no money to buy even the tiniest bag of flour to bake anything.'

'You can't get a loan or anything?'

'I don't think so. I've already borrowed quite a lot of money for other expenses around the move and I don't want to overstretch myself with no real income coming in just yet.'

Dylan took a gulp of his beer and looked at her thoughtfully. 'It's a tough one. I know how hard it was for Jas to find the start-up money for her business. It was only Mum and Dad… you know…' His sentence trailed off.

'I know,' Millie said gently. 'Of course, you'd both rather have your parents back than anything else in the world – anyone would. But I don't have an inheritance of any description on the horizon. I can't imagine where I could get that sort of cash from right now.'

'How about raising it by doing what you do best?'

Millie frowned.

'I mean,' Dylan explained, 'start selling your wares and turning over a bit of a profit to make the money you need.'

'How am I supposed to do that with no working bakery?'

'Bake here.'

Millie stared at him, her can halfway to her lips. '*Here?*'

'Why not?'

She took a sweeping glance of the tiny kitchen. It was a ridiculous idea but she was touched by the gesture. 'It's very kind of you, but your oven is far too small. I'd only be able to make little batches and it would hardly cover the cost of your gas, let alone turn a profit. No, I need to get the bakery running so I can bake in the quantities that will make me proper money.'

'Do you know what those quantities are?'

Millie tried not to be annoyed by the obvious practicality of his question. 'I know it's going to take more than a dozen fairy cakes.'

'I just mean,' Dylan pressed, seemingly oblivious to her irritation, 'have you actually sat down and worked out concrete figures?'

'Sort of…'

'Jasmine can help you there if you need it.'

'I know, she's offered already. But I know she's busy right now and I don't want to bother her with that.'

'If I know Jas, she'll love getting stuck in. She'll help anyone if she can.'

Millie shook her head. 'I can't ask her. She has her family and her own business to worry about.'

'Then let me help. You can't do everything on your own.'

Millie held him in a frank gaze. 'Why?'

'Why what?'

'Why would you help me? You hardly know me.'

He shrugged, a lopsided grin creeping across his face. 'I suppose I'm just that kind of guy.'

Millie took a thoughtful sip of her beer as she watched him take another gulp of his own.

'I just don't know what you can do,' she said finally. 'I don't even know myself what to do next.' She could feel tears burning her eyes. The bright new start she had dreamed of was crumbling around her. She swallowed the emotion back but not before Dylan was off his seat and on the chair next to her. He slipped an arm around her and she stiffened. Despite this, he pulled her closer. He smelt good – a clean, woody fragrance – and for a moment she could think of nothing but the image of them kissing.

'Everything can be fixed,' he said gently. 'My old dad used to say that there was no point in worrying about anything; as long as you hadn't killed someone, everything else in life could be mended.'

In an instant, her emotional defences shot up. Dylan was dangerous, no matter how attractive he was; he could easily screw her up – she had seen it in him the first time they met, and she had to remember that. She was letting him get too close right now.

'I think I would have liked your dad,' she said, trying to lighten a mood that was becoming far too charged for her liking.

'He was pretty cool.' Dylan stroked his thumb back and forth across her shoulder. Millie closed her eyes. God, it felt so good...

She shot up from her chair. 'I have to go. So much to do.'

Dylan looked up at her, a mix of surprise and mild annoyance in his expression.

'Right now? You haven't finished your beer.'

'You drink it. I need a clear head.'

She thrust it at him and then bolted for the door.

There was a knock at the front door of the old bakery almost before Millie had closed it behind her. *Oh God, please don't let Dylan have followed me across...*

She stood and stared at it, holding her breath. Maybe if she didn't answer he would go away.

'Are you in there, Millie?'

Millie let out her breath as she recognised Ruth Evans's phlegmy voice. With a rueful half-smile, she opened the door. Now that she thought about how she had reacted to Dylan's friendly concern, she felt a bit idiotic. She had to learn to stop letting the past haunt her.

'Hello, Ruth.' Millie forced a brighter smile for her neighbour. 'What can I do for you?'

'I saw you come across from Dylan's house,' Ruth said, eyeing Millie keenly.

'His builder friend had just been round to give me a quote. We were discussing it.'

'He doesn't have a girlfriend you know. No betrothed...' Ruth elaborated. 'So he's perfectly available.' She let out a wistful sigh. 'If only I were a few years younger... I'd love to get a good rogering from that one. I hear he's quite energetic.'

Millie's mouth fell open as she stared at Ruth.

'Aren't you going to invite me in?' Ruth continued, as though her wishful musings were nothing out of the ordinary at all.

'I do have rather a lot of work to get on with,' Millie replied, still staring at Ruth.

'I won't get in your way,' Ruth said briskly as she sidled past Millie, who watched as the old woman took the window seat and folded her hands across her lap. 'You can tell me all about it easily enough while you get on with your chores. I'll just sit here.'

Ruth Evans had proved as easy to get rid of as a rampant colony of nits. No matter how many hints Millie dropped, or how busy she made herself look, Ruth simply sat with her hands folded in her lap, firing question after question at her. Thankfully she didn't wait for replies, but instead used the gap before Millie's guarded responses to launch into convoluted anecdotes of her own. Eventually Millie stopped trying to reply and carried on with her work, Ruth's chattering slowly morphing into a featureless background drone. Occasionally she made a small noise of agreement, or looked up and smiled absently at her elderly neighbour, but mostly her thoughts were pulled to a place she really didn't want them to be. Two places, to be precise:

Dylan, and the old bakery, otherwise known as the millstone round her neck.

Where on earth was she going to find the money she needed to get this business off the ground? Dylan had offered help, as no doubt others would, but although there was a part of her that was desperate to accept it, the stubborn part of her wanted to owe favours to no one. This was her venture, and hers alone to succeed or fail in. Bitter experience had shown that letting people get too close led only to heartache.

'So I told him...' Ruth stopped mid-sentence.

Suddenly aware of silence filling the room, Millie looked up sharply.

'Are you alright, dear?' Ruth asked.

Millie shook herself. Lost in her tumultuous thoughts, she hadn't realised that she had stopped working and was staring out of the window. She hadn't even noticed her eyes glazing over with unshed tears.

'I'm fine, Ruth.' She forced a smile. 'Do you know what, I'm dying of thirst. I don't suppose...'

Ruth pushed herself slowly to a shaky standing position. 'Why didn't you say so? I'll go and make us a nice cup of tea. Back in a tick.'

As Ruth left, Millie sank to the floor and held her head in her hands.

Chapter Five

'It's brilliant news, sis. I just hope you and Rich don't forget your little brother when you're living the high life on his blockbuster film earnings.' Dylan was lounging on a mess of huge floor cushions on the bone-dry lawn of Jasmine's back garden. The heatwave had continued all through the previous week and this evening was still sultry despite the lateness of the hour, the air heady with the scent of Jasmine's namesake flowers crowding a trellis at the back door. Dylan took a sip of his beer.

Jasmine smiled at him, sitting on a pile of cushions herself and hugging her knees to her chest, a mass of curls tumbling around her bare shoulders. 'I won't hold my breath for the huge earnings. And I can't imagine anyone could forget you, least of all me and Rich.'

'I'll take that as a compliment. You'd be hard pressed to find a better brother, to be fair.'

'And so modest too…'

'Naturally.'

There was a pause. And then the thing that was on Jasmine's mind tumbled out. 'Do you see much of Spencer since he came back?'

'Not this again. Yeah, I see him all the time.'

'Not just around. Do you actually stop and talk to him?'

'I'm not sure that's a good idea.'

She shrugged. 'Just that you used to be so close and now…'

'Now what? He's busy all the time with his career anyway. He's Mr Workaholic and all he talks about is school.'

'That's not true. And how would you know if you've barely spent any time with him?'

'I've seen him in the pub.'

'Aha!' Jasmine gave a little cry of triumph. 'So he doesn't spend all his time marking books and thinking about school if he's in the pub!'

Dylan gave a quick grin, but it faded almost as soon as it had begun. 'We've both changed,' he said.

'It feels like more than that.'

Dylan raised his eyebrows in disbelief.

'Ok, the fight, I know. But surely you're grown up enough to get past that. You were so close once, and you said yourself it was a hot-headed mistake, and Spencer has never breathed a word to me since he got back about… Well, you know. Can't we all just move on?'

'We have.'

'So you say.'

'Can we drop this now? Spencer has moved on and so have I. There's no animosity now, but don't expect us to be best mates anymore.'

'Not even for me?'

'Why the sudden interest in Spencer?' Dylan returned sharply. 'What's he said to you?'

Jasmine stared at him. 'Nothing. Really. I just get the impression that he misses you.'

'You're kidding! He doesn't care one way or another and I don't blame him.'

'I think he does. I think he's lonely since he came back to the village and he could do with a friend.'

'He's got tons of friends. Everyone here loves him.'

'It's not the same as having a proper friend.'

Dylan tipped his head back and stared into the sky. 'Right,' he sighed, 'well, if it means that much to you when I next see him around I'll buy him a drink or something. Would that make you happy?'

Jasmine couldn't decide if he was being sarcastic or not. 'It would make me happy,' she replied.

'Good. I know you think love makes the world go round and we all need to live in peace and harmony or some such crap, so I'll do my best.'

'Ok,' she said. 'That's all I'm asking for.'

Rich strolled from the house and out onto the lawn with a glass of beer. 'Took me ages to get the kids to go down. They weren't very impressed that they had to go to bed while Dylan was still here.' He flopped next to Jasmine and kissed her on the forehead.

'See,' Dylan grinned, back to his usual self. 'What's the point of false modesty when everybody loves me?'

'Dylan was just telling me that we mustn't forget him when you're rich and famous,' Jasmine said, leaning her head against Rich's shoulder.

'I'm sure we can throw him a crust of bread from our golden chariot as we drive past. If he's really good we'll ask the driver not to splash him with mud like we do the other peasants,' Rich replied.

Jasmine giggled. She reached for the glass of orange juice on the ground beside her.

'So, what's been going on in the world of Dylan?' Rich asked. 'Now the kids are in bed, you can give us the full adult version.'

'Rich!' Jasmine elbowed him. 'I don't want to hear those sorts of details about my brother!'

Dylan laughed. 'I have no idea what you're both talking about. I've been perfectly hermit-like in my little house – reading, cooking, cleaning, like a good Christian boy.'

'So you've not attempted to charm your way into the affections of a certain new owner of the old bakery?' Rich asked over the top of his glass.

'There's not much that stays secret around here, is there? She seems to have other things on her mind right now, though,' Dylan said.

'You mean she doesn't fancy you?' Rich asked. 'Oh my God, we've fallen into some parallel universe where women don't drop their knickers at the mere mention of Dylan Smith's name!'

'Unbelievable, isn't it?' Dylan grinned. 'But,' he continued, his expression more serious, 'I think she's in way over her head taking on that old wreck of a building… and I think she's realised it too.'

'You don't think she can fix it?' Jasmine asked, frowning. 'But she seems so confident whenever I see her.'

'I know. But my mate Bony had a look and he reckons there's some serious structural work to be done on the place. I don't think Millie bargained for that. She told me she didn't even have a survey done – sold her old place, paid cash for this and packed her car up without a second thought.'

'Ruddy hell.' Rich took a gulp of his beer. 'That woman has a set of balls bigger than mine.'

'And that's saying something,' Dylan laughed.

'She must be regretting that now though,' Jasmine mused.

Dylan nodded. 'I think so.'

'But it can be done? The building's not beyond repair?' Jasmine asked.

'No, but beyond her budget.'

'Poor thing…' Jasmine tugged a hand through her curls.

'Poor thing?' Rich scoffed. 'She should have got a survey done. All her problems could have been avoided for the sake of a few hundred quid.'

'Don't be mean,' Jasmine chided. 'You've never made a silly mistake in your life?'

'I didn't mean that—'

'Well what then?'

'It's a pretty big thing, buying a building, especially one you plan to live in and earn your living from. You'd think a survey would be the first thing to do.'

Jasmine gazed quietly across the lawn for a moment. 'I'm going to see her tomorrow,' she finally announced. 'She's part of our community now, and if we can help we should.' She narrowed her eyes at her husband. 'No matter how silly you think she is.'

'You can try,' Dylan cut in, 'but she doesn't seem very keen to accept help. I already told her that we'd do what we could, and she pretty much refused point-blank.'

'She won't think *I've* got an ulterior motive though, will she?' Jasmine smiled wryly.

'I don't know what you mean,' Dylan replied with mock innocence.

'Did you wash your hair?'

'Yes…'

'That's all anyone needs to know.'

Rich interrupted their verbal sparring. 'I still don't see what we can do for her though.'

'In this village, there must be loads of people with different skills who can lend a hand. We just need to ask around, barter with them, see what we can get done for her for free or at a reduced price.'

Rich grinned. 'A bit like one of those TV shows where the whole community fixes a playground for the kids out of bits of old rubbish.'

Jasmine laughed. 'Sort of.'

Rich pulled her close and kissed the top of her head. 'That is a very good idea. I married such a clever little girl, didn't I?'

As Jasmine turned the corner, making her way to the old bakery on a meltingly hot Saturday morning, she was distracted by the sound of raucous laughter coming from Dylan's garden. Changing her route, she peered over the hedge to find Dylan and Spencer sitting on the front step.

'Hey,' Jasmine called. She pushed open the gate and strolled towards them. 'Something sounds funny.'

'Jasmine!' Spencer leapt up to fling his arms around her and kiss her on the cheek. But he pulled away quickly, and Jasmine caught a frown on her brother's face. It was so fleeting that Jasmine wondered whether she'd seen it at all.

'We're just catching up,' Dylan said, shading his eyes as he squinted up at his sister from the step.

'We've got a lot to catch up on, too,' Spencer cut in. 'I was just passing, to be honest, when Dylan shouted me over. I was only going to stay ten minutes – that was about an hour ago.'

'Have you come for anything in particular or is it just a social visit?' Dylan asked Jasmine.

'Actually, I was on my way to the bakery to see Millie.'

'Charming. So your little brother was second best?'

'I thought you'd still be snoring at this time of the morning.'

'What do you take me for, some sort of layabout?'

'Yes.'

Spencer grinned at her. 'I must admit, I did have to check my watch twice when I came past and saw he was in the garden.'

'Oi!' Dylan pouted at Spencer. 'I thought we were mates!'

'We are. Which is why I know that something is wrong with the world if you're up before midday.'

'If you must know, I thought I would go across this morning and see if she needs any help with anything,' Dylan said.

'She must be hot then, to get you out of bed this early… Or were you hoping to get back in and take her with you?' Spencer fired back with a mischievous glint in his eye.

'Why does everyone think I only have one thing on my mind?'

'Because you do,' Spencer said. 'Don't think your sensitive act fools anyone.'

Jasmine laughed. 'Have you met Millie yet?' she asked Spencer.

'I was thinking I'd put my head in at some point, but I don't want to seem too nosey or crowd her out. I know how stifling the community here can be, especially if you're new to village life and not used to it.'

'I don't think it's stopped anyone else,' Jasmine replied. 'Ruth Evans has moved in to the bay window seat.'

'That's exactly what I mean,' Spencer laughed.

'It hasn't stopped Dylan making a regular appearance over there either.'

'I'm just trying to be neighbourly,' Dylan said. 'Anyway, you were the one who suggested we get everyone involved in the renovations.'

'I need to talk to Millie first, though, before I invite the whole village into her home.'

'If you're going over now, why don't I come with you and introduce Spencer?' Dylan suggested.

'And why do I need you for that?' Jasmine raised a questioning eyebrow. 'I'm perfectly capable of taking Spencer myself if he wants to go.'

Dylan grinned. 'Yeah, but if I go across with weedy Spencer, I'll look all butch and then she'll definitely fancy me.'

Spencer grinned. 'I'll have you know that I'm all lean muscle and built for speed under this puny-looking exterior.'

Dylan stood up and clapped him on the shoulder. 'I believe you, mate, though thousands wouldn't.'

'I've seen him in the three-legged race on sports day,' Jasmine cut in. 'It's like watching a cheetah in action.'

Over the top of Dylan's hedge, Jasmine saw the door to the bakery opening and Millie emerging with a rubbish bag. She set it against the side of the building and wiped a hand across her brow.

'Looks like a good time to catch her if we're going to,' Jasmine observed.

'Come on.' Dylan rubbed his hands together like a panto villain. 'Time to meet the neighbours…'

Spencer raised his eyebrows at Jasmine as she let out a huge sigh. Dylan bounded down the path and they followed him out of the gate as he jogged across the road.

'Morning!' he called.

Millie looked up with a small smile, which spread as she noticed Jasmine behind him. 'To what do I owe the pleasure?' Millie asked as they arrived at the door of the bakery.

'Lots of things,' Jasmine said brightly. 'Most important of all, though, we wanted to introduce a dear friend, Spencer Johns.'

Spencer smiled shyly and put his hand up in greeting. Millie took the briefest moment to appraise him. He was slim, but strong looking, with thick, black hair that seemed to defy any attempt to style it and bright blue eyes. His intelligent features crinkled into a smile that betrayed a dimple in each cheek. Where Dylan was all rugged outdoor sexuality, Spencer looked as though he might read poetry and discuss the meaning of life with you. Millie decided quickly that she liked him.

'You're taking on the old place?' he asked with a nod at the building. 'I had heard. It's about time someone was brave enough to put the soul back into the bakery. It used to be a wonderful asset to the village.'

'I don't know about brave,' Millie said, glancing back at her ramshackle home. 'Stupid seems a lot more like it.'

'That's the other thing we wanted to talk to you about,' Jasmine said. 'How do you feel about coming for lunch? A sort of business-meeting lunch? We've got some ideas to put to you.'

Millie scratched her head through the floral headscarf she had tied over her hair. 'I'd love to, but I have so much to do here...' She glanced uncertainly at each of them in turn.

'I've got time on my hands,' Dylan replied cheerfully. 'I can help you this morning, and then you'll be able to come.'

'It's kind of you, but I couldn't...' Millie looked at Spencer hopefully as her sentence trailed to nothing, but he simply shoved his hands in his pockets with an amiable smile. Perhaps it wouldn't be so bad having Dylan around to help, but she didn't think she could cope with him alone. Somehow, Spencer seemed a lot less threatening. She wondered whether he would offer his services too.

'Ordinarily I'd love to help, but I have a thousand details to plan for a school trip next week,' Spencer said, seeming to guess her thoughts.

'Spencer is also known as *Mr Johns*,' Jasmine said. 'He teaches at the school, and more specifically, he teaches my triplets.'

'We're going to Stonehenge with the children, so I have loads of research to do about the place before we get there.' Spencer ran a hand through his hair. 'Kids are full of questions and I'm determined that they won't catch me out with something I don't know the answer to. It hasn't happened yet, but it probably will.'

'Stonehenge is a wonderful place, full of magic,' Millie said earnestly, forgetting herself for a moment. 'I mean, if you believe in magic,' she added, blushing slightly.

'I happen to think so too,' Spencer said. 'I don't necessarily know a lot about it but I think that anything so spiritually important to the people who built it has its own kind of magic, y'know?'

Millie beamed at him. It was as though a light switch had gone on inside her. This was safe ground. Surveys and building work and bookkeeping were a mystery to her, but the things under the surface of the world that others didn't see, these were the things that felt like old friends. 'I haven't been to Stonehenge in years,' she said warmly.

'Spencer needs help on the trip,' Jasmine cut in. 'You said so, didn't you, Spence?'

'The more the merrier as far as I'm concerned,' he replied. 'We always need all the help we can get.'

'I don't know…' Millie began. 'I have a lot to do myself.'

'I'm going,' Jasmine said. 'And it would do you good not to think about the bakery for a few hours.'

'Why don't I strike you a deal?' Spencer offered. 'What if I pop back when I'm done planning, to help you clear out, and then you come with us next week? I can't promise I'll be *strong like lion*,' he said, putting on a fake macho voice, 'like my mate Dylan here, but I can scrub a floor with the best of them.'

'Or, how about you stay and help now,' Jasmine cut in, 'and I'll print you some stuff off about Stonehenge at home and bring it to the pub for you? I'm at home knocking about with the kids anyway and Rich will be locked away in the study working his musical magic. I might as well be doing something useful.'

'That is tempting...' Spencer smiled. 'Honestly, Jas, where were you when I was at uni? I could have done with someone researching for me then.'

Jasmine laughed. 'I'll bet you could.'

'Sounds like a plan to me,' Dylan agreed.

'And if the boys are helping you today, Millie, that means you can join us on the trip to Stonehenge,' Jasmine continued.

Mille paused for a moment before letting out a sigh. 'I suppose I can't refuse an offer like that.' She frowned. 'Won't I have to have police checks and things if I'm out with the children on your trip?'

'As you're not alone with them there's no need for all that. We just need your address and date of birth and we'll be good to go.'

'Maybe *I* should come to Stonehenge...' Dylan said thoughtfully.

'*You'd* need police checks,' Jasmine shot back. 'And they'd all come back with a great big red *no way* stamped on them.'

Dylan's face split into a huge grin. 'The kids would come back from the trip way cooler than they went.'

'That's what I'm afraid of,' Jasmine said with a sideways glance at her brother.

* * *

Three hours later and the ground floor of the old bakery was a lot clearer than it had been when Millie arrived. She could see the actual stone flags of the floors, and upstairs, although her bedroom was still a luxury spider retreat, at least she had progressed from mattress on floorboards to the outrageous decadence of an assembled bed, complete with legs and headboard. Not only that, but she also had a flat-pack wardrobe that was no longer flat; if only, she mused, she could find the boxes that contained the majority of her clothes and shoes to fill it. So far, the few clothes she had stuffed into a small suitcase had been enough to tide her over.

Having Dylan and Spencer over had also meant that she didn't have to listen to Ruth Evans prattling on when the old lady called just after eleven. Dylan had charmed the old woman into submission, and she had fallen into silent and awestruck contemplation of his perfect form as he moved debris and boxes and fixed bits of furniture together, whistling and shouting instructions to the less capable Spencer. Despite his practical shortcomings, Spencer was a welcome addition to the crowd that filled the old bakery that morning, for what he lacked in practical skills, he more than made up for in intelligent conversation. Millie could have listened to him talk about books he had read and films he had watched all day. Spencer was the bridge between the three. While he was there, Millie felt safe having Dylan around, like Spencer was a filter who neutralised all the sexual angst that invaded her thoughts when her neighbour was near. And Spencer was attractive, in his own way, but it was something altogether less frightening. He didn't stare at her in the hungry way that most men did.

'So, Spencer,' Millie began as they stopped to down the cups of tea Ruth had carefully brought over on a tray. 'You haven't told me about yourself.'

Spencer shrugged. 'There's not much to tell. I'm a teacher by day and a boring git by night.'

'There must be more than that,' Millie laughed. 'What do you do to relax? You must have hobbies. Is there a Mrs Johns?'

Dylan looked up sharply, but neither Millie nor Spencer seemed to notice.

'No Mrs Johns. No prospective Mrs Johns. And before you ask, no *Mr* Johns either.'

'Not still pining after Lucy Pryce are you?' Dylan asked. Millie couldn't be sure, but there was something like a note of forced jollity in his voice.

'No,' Spencer replied quietly. 'I don't have time to *pine* after anyone these days.'

'Me neither,' Millie said briskly, suddenly aware of a tension in the room. 'All work and no play makes Millicent Hopkin a very dull girl indeed.'

'Oh, I'm sure you could never be dull,' Dylan said cheerfully.

And then, almost in the same instant, everything was back to normal. Had Millie imagined that sudden chill between Dylan and Spencer? It was as if the moment had never happened.

Spencer looked at his watch. 'We should get cleaned up; Jasmine will be at the pub soon.'

Jasmine and Rich were in the Dog and Hare, both with pint glasses in front of them half filled with bitter. If Millie hadn't thought them to be the happiest, most perfect couple she had ever met, she could have sworn their body language betrayed an interrupted argument. Dylan didn't seem to notice anything, however, and simply berated his sister as he, Spencer and Millie approached their table.

'I thought you were detoxing?'

Jasmine laughed. Whatever words she might have been having with Rich obviously hadn't affected her too much. 'I am. But you can't come to the Dog without having a little taste of its finest, can you? I mean, it would offend Doug.' As if to prove her point, she lifted her glass and took a long draught, placing it back on the table again with a satisfied smack of the lips.

Millie threw her a slightly awestruck look. She had never met a woman who managed to look so pretty and womanly downing a pint of bitter before.

'I'm beginning to think this detox of yours is a myth,' Dylan replied, eyeing her up with a wry smile.

'Me too,' Rich said. 'I bet she's stuffing ice cream morning and night when I'm not there.'

Jasmine gave him a playful slap.

It was the first time Millie had been in the pub. It was just how she imagined a village pub should be: warm wooden panelling lined the room, hung with portraits of local dignitaries from days gone by along with watercolour landscapes; the bar area was shelved – row upon row of pewter and glass tankards sitting alongside various bottled spirits. The sun slanted in through sash windows, dust motes dancing in the beams of light like tiny galaxies. There was a rich, beefy smell, and Millie guessed that some sort of meat and ale pie was on the lunch menu. Her stomach growled as she suddenly realised how hungry she was.

'I'm starving,' Spencer said, voicing Millie's thoughts, 'how about we grab menus before we do anything else?'

'That's the best idea you've had today,' Dylan said.

* * *

With fragrant plates of hearty pub food in front of each of them, Jasmine called for the table's attention.

'Millie,' she began, 'I know that you're going to say no to all of my suggestions. So let's get it straight right now that I am not going to take a blind bit of notice of any refusal you make.'

Rich cocked an eyebrow. 'Trust me, she's not lying, Millie – I've seen it in action.'

Jasmine nudged him. 'Oi!'

'Just saying…'

'He's got a point,' Dylan put in.

'Shut up!' Jasmine scolded. 'I'm trying to chair a serious meeting here.'

'*Chair a meeting*? You've been watching too much *Apprentice.*' Dylan rammed a forkful of chips into his mouth with a grin.

Jasmine sighed and turned to Millie again. 'Me and Rich were talking it over this morning and we made a list of everyone we could think of who might be able to help with the bakery renovations, or anyone who might know someone who could help. And we think a lot of them would be happy to help for reduced rates, maybe even in return for services or pledges of payment later on, when you're on your feet…'

Millie held her hands up to halt the discussion. 'Please, I can't ask people to do all this for me. I'll sort things at the bakery myself. It might take a little longer, but I won't be a charity case.'

'It wouldn't be charity. You'll still pay people, but in different ways.'

Millie took a sip of her juice. 'How?'

'Well,' Jasmine resumed patiently, 'what about this, for instance: we were chatting to Doug the landlord here, earlier, and he said he could do with help in the kitchen at dinnertimes. In return, he knows someone who might be able to restore your windows. You can cook?'

'I can *bake*,' Millie replied. 'But it's not the same as cooking. And I imagine I'd have to make an awful lot of meals to repay a service like that.'

'What about if you make pies and puddings and sell them to him, then you can pay his friend with the money you make?'

'Which brings me back full circle to the original problem – I have nowhere to bake in that sort of quantity.'

Jasmine continued unperturbed. 'There are plenty of people with kitchens who could let you use them.'

Millie thought for a moment. 'I don't want to sound ungrateful, really I don't, but I need a well-equipped, decent-sized kitchen to make anything commercially.'

'We've got a huge kitchen, haven't we, Rich?' Jasmine turned to her husband, who nodded slowly. He stole an uncertain glance at Millie. 'And I'm sure whatever equipment you need you must have in your boxes at the bakery. Could you transfer them to ours for a while? You can use the kitchen during the day when I'm in the workshop and Rich is in his music room.'

'I couldn't impose on you like that. And besides,' Millie added, doubt in her tone, 'I still don't think it's quite the sort of kitchen I need.'

'What about if you use Doug's kitchen? I'm sure he wouldn't mind.'

Millie shook her head. 'Even if we did that it's still a drop in the ocean compared to what I need to get the bakery shipshape.'

Jasmine looked at the others, who were all silently tucking into their meals as they followed the conversation.

'Any ideas from the boys?'

Spencer shrugged. 'We always need help in school, but I can't think of any way that could benefit the bakery.'

Dylan's face suddenly lit up. 'What about a crowdfunding scheme?'

Millie frowned. 'What's crowdfunding?'

'You know, like people do for films and music. You set up an internet account –in our case, we could keep it local – and people pledge money if they think it's worth supporting. You set a target of how much you need. Getting the bakery back would benefit the whole community and this way would be a much more businesslike approach.'

Millie glanced uncertainly at each of them. 'What if people don't want to pledge, or we don't raise enough?'

Jasmine nibbled on a chip. 'You must be able to do things other than bake?'

Millie could do things, things that none of them could do, things she suspected not many would even consider were possible. But they were things that she wouldn't dare share with them – she didn't want the people of Honeybourne to have any reason for mistrust, she'd had quite enough of that back in her old life.

'I suppose…' she began slowly, 'I can make remedies and things. You know, from old, trusted herbal recipes. And soaps and lotions – all natural. People tell me they work. And I would need somewhere to make them, but it wouldn't require enormous ovens.'

Jasmine's eyes widened, another chip held halfway to her mouth. 'You can? But that's brilliant!'

'It is?'

'I've been thinking about expanding the craft business to sell natural toiletries and things. I had thought I would learn how to make them, but never seemed to have the time. We could work together, it would be perfect.'

Rich looked up from his meal. For a moment, it seemed he would offer some argument, but as Jasmine shot him a warning glance, so subtle that only the two of them would understand what it meant, he put his head down again and shoved a forkful of steak into his mouth.

'It would make craft fairs and markets a lot more fun if someone came with me,' Jasmine continued. 'I'm always bored standing there all day on my own, especially if we have a quiet one. You could sell your stuff alongside mine and we each keep what we make. We can split the hire of the stall between us.' She smiled brightly. 'You get to earn towards the bakery renovations, I get some company and halve my overheads in one fell swoop – everyone wins!'

'It still won't earn enough,' Millie insisted.

'Have you seen what people charge for that stuff?' Dylan put in. 'I'm sure you could turn a profit from some old bits of weed found in your garden.'

'I don't think it's as simple as that,' Millie laughed, in spite of herself.

'What about internet sales too?' Jasmine offered. 'I sell my stuff on my own website, but also on eBay, Amazon Marketplace, Etsy – there are loads of outlets.'

Spencer raised his hand. 'Is this as well as the crowdfunding and calling in favours from villagers?'

'I don't see why not,' Jasmine said. 'Every avenue should be explored.'

'Only,' Spencer continued, 'that's an awful lot of balls to juggle for Millie.'

Millie shot him a look somewhere between gratitude and annoyance. While she was grateful for Jasmine's enthusiasm, she couldn't help the foreboding now creeping over her that this venture was going to end badly. Spencer's well-intentioned argument might have seemed misguided, but it could get her out of a potentially sticky situation.

'I think it's perfect,' Dylan offered.

Jasmine beamed at him. 'Of course it is,' she replied airily. 'It was *my* idea, after all…'

Chapter Six

Millie sat on the cool floor of the bakery in the chalk circle she had drawn for herself. It wasn't that she was in danger, but she was feeling vulnerable. As she sat surrounded by candles, their golden light flickering on her anxious features, the circle made her feel safe.

How was it that she had agreed in the end to Jasmine's plans? Jasmine had once said that Dylan was the sibling with the gift of the gab, but now Millie wasn't so sure. Whatever had happened, they had parted company at the doors of the pub, Jasmine a little flushed from her afternoon tipple and in something of a rush as she and Rich realised that the triplets were overdue to be picked up from their playdate at the house of school friends, with promises to start work on their new schemes the following day. Dylan was overseeing the online campaign, while Spencer and Rich would use their connections in the village to see what help they could source, leaving Jasmine and Millie to formulate a business strategy that would enable them to work successfully together. Working with Jasmine was the one aspect of the whole thing that Millie was really looking forward to. Already, ideas for new products were bouncing around her head. The first thing she had done when she got back to the bakery was to search her boxes for the books that contained all the knowledge she would need to make them.

Open in front of her now was one such book. But although she was diligently trying to read the page that explained how to recognise and use various British hedgerow plants in skin ointments, all that filled her mind was the dread of getting too close, of ruining more lives as she had done before. She really liked Jasmine and her family and friends, saw in her someone who could be a confidante and friend for life. But that made the fear greater still; it was an irrational fear, she knew that, and they said that lightning never struck twice, but it was hard to shake when letting people get too close had been so catastrophic before.

Jasmine woke early the next morning. The sun broke in through a gap in the curtains, throwing a slice of yellow light across Rich's sleeping form. The day looked as if it was going to be as hot as the ones that had gone before. There had been drought warnings over the last couple of days, but no one took them seriously – after all, weren't there drought warnings every summer? This time, Jasmine mused as she swung herself out of bed, if they didn't have rain soon, the warnings might not be so empty.

It wasn't until she was sitting at the kitchen table with a cup of green tea that she thought to look at the clock. It had just gone five thirty. She raised her eyebrows, inwardly chiding herself for wasting another precious Sunday lie-in. It was always the same, whenever the excitement of a new adventure gripped her. Because that was what her plans with Millie represented – an adventure – and Jasmine secretly couldn't wait to throw herself into it.

Her pencil tapped against the blank page of a notepad as she mulled over some ideas. She lifted her eyes to the kitchen window to gaze on the bright morning outside. What were the most important considerations of partnering with Millie? How would they organise themselves? Would they get along as business partners? Jasmine doodled on the paper, little balloons of thought that she connected with a scrawling mass of pencil lines. It was the way she thought best, through pictures and form rather than long, dry lists. There would be a list eventually, but for now it was all about inspiration.

Her thoughts were interrupted by Rich shuffling through the kitchen door, rubbing his eyes.

'What's wrong?'

Jasmine shrugged slightly. 'I woke up early and couldn't get back to sleep. Nothing to worry about.' She cast an appraising eye over him as he yawned and dragged a hand through his messy hair. 'You should go back to bed.'

'Nah…' Rich smiled as he dropped into a chair. 'Sleep is for wimps.' He stretched into an exaggerated yawn. 'They say dawn is a good time of day to be inspired.'

'You won't agree with that come three o'clock this afternoon when you're falling asleep at your keyboard.'

'Very likely.' Rich peered at his wife's cup with a frown. 'No coffee on?'

'I just fancied something a bit fresher.'

'I suppose I'll have to make my own pot then.'

'I'm sure you can manage – you are such a clever boy, after all.'

Rich smirked as he got up to fill the kettle. 'So what woke you?' he asked as he ran the tap.

'This and that. Mostly that.'

'*That* being Millie?' Rich raised a questioning eyebrow.

'That obvious?'

'You're forgetting how well I know you, Jasmine Green. I knew you when you were Jasmine Smith and you haven't changed a bit. I know how excitable you get at the merest whiff of a new adventure.'

Jasmine laughed lightly. 'Ok!' She held her hands up. 'You got me!'

'I just…' Rich turned to her and leaned against the sink. His expression became serious and he seemed to be weighing his words carefully. 'I just want you to be careful.'

Jasmine took a sip of her tea and frowned.

'I know you like Millie. But she's only just arrived in Honeybourne and you hardly know her.'

'I know enough.'

'There you go!' Rich rubbed a hand across his stubbled chin. 'I love you for your willingness to see the good in everyone you meet, but…'

'What?'

'It's not important.'

'What?' Jasmine's voice rose, but then she glanced at the doorway and lowered it again. 'You might as well tell me now, because it's obviously bothering you.'

Rich swallowed. 'We don't know anything about the woman. We don't know where she's from, what she did before she moved here – I mean, we don't even really know *why* she moved here—'

'To reopen the bakery, of course.'

'But that's not it, is it? Not really. The fact that this bakery was available at just the right moment might have brought her to this village out of a hundred others like it, but that's not the reason she ran away from her old life.'

'*Ran away*? That's a ridiculous thing to say.'

'I'm sorry, Jas, but everything about her says to me that she's running from something. For a start, who buys a building that they've never even visited without at least getting a survey of some sort? That's someone panicking. Which means she's either done something really bad, or someone is out to get her, or both.'

Jasmine folded her arms tight. 'Wow,' she said coldly, 'your capacity for instant psychological profiling is truly astonishing, *Sherlock*.'

'Scoff all you want,' Rich fired back, his hackles rising now, 'but I know I'm right this time.'

'You know nothing about her.'

'And neither do you, but it hasn't stopped you making judgements.'

'I'm not the one passing judgements!'

'But you have made a snap decision to trust her… with your livelihood, no less.'

Jasmine forced a short laugh. 'It's hardly my livelihood. She's going to sell a few perfumes on a stall with me.'

Rich stared at her for a moment. 'But it won't end there, will it? You'll get the bug and then there'll be no stopping you until she's fully embedded into our lives.'

'*Bug*?'

Rich's tone softened. 'That bit of you – that wonderful, beautiful bit of you – that compels you to help every lost cause, take in every waif and stray, that makes you want to save everyone you think needs it…'

'You knew what you were getting when you asked me to marry you.'

'I'm not saying it's a bad quality. But sometimes you need to step back and really examine the whole picture before you commit to helping someone.'

'Well, I can't do that now. I've already told Millie that we'll help and I can't go back on my word when she so clearly needs friends around her. The poor woman is all alone here.'

'That was her choice.'

'And that means she should suffer?'

'I didn't say that. But she knew what she was doing when she moved to a new village alone.'

'Maybe she didn't. Maybe she didn't quite realise how hard it would be. You've never made a mistake?'

'Not one that stupid, no.'

'Argh! What the hell is wrong with you? It's not like you to be this judgmental!'

'I just don't have time for idiots.'

'You could have said as much over lunch in the pub. It would have saved me this argument now.'

'That would have been a great idea. You'd have loved me questioning Millie in front of everyone. Don't be so ridiculous. How could I have said anything there? You never give anyone a chance to express an opinion anyway.'

'You were fine about helping Millie when we talked about it in the garden with Dylan.'

Rich ground his teeth. 'That was then.'

'What's changed your mind?'

'I'm too bloody busy trying to make money for this family, that's what's changed my mind.'

'And I'm not?' Jasmine shot him a challenging stare. She had made a promise to Millie, and she never went back on a promise. 'If I have to do this thing alone, then I will. But I'd rather have you with me.'

Rich sighed. 'I'm not going to sway you one bit on this?'

Jasmine folded her arms and shook her head. 'No, you're not.'

He made a move towards her but then stopped, letting his arms fall back down by his sides.

'Just be careful how deep you get,' he said quietly. 'That's all I ask.'

Jasmine pulled her denim jacket tighter as the wind roared across Salisbury Plain.

'No matter how hot it is anywhere else, it's always ruddy freezing up here.'

Millie laughed as she hugged herself. 'I know what you mean. I never thought about bringing a jacket because it was so hot at home.'

'It's a wonder the druids didn't have permanent hypothermia wearing those big dresses.'

Millie laughed harder, despite the chill that made her shiver. But then she stopped and stared, awestruck, as the path curved and ahead of them on the plain rose the majestic grey pillars of Stonehenge against the cornflower sky. 'It never fails to make me feel strange, seeing them standing there all tall and mysterious, no matter how many times I see them,' she murmured.

There was a chorus of 'whoa' and 'amazing' and sharp intakes of breath from the small group of children surrounding them.

'It looks as though it's having the same effect on the kids,' Jasmine smiled.

Spencer bounded to the front of the group and faced them with an enthusiastic grin. But he wiped it from his face as he addressed them.

'Ok… We have rules and I need you to listen up before we go on. If we stick to the rules, nobody goes wrong, nobody gets in trouble and everyone has a nice day.' He glanced around, his stern-but-not-really gaze resting on every child's face for a fraction of a second. 'Everyone ok with that? Because anyone who isn't can go and sit on the bus now and save me a job later.'

'Ooh, get *Mr Stricty-Pants Johns*,' Jasmine whispered to Millie with a giggle. 'I'm almost tempted to go and sit on the bus myself, just in case I'm naughty by accident.'

Millie stifled a giggle of her own. Some of the children nodded; some replied, 'Yes, Mr Johns.'

'We are representing Honeybourne School,' Spencer continued, 'and we want people to think it's a good school full of good children. So we don't shout, we're not rude, we don't race about like idiots, and we don't drop litter. We don't touch the stones either…' A slightly playful smirk crept across his face. 'They've been standing here for thousands of years. It would be just my luck for a couple of my year fours to wrestle against one and topple the whole lot over.'

Some of the children dared a self-conscious laugh, but most of them looked at their teacher blankly.

'Ok then…' Spencer turned towards the path again, 'follow me and we'll go and see what our ancestors got up to in their spare time.'

The group followed as Spencer led with leggy strides, some of the children almost jogging to keep up. As they approached the stone circle, Spencer stopped and halted the group. He hopped from foot to foot lightly like a boxer getting ready for a sparring match – every inch of him seemed to be full of nervous energy.

'Now, who can tell me anything about where the stones came from?'

Instantly, hands shot up in the group. Spencer pointed at a blonde girl. 'Grace?'

'Was it cavemen?'

'It has been here for a long time,' Spencer replied patiently, 'but although that's a good answer it's not right. I'm looking for people not quite so far in our past.'

Hands shot up again.

'Reuben…' Spencer said, glancing for the briefest moment in Jasmine's direction. Millie caught the strange, forlorn expression that was there and gone again in the same instant. Had she imagined it?

'Merlin put them here,' Reuben said, puffing his chest out, certain that his answer would be right.

'Well… that is one legend around the stones. Some say Merlin moved them here from Ireland by magic. It's one of many ideas over the years about the stones and how they got here.'

Reuben's face fell.

'It's not a wrong answer, Reuben,' Spencer said kindly. 'Just not the one I'm looking for.'

'Bless,' Jasmine whispered to Millie. 'We've been reading legends of King Arthur together before bed. I think I need to explain to Reuben that it's not real.'

'I think it's a brilliant answer,' Millie said with sudden belligerence. 'There's nothing wrong with a mythical explanation for something. It's not your son's fault that the rest of the world is too short-sighted to see anything other than cold, hard logic as a reason for everything that happens.'

Jasmine stared at Millie, who simply fell silent and turned her attention to Spencer again, gazing at him as though her very existence depended on his next sentence.

'When we get closer, I have some information that we'll discuss, which might help us to uncover the mystery a bit more. We'll go around the circle and look at every stone in turn. Each stone has a story…' He stared at a dark-haired boy who had nudged his friend and laughed. 'It might sound boring to you, Tom, but each stone *did* have a special meaning for the people who put them here. And we're going to talk about that and what it means to us, even in today's society.'

The boy stopped grinning and tried to look repentant as Spencer continued.

'So, we'll continue up to the path around the stones. When we get there, *don't* go beyond the barrier keeping them safe!'

He began to walk again and the group trekked after him. Jasmine kept a close eye out for stragglers as they followed, while Millie was mesmerised by the circle that grew closer with every step. She'd always felt a deep connection to the spiritual side of life, and it was a part of her that defied explanation, though it was there all the same. Whenever she was faced with a sight like this, it overwhelmed her.

Her thoughts were interrupted by a tug on her sleeve. She looked down to see that Rebecca was gazing up at her. 'Can I walk with you, Miss?'

Millie was a little taken aback by the request. She glanced up at Jasmine, who simply smiled. 'Of course, but you don't have to call me Miss.'

'But we're at school. We have to call all the grown-ups Miss or Sir.'

'Well…' Millie leaned forward and lowered her voice. 'When nobody's listening just call me Millie and it will be our little secret.'

Rebecca giggled. Rachel, who was a few steps in front, whipped her head around. As soon as she noticed her sister slip an arm through Millie's, she shot back to join them, linking her own through Millie's other one.

'It looks like you have a fan club,' Jasmine observed. 'Don't worry – when you're a mother you quickly come to accept that just about everyone is more interesting than you.'

'I'm sure that's not true,' said Millie, laughing self-consciously.

'We still love you, Mum…' Rebecca said awkwardly. 'We just thought we'd walk with Miss – Millie – today. She doesn't have any children to keep her company usually.'

Millie had never considered herself the maternal type, but she couldn't deny the warm feeling it gave her to have a child on either side showing her such pure and honest affection, untainted by desires or ulterior motives. If only the rest of her relationships could be this simple and rewarding.

Chapter Seven

Millie sat nursing a warm cup of chocolate. Things had progressed significantly in the bakery in a little under a week; she now had a rudimentary electricity supply from a generator to tide her over until the rewiring was done, along with a water supply. Her paltry savings had taken a bashing, she reflected ruefully, but at least she could now boil the kettle. A little more furniture had also been unpacked and, compared to the first few nights, her home felt like a five-star hotel. She was in the cosy back room behind the ovens and shop floor, which she had turned into makeshift living space. She didn't imagine it would be very practical once the bakery was functional, and she would probably have to rethink the living quarters, but for now it felt cosy and just, well, right.

The day trip with the school to Stonehenge had been more enjoyable than she had imagined. She had never considered herself to have a natural affinity with children, and spending the day with a group of them had been a scary prospect. But she had found them all fascinating and delightful; their curiosity and wonder at everything they were shown was infectious. And it helped that Spencer was so brilliant with them. He was patient and gentle, but never a pushover, and Millie mused that if she'd had teachers like him at school, she might have achieved much more, academically, than she had done – maybe even gone on to higher education.

After they had returned from school and Jasmine had dropped off her brood with Rich, she and Spencer had taken Millie to the Dog and Hare for a well-earned drink and a pub tea, where they had discussed how the plans to get the bakery fixed up were progressing. Since their Sunday lunch, Jasmine had been full of ideas – pages and pages of them that she had showed Millie at every opportunity. Some were genius, some a logistical nightmare, and some downright silly, but they had thoroughly discussed every one in earnest tones no matter how improbable they seemed at first. The ritual was binding their friendship a little tighter each time. Millie was beginning to feel that she had found her rock, someone she could rely on in life. After all, it wasn't like she had a man to take that title, and the way she had messed up in the past, it wasn't likely she was going to get one any time soon.

There was a tap at the front door. It wasn't particularly late, but the sun was sinking and being alone in her ramshackle home made her feel more edgy than usual, acutely aware of just how easy the place would be to break into and how little she could do to defend it or herself.

Before she'd even managed to leave her chair, there was a second, more insistent knock. Millie pushed herself up, now wondering whether there was some sort of emergency. But then Ruth Evans's faint voice calling through the letterbox made Millie break into a wry smile.

'It's only me, dear. Just came to see if you needed anything.'

Ruth already knew that Millie now had electricity and water, but still insisted on calling round to see whether she could make her more tea, or offer warm water for a wash, or some other kindness. Millie politely declined and tactfully pointed out each time that she could now do those things for herself, but she understood that Ruth was only making excuses to seek company.

'Give me a second, Ruth,' Millie called as she snatched the front door keys from a hook on the wall.

The door opened with a creak.

'I'm alright, Ruth, thank you.'

'Oh…' Ruth looked up at her expectantly.

Millie sighed. 'But would you like to come in?'

'Oh, well, I could just stay for ten minutes or so.' Ruth tottered over the threshold as Millie stepped back to let her in.

'Come through to the back room,' Millie offered, leading the way. 'It's much cosier in there now I have armchairs.'

'Oh, you do have it nice now,' Ruth agreed as she ran an approving gaze over the place. Millie had lit candles so that despite the fading, dusty décor the room looked warm and inviting. Two plump armchairs dominated the space, arty knick-knacks lined the ancient stone mantelshelf over an unlit open fire and a jug of fresh wildflowers gave the room a subtle scent. It was easy to imagine that this was how the room must have looked all those hundreds of years ago when the bakery had first been built.

Ruth eased herself into one of the armchairs, a slight frown crossing her expression as she did so.

'Can I make you a cup of tea?' Millie asked. 'Return the favour for all the ones you've made me?'

'That would be lovely,' Ruth said. 'Milk, one sugar please.'

'It's been another beautiful day.' Millie went over to the kettle sitting on an upturned crate in the corner of the room and flicked it on. 'I've been up to Stonehenge today with the school trip.'

'I wondered where you were. I called this afternoon… Just to see if you needed anything, of course.'

'Of course,' Millie smiled as she sat on the remaining armchair. 'It's very nice of you to keep checking.'

'Just doing my neighbourly duty.'

'And how are you?' Millie bit her lip. The question was out before she had thought it through. It was a socially conditioned thing.

Ruth pulled a suitably martyred expression. 'I wish I could say that I'm well, but really I'm not.'

'Oh…'

Ruth massaged her knuckles in a slow movement. 'I think we've a storm heading in.'

Millie nodded uncertainly, wondering what this sudden observation on the weather had to do with Ruth's health. 'I suppose we've had such a long, hot spell, it must be due to break soon.'

'Very soon, if my joints are anything to go by.'

'Your arthritis?' Millie said, understanding illuminating her features. 'It's giving you trouble today?'

Ruth nodded. 'When I was young my grandmother was plagued with it. I used to think she was exaggerating when she complained. If you've never suffered, you can't imagine how miserable it makes you – the constant pain, gnawing away at you, no rest, no comfort…'

Millie stared at her. Her neighbour had always seemed so bullish, so full of spark. Now that Millie looked closely, Ruth seemed very old and fragile. Millie found herself seized with a sudden melancholy.

'Ruth,' she said, 'have you ever been married?'

For a moment, Ruth seemed surprised at the question. But then a quiet look of pleasure crossed her expression.

'There was a man once,' she said. 'We were engaged.'

'But you never married him?'

'He joined the navy. Promised to come back and marry me when he was earning a decent wage.'

'What happened?'

'He drowned. Out at sea.'

Millie clapped a hand over her mouth. 'Oh God!'

Ruth smiled sadly. 'It was a long time ago now.'

'And you never found anyone else?'

'No one who compared to my Alf.'

'So you've always lived alone… Nobody to take care of you?'

'Oh… I don't need taking care of, I'm perfectly capable.'

'Don't you get lonely?'

'With this whole village to talk to?' Ruth forced a laugh, but Millie wasn't fooled by her bravado. 'How could I be lonely in Honeybourne?'

Millie fell to brooding. Perhaps she and Ruth were more alike than she realised. Perhaps, if Millie didn't pull herself out of this destructive spiral of guilt and regret and get on with her life, she would become like Ruth – a sad, lonely old lady dependent on the fleeting kindness of strangers. It was an odd and slightly terrifying epiphany.

The kettle clicked off. Millie shook herself, hastily rubbing at her eyes as she got up. 'I'll just get you that cup of tea.'

The room fell silent as Millie busied herself, an unspoken tension suddenly in the air. Something had happened in that room and their relationship had changed.

Millie brought a steaming mug over and handed it carefully to Ruth.

'Thank you.' Ruth gave a brief smile as she took it from her. 'If you have a quick look in my bag,' she said, nodding to a huge shopper at her feet, 'you'll find a hip flask. I think I could do with a tot of something tonight.'

Millie nodded and rifled around in the bag until she found the small steel bottle. Unscrewing the lid, she sniffed the contents. 'Whisky?'

Ruth held out her mug with a wink. 'Just the thing to chase away the blues.'

Millie poured a slug into the old lady's tea.

'Have some yourself,' Ruth added.

'I don't think—'

'Nonsense,' Ruth insisted. 'A little bit of whisky never hurt anyone. Thins your blood, don't you know.'

Millie hesitated, and then smiled. 'I could have a drop in my hot chocolate.'

'Best in a lovely cup of tea,' Ruth replied, smacking her lips as she took a sip of her own.

'I'd better make another one then,' Millie laughed.

For the next hour, Millie listened attentively while Ruth told her stories about her life with Alf, the village and the people who had come and gone, and about why she had chosen to remain alone when Alf had not returned from his doomed voyage. And for the first time since she had arrived in Honeybourne, Millie didn't want to run away from Ruth's chattering. Once or twice, Ruth had alluded to Millie's own past, in her unsubtle way trying to prise facts from her, but Millie tactfully steered the conversation back to Ruth's life – something Ruth was only too glad to discuss and Millie only too glad to listen to.

Millie shivered slightly as a natural pause found its way into the conversation. 'It's getting a bit chilly,' she commented, her gaze travelling to the darkness beyond the windows.

'Probably time I was letting you go to bed,' Ruth smiled.

'I am a bit tired.' Millie peered at Ruth more closely. 'You look tired too.'

'I doubt I'll get much sleep tonight.'

'Why? Usually whisky knocks me spark out.'

'Not with these old joints. It'll take more than a nip of whisky.'

'Don't you have painkillers?'

Ruth blew out an impatient breath. 'Don't touch the sides. Load of rubbish if you ask me.'

'Does it happen a lot?'

'Most nights. I suppose I'm lucky that I can take naps during the day.'

Millie wondered when, exactly, Ruth took naps. As far as she could see, the woman was always around and about in the village, chattering away to anyone who would listen. She let the comment pass, though. Instead, she was gripped by the urge to help, despite it bringing to Ruth's notice skills that might attract unwarranted attention.

'I might be able to make you a herbal draught,' Millie blurted out. 'It would ease you a little so that you could sleep.'

Ruth looked doubtful. 'New Age nonsense? Sounds like something Jasmine Green would try to palm off on me.'

'Not New Age. Very Old Age actually,' Millie smiled. 'As remedies go, this one's as old as the Earth itself. But I'm fairly confident it will help you. And if it doesn't, there's nothing in it that will do any harm.'

'It does sound tempting.'

'Of course it does. Why don't you sit tight? I'll be ten minutes; I just need to find some bits and pieces to make it.'

Without waiting for Ruth's reply, Millie raced through to the main shop. She knew where all her books were, as she had sat and read them only a few nights earlier. But there were other things to find too. Rifling through a couple of boxes, she found one that contained candles – blue and green for healing. She pulled a handful out and laid them on the counter as she continued her search. Now she needed a medium, some sort of tonic to channel her healing into. Flicking through the nearest book for inspiration, she found the perfect thing – a remedy to induce peaceful sleep. Running a finger down the list, she rooted in another box for the right herbs. A pan was lit on a little gas stove and Millie set some water to boil, tipping the carefully measured mix of herbs into it.

As the solution cooled, she lit the candles and breathed in deeply, focusing her power. She had felt a little tipsy with the whisky, but her mind was now sharp with a sense of purpose – she only hoped that it was sharp enough to fully visualise the power she would need to make her healing draught work. She had spent too long feeling like a useless failure, and it was time she did something positive, even if that thing was a small gesture to help a suffering neighbour. Once she felt she was ready, she poured the mixture into a tiny bottle, whispering to it as she did. Then she stoppered it with a satisfied smile and took it through to where Ruth waited with uncharacteristic quiet and patience.

'What's this?' Ruth took the bottle and unscrewed it, sniffing.

'Careful not to spill it,' Millie said. 'It's just something to help you sleep a bit easier.'

'Smells like lemon balm.'

'There is some of that… amongst other things.'

'You're not after my money?' Ruth laughed. 'Because I haven't changed my will to include you just yet.'

Millie gave her an indulgent smile. 'Don't worry. We won't need to call Miss Marple in the morning.'

Ruth grasped Millie's hand and looked her squarely in the eye. 'Thank you.'

When Millie looked at the expression on Ruth's face, she knew that the old lady was thanking her for much more than a bottle of sleeping draught. Millie wasn't sure if her potion would work but she sincerely hoped that it would give Ruth some comfort. If anyone deserved some peace, poor old Ruth Evans did.

Ruth's prediction had been right and Millie was woken at dawn by a rumble of thunder that seemed to shake the whole frame of the precarious building she now called home. Millie got up, hoping that her concoction the night before had given Ruth a little respite from her constant pain. And if that was all Millie was doing, then surely things couldn't get out of hand, could they? She had come to Honeybourne intending to keep a safe emotional distance, and already she knew she was getting too close to everyone. But the village was such that it was hard not to fall in love with the residents, and she wanted to help if she could.

One mistake… It had been a huge mistake with terrible consequences, but it was only one. She had come to Honeybourne to put the past firmly behind her, and that meant putting that mistake behind her too. If she couldn't get over it and go back to the things that made life worth living, like good friends and a sense of belonging, then she would never truly be able to move on from that one lapse in judgement that continued to haunt her.

The thunderstorm proved to be violent, but it was also mercifully short. A handful of thunderclaps that felt as though they shook the very earth, lightning that tore a blazing path across the sky as Millie watched from the safety of her bedroom, a sharp deluge, and it was all over. An hour later, the day was still overcast, but the heat that had baked the village over the previous weeks was building up again. Everyone had been talking about the summer of '76 since the heatwave began, and for the last few days, every newspaper had reported that this summer had broken the record of that quite remarkable year. From the way the sky was clearing up now, it didn't seem as though the sun was finished with Britain yet.

By about ten o'clock the sun began to climb back into the sky, Millie glanced at her watch for what felt like the hundredth time that hour. Ruth hadn't called this morning, and Millie's mood had gone from one of optimism to a crushing fear. What if her potion had done something it shouldn't have done? What if Ruth was unwell, unable to wake... or worse? Dragging a pestle and mortar from a cupboard, she began to crush a mixture of leaves into a paste, working with fierce concentration in a bid to cleanse herself of these unhelpful thoughts. She had work to do, lots of toiletries and potions to make for her first craft fair, and moping wasn't going to get any of that done. The draught she had given Ruth was a simple remedy, one of the first she had learned to make – of course nothing had gone wrong. But if that was true, where was Ruth?

'Hello? Millie, are you home?' Jasmine called through the letterbox.

Millie clicked her tongue, annoyed at herself for being so melodramatic, and went to find her friend. Jasmine stood on the step, looking adorable in a pair of loose-fitting floral trousers and a long-sleeved cheesecloth blouse, her hair piled on her head with a huge clip. Her cheeks wore a natural blush that made Millie feel very grey indeed, her morning of worry and lack of make-up not helping to dispel that feeling.

'Did you hear that thunder this morning?' Jasmine asked, following Millie back into the main shop.

Millie nodded. 'It was mad, wasn't it?' She took her place behind the counter again, clearing away some of the debris.

Jasmine ran her gaze over the detritus of her morning's work. 'You have been busy. It smells amazing in here. What are you making?'

'I thought I'd start with hemp soap. It always seems to go down well.'

Jasmine grinned. 'Don't let Dylan know you've got hemp in here. He'll be trying to smoke it.'

'I'm not sure it's quite the right hemp. Besides, he can't smoke a bar of soap.'

'Trust me, he'd try.'

Millie gave her a small smile.

'What's the matter?' Jasmine asked.

'Have you seen Ruth this morning?'

Jasmine frowned slightly. 'You mean she wasn't here at the crack of dawn plying you with tea and toast?'

'No. She normally comes way before now.'

'Want me to go and knock at hers?'

Millie shook her head. 'I'm sure it's nothing.'

Jasmine's frown deepened. 'Are you certain you're alright? You seem more worried about this than it probably warrants, if I'm honest. Has something happened?'

'No… She came over last night and stayed until late. We drank some whisky and she told me about all her illnesses. I thought…'

Jasmine smiled. 'Let me tell you that Ruth Evans can drink us all under the table, even though she looks like a frail little old lady. I'm sure she's fine, probably just sleeping off a hangover.'

Millie forced a smile of her own. 'I'm sure you're right. So… what brings you over?'

'I'm taking you out.'

'I can't... Where?'

'There's a bakery in Ringwood I want to go and have a look at. They do some amazing cakes and savouries and they also do a roaring trade. I thought we could go and check it out, see what sort of thing sets them apart from other bakeries.'

'Like industrial espionage?'

'No!' Jasmine laughed. 'Like research. You won't be in competition with them, but you might pick up some useful tips. I'm sure they won't mind if two very nosey and not remotely invested tourists quiz them a little about their business.'

Millie paused, glancing around at the mess she had made and the work she still had to do. 'I don't know...'

'Won't all this wait?'

'I don't think so. It might spoil if I leave it unfinished.' She looked up to see that Jasmine's expression was a little hurt. For a moment she felt cruel, but Jasmine had given her no warning. What sort of person expected you to drop everything at a moment's notice and go out? 'I can't go today,' she added stubbornly.

'I know it's last minute, it's just that I had some free time. But I should have realised that you might not. Don't worry about it.'

Immediately, Millie hated herself for her thoughts. How could she have been so mean spirited? She smiled brightly. 'No, don't apologise. I'm being ungrateful and it's lovely that you want to help. Let me clear up and set what I've done. It might take an hour or so... Will that be ok?'

'Brilliant,' Jasmine squeaked. 'I'll help if I can. Just point me to things and tell me what to do with them.'

* * *

The trip out to Ringwood had turned out to be a welcome distraction from the increasingly morbid fears plaguing Millie. They hadn't been alleviated by the fact that Jasmine insisted on knocking on Ruth's door on the way to get her car, only to find that the old lady didn't answer. But as Jasmine gently reminded Millie, Ruth was often out and about all over the village, bothering anyone who had a spare moment to listen, so it didn't mean anything. In all likelihood, Jasmine laughed, she had invented a new and hideous ailment to go and see Dr Wood about. She told Millie not to worry, they should go for their afternoon out as planned and she would call later to see if Ruth had returned. If she still didn't answer her door, Millie had permission to start worrying. Reluctantly, Millie had agreed, and as the distance from Honeybourne increased, she had started to feel better.

The Riverside Bakery was a delightful place. It was decorated in mouth-watering pastels, a small array of elaborate wrought-iron tables and chairs outside in the sun. Inside, it was a delight of vintage posters and floral patchworks, with the most divine fragrances filling the air from the kitchens. The owner had been only too happy to chat to them about new and unusual recipes that had been a hit with their customers, such as rhubarb-and-custard pasties, sugar-coated Yorkshire puddings with toffee sauce, and pies stuffed with pulled pork and plum sauce. The conversation was punctuated with a steady stream of customers, but not once did the owner, a small, dapper man who seemed like something from an Agatha Christie novel, feel the need to excuse himself from his enthusiastic accounts of how he got started in baking and how wonderful the staff, consisting entirely of family members, were. Emboldened by his easy-going and friendly manner, Millie told him a little of her own hopes and fears for her village bakery. Whilst she knew that the success of his enterprise was always going to eclipse her own – it was in a much bigger town – the visit still filled her with hope and a new enthusiasm. They left with a bag of cakes and pies almost large enough to feed their own village and promises to come back once they were up and running to share how they were getting along. And the owner of the Riverside Bakery had promised to call in next time he got a free day and was in the area.

But as they returned to Honeybourne and to Millie's tumbledown bakery, it seemed that the very structure itself had been incubating Millie's fears, so that they came back to assault her, sharper and more painful than they had been before.

'I'm going to check on Ruth again,' she said, placing the bag of treats on the counter.

'Let me do that,' Jasmine said. 'If she's still missing we'll take it more seriously.'

Millie paused before nodding shortly. 'Thanks. I'll put the kettle on while you're gone.'

A few moments later Jasmine returned with Ruth in tow. Millie heaved a huge sigh of relief as she saw that not only did Ruth look to be in very good spirits, but she looked a great deal healthier than she had done since Millie had moved to Honeybourne.

'Do you know what time I woke today?' Ruth asked, rushing over with surprising speed to grasp Millie by the hand. 'Two o'clock… in the afternoon! I've never slept that long and that well – not for years. I feel twenty years younger today!'

Millie smiled as Ruth pulled her into a kiss on the cheek. 'That's good. So the sleeping draught worked?'

'Sleeping draught? It's like an elixir of life or something! I feel as though every ailment I had is cured.'

'Dr Wood won't know what to do with himself,' Jasmine put in with a wry smile.

'Honestly,' Ruth continued, unperturbed, 'you could sell that potion and make a fortune.'

The old darkness crossed Millie's features again. 'I could never sell it. Those remedies are ages old and the knowledge needed to make them is something valuable that demands respect, they're not for personal gain.'

Jasmine and Ruth exchanged troubled glances.

'She didn't mean anything by it,' Jasmine said.

Millie turned her back on them in a bid to compose herself. 'I know you didn't, Ruth,' she said, facing them again. 'It's been a long day and I still have a lot to do.'

'We'll go,' Jasmine said, nodding at Ruth.

'No… not yet. I have all this cake from Riverside to eat and I certainly can't manage it alone.' Millie forced a smile for them.

'If you're sure,' Jasmine said uncertainly, but then turned to see Ruth already settled in her usual place in the bay window seat.

'Of course I'm sure.' Millie smiled, a little too brightly.

Millie had bottled the last of her almond oil moisturisers, along with fennel shampoos, witch hazel cleansers and various soaps. She stood back and surveyed the crates, a great feeling of achievement prompting a secret smile. When Jasmine had suggested she make products to sell, she had been doubtful that she could do it on such a commercial scale. When Jasmine had then announced that a big craft fair was coming up in Salisbury in two weeks and that it would be a good idea for Millie to have her stock ready, it had seemed impossible to do it at such short notice. But here she was, the night before, and thanks to her hard work for every evening of that two weeks, everything was ready. As she progressed, working like a woman possessed and enjoying it, she had thought long and hard about whether, in fact, she might be better off changing her business plan, forgetting the bakery and doing craft fairs with Jasmine full time. But every time she came close to making that decision, she remembered the irrational pull that had brought her to Honeybourne, and the voice in her head that had nagged her to buy the old building. What if she forsook that now? The old place deserved to be restored; every brick, every beam, begged for it, and Millie could not allow herself to be distracted from the task she had promised to undertake. There was something strange and spiritual about it that she couldn't explain. But the feeling was there all the same. As it haunted her again, she made a note to ask Jasmine about who had owned the bakery and what had happened to them.

Letting out a huge yawn, she checked her watch. Tomorrow would be hectic, and although it was only just gone nine, her bed was calling. Perhaps it would be a good idea to get a proper night's sleep for once. Just as she was about to lock the front door and blow out the candles dotted around the room, there was a tap at the window and there was Ruth.

'What can I do for you?' she asked as she opened the door to let her in.

'I wanted to come before you locked up for the night... I don't suppose you have any more of that wonderful sleeping draught, do you?'

Millie's smile slipped. 'You won't need it again.'

'But I can't sleep without it.'

'Ruth... you've only used it for one night. How do you know if you don't try?'

'Please. I won't keep badgering you. How about you make me an extra big bottle and then I won't need to.'

'I can't, Ruth.'

The old woman cast her gaze to the ground. 'I only wanted a little,' she mumbled. 'I had such a wonderful night's sleep – the best I've had in years…'

Millie placed a hand on her arm. 'Have you had any trouble from your joints today?'

Ruth looked up at her, confusion colouring her features. 'Come to think of it, I haven't.'

'Didn't you notice?'

She shook her head. 'Having such a good sleep must have made me forget somehow, but I suppose I should have. It is strange.'

'Trust me; you'll sleep tonight without the draught. In fact, you won't ever need it again. And you won't be troubled by your arthritis either.'

Ruth stared at her. 'Won't I?'

Millie shook her head with an indulgent smile.

'I'm cured? But… how?'

'An ancient remedy that most people have forgotten. If you ask me, that's probably as it should be.' Millie began to usher Ruth to the front door. 'We should keep this between you and me.'

'Should we?'

'Yes. When people don't understand things it can lead to awkward questions and mistrust.'

'Can it?'

'Yes. Do you mind terribly if I don't ask you to stay tonight? Only I have an early start with Jasmine.'

'Jasmine Green? Works at the pub?'

Millie sighed. There were some things she could cure, but, it seemed, Ruth's memory was not one of them. 'Jasmine Green, yes, but she doesn't work at the pub anymore.'

'That's right, I know that.' At the doorstep, Ruth stopped and turned back. 'So, I really am cured?'

'I hope so,' Millie replied. 'But remember, it's our little secret.'

'Our little secret. Righto.'

Ruth tottered out into the balmy evening air. Millie watched her head in the direction of her own cottage. She wondered whether Ruth even knew what the meaning of the word 'secret' was. She just hoped her memory would be bad enough that she would forget about a funny little sleeping draught her neighbour had given her during a moment of weakness. While she was happy to see Ruth was much better, the last thing she needed now was curious Honeybourne residents coming to see what it was that had the village gossip walking taller than she had done in years.

Jasmine stretched her legs out across Rich's lap as they sat on the sofa together. She was feeling particularly smug, but then she had a lot to be smug about. The craft fair had been a huge success, particularly Millie's natural toiletries. Not only had it been a good business decision, but Millie's presence on the stall had meant that Jasmine really enjoyed herself. She had arrived back home tired but happy, and excited for the next one.

The triplets were safely in bed now and Jasmine was cradling a well-earned glass of wine.

'And before you say anything,' Jasmine continued, 'we will be doing it again. I really enjoyed having her there today. I feel like I've got a real business partner.'

'But she's not your partner,' Rich reminded her. 'And I think it's safer that way, so don't put ideas in her head.'

'I know that. And I'm old enough and clever enough to make my own business decisions, thank you, Lord Sugar. I don't know what you've got against her anyway.'

'I don't know either. Everyone in the village thinks the sun shines from her nether regions but that alone makes me uneasy. I saw Ruth Evans today when I was fetching the kids from school. She was spouting some nonsense about a miracle potion Millie had given her to cure her arthritis. Half the time that woman doesn't make much sense, I know, but Millie must have given her something or said something to plant that idea.'

'And that's bad because…?'

'I don't know. It's just a feeling I get about her. Don't shout when I say this… But I still think she's got some secret past that's not altogether as rosy as we might want to believe.'

Jasmine paused for a moment. But then she let out a sigh. 'If I'm honest, I get that from her too. But not in the same way you do. I feel like there's some darkness inside her, some great tragedy. When you said the other day that she was running from her past, I think you might be right. But that doesn't make her a bad person, just damaged.' She took a sip of her wine. 'And let's face it, we've all been damaged by life at one time or another.'

'I just don't want you getting too involved and dragged into something that will affect you. I know how sensitive you can be.'

'Don't worry… If she ties me up and keeps me in her loft as a sex slave I'll ask her to let you come and watch from time to time.'

'I'm being serious, Jas.'

'I know you are. And I love that you care but you really are seeing problems that aren't there. At the first sign of trouble, you have my word that I'll be straight out of the way.'

'Hmm, why don't I believe you?'

Jasmine grinned. 'Shut up and kiss me. Maybe I'm not so tired after all…'

Rich broke into a broad grin and reached for her. As he did there was a quiet knock at the front door.

'Ignore it,' he said. 'Whoever it is can wait until tomorrow.'

'Don't be silly,' Jasmine replied, handing him her glass and getting up from the sofa. Smoothing down her skirt she padded, barefoot, to the front door while Rich gave a frustrated grimace as he watched her go.

She returned a moment later with Dylan and Millie.

'I was on the way over to give you this back…' Millie handed Jasmine a money bag. 'You left it in one of my crates. And Dylan was coming over to see you too so he walked with me.'

Jasmine tried not to frown at her brother, who simply shoved his hands in his pockets with an amiable smile. He never came to visit them unless she nagged him to and he certainly never surprised them. He had obviously been waiting for Millie to emerge from her house and the fact that she was on her way to see Jasmine was a valid enough excuse for him to tag along. This worried her. Millie had been hurt in the past. It was easy to see once you got close – the moments of sadness and introspection, the distance in her stare when she thought no one was looking, her unwillingness to share more than the barest of details about her life before Honeybourne. She had come to their village to get over it, and that was ok with Jasmine. But as much as she loved him, Dylan was not the man to have around at such a time. He was like opium – he made you feel wonderful, but too much of him would break you. Jasmine had seen it happen dozens of times before. Millie looked to Jasmine like a woman who wouldn't take too much breaking. It was a mess that she didn't fancy being caught in the middle of.

'Aren't you going to offer us a glass of that rather fine-looking wine you're drinking?' said Dylan, interrupting her thoughts.

'How do you know it's fine?' Rich cut in. 'I'll have you know we're on a budget. It's Aldi's finest or none at all in this house.'

'As long as there's an alcohol content I'm game,' Dylan fired back with an impish look. Jasmine caught Millie's glance at him, the look of desire mixed with what seemed to be almost fear, and her heart sank. Dylan was working his magic and Millie was already a lost cause. She couldn't just sit by and wait to pick up the pieces of Millie's heart once he was done smashing it to bits. And she couldn't risk losing someone who was becoming a dear friend into the bargain.

'Take a seat,' Rich said, glancing at Jasmine, whose defeated shrug was barely perceptible to anyone but her husband. 'I was about to open a new bottle anyway.'

'Good man,' Dylan said, vaulting over the back of the sofa like an Olympic athlete and patting the seat next to him. 'Ladies… Come and tell me about your day.'

Jasmine rolled her eyes but made a point of sitting right next to him so that Millie couldn't. 'My days involve work and the mere mention of that nasty four-letter word makes you hyperventilate.'

'That's a bit harsh,' Dylan laughed. He leaned across to where Millie had taken an armchair. 'Ignore my sister. She doesn't realise that a life plan takes time to perfect. I'm figuring out how to make my fortune before I dive in and make a hash of things.'

'You're saying I made a hash of things?' Jasmine replied.

'Only at the beginning, which you do admit yourself anyway.'

'So, come on then, please share your grand plan to make your first million.'

'I can't tell you. If I did I'd have to kill you.'

'That means it doesn't exist,' Jasmine said to Millie with a wry smile.

'Just because you think you know everything about me, sister of mine, doesn't make it so.'

'Enlighten me then.'

Dylan looked up with a nod as Rich handed him a glass of wine. 'Actually, a very interesting proposition has come my way.'

'Sounds intriguing,' Rich said as he handed Millie a glass and then took the last remaining armchair.

'I'm going into business with Bony.'

'The builder?' Jasmine said, her eyebrows flying up her forehead. 'You're going to be a builder?'

Dylan nodded. Rich let out a guffaw but Dylan seemed unconcerned by the reaction to his news.

'What in the world made you decide this? You've never shown the slightest interest in building before.'

'Bony's a mate, and we've talked about it a few times. I just wasn't in the right frame of mind to take it seriously before. But I'm twenty-eight now and I feel like I need to start making something of myself. We've got plenty of work lined up too so he's more than happy to have me on board.'

'You have? But you don't know the first thing about the trade.'

'I've got muscle and I'm a fast learner. I don't see what's so hard about it.'

'I'll remind you of this conversation after your first week on the job,' Rich said. 'So when do you start?'

'Bony's sorting it out. Maybe next week.'

Jasmine smiled at Rich. Perhaps Dylan was finally growing up after all. 'If you're serious about it then I think it's great.'

Dylan looked across at Millie, who had been silently following the conversation, her expression closed. He gave her a huge smile. 'And it also means that I'll be able to help you out with getting the bakery shipshape. I'll talk to Bony about doing it at cost.'

Jasmine's expression darkened. And there it was: the ulterior motive. How could she have been so silly? Dylan was still Dylan... charming, fun and handsome – but always looking for the next conquest. She was about to open her mouth when Rich glanced across at her, gave his head the tiniest shake, and then began a new conversation with Millie.

'So, Ruth Evans was telling me today that you're some herbal remedy whiz.'

This time the shadow crossed Millie's expression. 'It was just a sleeping draught... something very simple that beginners in apothecary skills could make. It was nothing to get excited about.'

'Ruth certainly seemed to be excited.'

Millie took a gulp of her wine. 'This is lovely,' she said, forcing a smile. 'What is it?'

'I've no idea,' Rich laughed, 'I just open the bottle and drink it.'

The tension in the room suddenly became palpable. Jasmine sensed another change of subject was needed, but no conversational territory seemed safe.

'Who's hungry?' she asked brightly, jumping up from her chair. 'I'll get some nibbles on the go.'

Jasmine heaved a sigh as she stuck her head in the fridge to see what she could rustle up. As she brought hummus, salads, pitta bread and cheese over to the counter, she painted on a smile. 'Rich, why don't you get the Scrabble out? We might as well have a laugh watching Dylan try to convince us that words that don't actually exist are real, as he usually does.'

Dylan let out an exaggerated guffaw. 'You're just jealous because my vocab is so much bigger than yours.'

'I don't need a dictionary to tell you to bog off, loser-boy.'

Rich went off to a cupboard and Jasmine smiled at her brother. She was going to salvage what she could of this night if it killed her.

Chapter Eight

Jasmine woke the next morning with a mouth like a sandpit and a head full of rocks. She had been determined to turn the uneasy mood of the previous night and judging by the amount of wine they had got through – the evidence of which lay along the kitchen counter in the form of empty bottles – she had succeeded with far more aplomb than she had intended. It was lucky she didn't have to get the kids up for school; she didn't think her delicate state would survive their morning squealing and bickering. As it was, Jasmine had woken early, a wave of nausea dragging her from her bed, and raced to the bathroom; the triplets slept on, for now at least.

She sat with a cup of hot, sweet tea, staring out at the rising sun that coloured the sky rose and gold. She needed to see Dylan as soon as she was able to pull herself together. Last night they'd simply had good, clean (relatively clean, anyway) fun. But the threat of disastrous sexual conquests wouldn't have been banished so easily.

She bolted upright in her chair, recalling now that Dylan had staggered away from their house, bound for his own, some time after one. He had refused their offer to sleep on the sofa, as had Millie, who had left with him. How could Jasmine have been so stupid? What if they had gone home together?

Jasmine raced up to the bedroom and gently nudged Rich awake.

'What's up?' he mumbled, releasing a cloud of wine-fuelled breath into the air.

'I've got to see Dylan.'

Rich pushed his eyes open to peer at her. 'Right now?'

She nodded. 'He went home last night with Millie.'

'He didn't go with Millie; he walked her back to her place. He does live right across the road from her, you know.'

'They were both drunk.'

'And they're both consenting adults.'

Rich pushed himself up and patted the edge of the bed for Jasmine to sit down. He stroked an errant curl away from her face. 'You worry too much. Besides, one of these days Miss Right will come along and Dylan will settle down. I think he likes Millie a lot. Perhaps she's his Miss Right.'

'This is my brother we're talking about.'

'All men want to spread their seeds when they're young. But in time they find the perfect field to sow them in and they build a farm-house there.'

'Sometimes…' Jasmine said with a wry smile, 'I have absolutely no idea what you're talking about.'

'Well, you did wake me up at the crack of dawn with a raging hangover.'

Jasmine got up from the bed and pulled a blouse over her head without reply.

'If you ask me, it's Dylan who needs protecting from her, not the other way around,' Rich said.

'What? You're not still going on about that?'

'I'm just saying, we know him a lot better than we know her.'

'I've spent time with her and I am an excellent judge of character.'

He gave her a lopsided grin. 'Not that good – you married me, didn't you?'

'Everyone is allowed the odd lapse in judgement,' she replied, poking her feet into a pair of silver flip-flops.

'Just promise me you won't make a big fuss if they have… you know… done the deed. Dylan won't take kindly to you shoving your nose in his personal life, no matter how well intended it is. Remember how shitty he got last time you did it.'

'If he behaved like a decent human being then I wouldn't have to.'

'Give the guy a break, Jas. He's your brother and your parents' loss affected him just like it did you. The difference is you both dealt with it in your own ways. Have you ever stopped to think that he might find it hard to form real relationships because of it?'

Jasmine paused at the door and sighed. 'I know. But this spiral of self-destruction isn't going to help him get over what happened. I know what you're saying and you're probably right, but there is more than one person involved in this mess and I have to think about her too. I just need to talk to him.' She skipped back over and kissed Rich on the forehead. 'I'll be an hour, tops. If the kids wake up, feed them and then reapply the restraints.'

Rich grinned. But it faded as quickly as it came. 'Seriously, I hope you don't make things worse,' he muttered.

But Jasmine had already gone.

Millie opened her eyes. Summer sun poured into her bedroom, as it had every morning since she arrived in Honeybourne but, somehow, the light seemed to be in the wrong place. Not only that, but her head didn't usually hurt this much. Her eyes roved around the room, taking in the unfamiliar furniture – an old mahogany wardrobe sitting incongruously alongside a flat-pack set of beech-effect laminate drawers, bottles of aftershave, many of them almost empty and coated in a thick layer of dust, ranged along its top. A wash basket overflowed with dark clothing interspersed with what looked like boxer shorts, the one pair she could see properly depicting Homer Simpson's distorted yellow face. Wherever she was, the owner had taste, she reflected with a wry sense of irony. Or she would have done, had her faculties been quite in the working order they usually were.

She screwed her eyes shut, burying her nose in a pillow that smelt as strange and different from her own as everything else. Snapshots of the previous evening bounced around her brain. She remembered arriving at Jasmine's with Dylan, both of them in good spirits. She recalled a lot of wine… Then they had made the decision to stagger home rather than take Jasmine and Rich's offered bed and then…

She bolted up in bed. *Oh God, she was in Dylan's house!*

What had happened when they got here? Millie threw back the bedcovers and heaved a sigh of relief as she saw she was still fully dressed in the clothes she had worn the night before. It was coming back to her, but hazily, and not nearly fast enough to ease her panic.

They had stayed up a while longer to drink some ancient alcohol he kept in a dusty cupboard, the identity of which they hadn't known or cared about, and had flirted like crazy, she knew that much. And she had liked it more than she ought to. Had they kissed? She seemed to have some recollection of the way his lips tasted: warm and spicy and deliciously pliant. His hands – firm yet playful and dextrous – had explored her breasts… Or was she embellishing the memory now? She shook her head, angry at herself. Where had they gone after kissing in the kitchen? He didn't seem the type to let an opportunity for sex to pass him by but Millie didn't feel as though she *had* had sex. She'd know, surely? That last glass of odd amber liquid had been a very bad idea. But unless he had shagged her whilst she was unconscious and then replaced her knickers – and he didn't seem very capable of either of those tasks the state he had been in – then perhaps she was overreacting after all. But she was still angry with herself for letting him get that close, for finding herself in his bed this morning.

Where had Dylan slept, she wondered, as she now pondered the fact that she was alone and the house was in silence.

Swinging her legs over the side of the bed, Millie scanned the floor for any sign of her shoes. Other than some rather fluffy, balled-up socks and a few men's interest magazines stacked in a corner, there was a distinct lack of familiar footwear. With a sigh, she nudged open the bedroom door, which gave with a stubborn creak, and ventured onto the tiny landing.

The only other rooms upstairs were a bathroom and a wee box room stuffed with exercise equipment and boxes of unidentifiable junk. The cottage really was the tiniest of places. Millie remembered Jasmine saying that their parents had left the house to her and Dylan in their will. She wondered if this had been the family home before that; it would have been an interesting, if somewhat cramped, living arrangement.

Not finding what she needed upstairs, or any sign of Dylan for that matter, Millie crept down to the ground floor. She poked her head into what she thought was the sitting room and found, instead, a musty bedroom, complete with a carelessly made bed. This explained the extra room the family must have needed… She crossed the hall to another door and found a tiny conservatory-style living space with a sofa and TV. There was a shout from what could only be the kitchen: 'The kettle is on!'

Millie shuffled, somewhat sheepishly, to the source of the noise. The room was flooded with early morning light and Dylan was grinning as he leaned against the worktop, arms folded across his broad chest.

'Who lives in a house like this?' he drawled in his best fake American accent. 'Did you enjoy your little tour? You only had to ask and you could have had the guided version.'

Millie scowled, half mortified that she had been caught snooping and half irritated at his eternal cockiness. 'I was looking for my shoes and I had no idea where you were to ask you.'

'They're under there,' he replied, nodding towards the kitchen table, his humour in no way diminished by her belligerence. Even more annoyingly, he looked fresh and rested, not like someone who had drunk his own body weight in alcohol the night before. Millie was fairly certain she didn't look quite as good. 'Coffee or tea?' he asked.

'You're making an assumption that I want to stay.' Millie ducked under the table and retrieved her shoes, slipping them on. 'I have tea and coffee across the road.'

'True. But not the riveting company. Or… a hot shower.'

As he said the words *hot shower*, he raised his eyebrows provocatively. It was meant as a joke but the subtext wasn't wasted on her. A proper shower did sound very tempting though. It was all very well feeling martyred as she roughed it in the old bakery, swilling down in bowls of water every day, but sometimes a girl needed a little luxury.

'You want it, don't you?' he grinned. 'My hot shower, that is… I knew you couldn't resist.'

'Dylan…' she began, 'about anything that might have happened here last night—'

'I know,' he cut in, 'you were drunk and it didn't mean anything. It's cool.'

Millie gazed at him. His words were flippant and yet behind his eyes there was something else. Was he hurt by her rejection? She nudged the thought from her head. It didn't matter either way – a relationship with anyone was not on her agenda and one with him would only end badly for both of them.

'I like you,' she said, aware that she was in danger of launching into a full-scale babble, 'but just as a friend. I'm not in the market for anything else right now and I can't say any more about it than that.'

Dylan tipped his finger to his forehead in a sloppy salute. 'Got it. Ask you no questions and you'll tell me no lies.'

The kettle clicked off behind him and he pulled two mugs from a cupboard, blowing into one of them. Millie tried to hide her grimace while he busied himself making tea.

'A shower would be fantastic,' she said into the silence.

'Not a problem. The bathroom door locks, by the way.' He turned to her, his familiar grin back in place. 'So you don't need to worry about being interrupted.'

'I wasn't worried,' she said, taking a mug of tea from him.

'I wasn't joking about the building work on your bakery either,' Dylan added as he took a seat across from her with his own mug.

'I can't expect you to take on a task like that. I—'

'I know you're going to refuse me, and I understand why. But you need all the help you can get and I want to. When you talked about your hopes and dreams for the future last night, well…' He stared at the opposite wall, and then seemed to shake himself. 'It made me think, that's all. It made me realise just how much it means to you, and I think the least I can do is help make your dreams come true.'

Millie stared at him. Where the hell did that come from? 'That's very kind of you.'

'But you're still going to say no?'

'I can't expect you to drop everything and besides, what would your friend say about it? Have you even asked him yet? It doesn't exactly make good business sense, and you know I don't have much money to pay you.'

'Bony will be alright. He'll probably leave most of your jobs to me and I can handle them if he gives me the right instructions and the odd helping hand with the bigger things. It'll be like an apprentice-ship – on-the-job training – and you won't have to pay me for it.'

Millie's eyes widened. 'You'd do it for free?'

'I'd need money for materials. But I'm in no rush for a wage. I still have a bit of inheritance to live on for now.'

'It won't last for ever and you won't make a successful business out of free work.' Millie frowned.

'I'll start to charge once I can justify it by having some kind of building knowledge. Jasmine will tell you that it's not very often I'm moved to help anyone, so why don't you let me?'

Millie smiled. 'I don't think that's true. I think you let people believe that so you don't seem as soft in the middle as you really are.'

He leaned forward with a conspiratorial air. 'Maybe. But don't tell anyone, will you?'

'Anyway, don't you have to go to college, do courses for this sort of thing?' Millie continued, biting back a huge grin.

'Nah, that's all a con to keep teachers in jobs.' He lifted his cup to his lips and took a gulp. 'How hard can it be?'

Millie thought about arguing for a moment but then let it go. She was quickly learning that Dylan inhabited his own peculiar planet with his own peculiar brand of logic and he was perfectly happy there. She was a little envious; Planet Dylan seemed like a nice place. She wished she could be equally divorced from the sharp edges of the real world; that she could sail through life without giving a damn.

Her glance travelled to the cooling mug of tea in front of her. It looked like dishwater and didn't really taste much better. Dylan might have been a man of many talents, but tea-making wasn't one of them.

'Maybe I can get that shower?' she asked, suddenly feeling awkward at the request and hating her weakness, her desire for so frivolous a luxury. She felt it put her at a disadvantage, that accepting Dylan's offer chalked up another debt to repay, and she was racking those up fast enough already since her arrival in Honeybourne.

He leaned back in his chair and appraised her with an easy smile. 'You already know where the bathroom is. There's a stack of clean towels in the airing cupboard. The soap's a bit manly, I'm afraid, but it does the job. Unless you want to nip home and fetch some of your homemade stuff to use?'

'Yours is just fine. And I sold all my natural stuff yesterday anyway.'

He raised his eyebrows and let out a low whistle. 'You sold it all? That's a cracking start for you.'

She smiled, the first proper one of the morning. 'It is. I can't wait to get started on a new batch.'

'What else do you make?'

'What do you mean?'

'Apart from soap and shampoo? Do you make medicine?'

Millie's smile slipped. 'Why do you ask that?'

He shrugged. 'Just what Rich was saying last night about Ruth Evans…' He leaned across the table and lowered his voice. 'Are you some sort of witch? Can you make potions and do spells and stuff?'

Millie stared at him for a moment and then forced out a laugh. 'Don't be daft.'

He leaned back and grinned. 'That's a shame. There are one or two uses I could find for a decent love potion.'

'It doesn't work like that,' she replied, aware of the heat rushing to her face. 'The knowledge I used to make Ruth's remedy comes from ancient recipes and it needs to be treated with respect.'

Dylan held his palms up in a gesture of surrender. 'Alright. I didn't mean to offend you. I just wondered if that was the only thing you could make. If everything works as well as hers seems to have done, you could make a lot of money. I mean, have you seen how much shops charge for that homeopathic shit? Your bakery would be paid for in no time.'

'I don't feel right making money from it.'

'Ok…' he replied slowly, 'don't make money from it, make favours.'

'You mean like we originally planned to do with my baking?'

'Exactly. You get people to do jobs for you in return for whatever remedy or cure it is they want.'

'Nobody would put their trust in a bottle of herbs,' Millie replied doubtfully. 'Not these days anyway.'

'Ruth did.'

'Ruth was desperate and she's… Well, she's Ruth.'

'She's also telling the whole village that you're a miracle worker.'

The flush drained from Millie's face and she paled three shades in as many seconds. 'She is?'

He nodded. 'You heard it from Rich last night.'

'I thought he was exaggerating.'

'He was straight up. You still have a lot to learn about Ruth, don't you?'

'Nobody believes her, though?'

'I don't know.' Dylan rubbed a hand across his chin. 'She looked pretty sprightly to me when I saw her yesterday. I haven't seen her look that well in a long time. I'm no sucker, so if even I'm convinced that there's something in it, then the less cynical residents will be lapping it up.'

'You believe her?' Millie squeaked.

He looked her square in the eye. 'Yeah. I believe her.'

Millie stared at him. She didn't know how to feel at this revelation. On the one hand, she was gripped by panic at the thought of her life unravelling all over again; on the other hand, she felt a swell of pride that Dylan actually took her seriously. Most people scoffed at the idea of her natural remedies, but Dylan seemed genuinely impressed and open-minded.

And at that moment, she didn't think she had ever felt more attracted to him.

'I don't know…' she mumbled, scraping her chair from the table. 'If it's all the same to you, I'll have that shower now.'

She had wanted to shower quickly and get out, but standing under the hot spray, Millie couldn't help but be seduced by the sensation. Before she knew it, she had been messing about in Dylan's bathroom for half an hour. It had been a long time since she had felt so clean and alert, she reflected, as she towelled herself dry and pulled on her not-so-fresh clothes again. Dylan's offer to get working on the old bakery was more tempting than ever, if only so that she could put a real bathroom in.

It was as she made her way downstairs, hair still wet and cool against her neck in the summer heat of Dylan's tiny cottage, that she heard voices in the kitchen and her stomach dropped.

Jasmine was having what sounded like a stern word with her brother. As Millie sheepishly pushed open the kitchen door, both occupants stopped mid-flow and turned to her. Both wore guilty looks and Millie guessed that she had featured strongly in their conversation.

'Millie!' Jasmine greeted, far too brightly. 'How are you? Nicely hungover from last night, I hope.'

'I'm better for a shower,' Millie replied carefully, glancing from one to the other.

'Jasmine has this outrageous idea that we spent the night rutting each other senseless,' Dylan cut in with a lazy grin at his sister, the cockiness he had abandoned earlier with Millie now returned with a vengeance.

Jasmine glared at him and Millie paled.

'Of course, I told her it was complete bollocks,' Dylan added. He leaned back in his chair and folded his arms, his grin at Jasmine spreading. 'I told her we had a perfectly innocent game of bridge before retiring to our own beds with a Horlicks.'

'You think you're so funny, don't you?' Jasmine hissed. 'Why can't you ever rein it in?'

'Charming,' Dylan said carelessly. 'And I was going to make you a cup of tea. You can forget it now.'

Jasmine turned to Millie. 'I'm so sorry… I didn't mean any insult towards you, not for a minute, it's just him…'

'It doesn't matter,' Millie said in a small voice. She rubbed at her temples, suddenly feeling exhausted and desperate for her own quiet space in the dust and cobwebs of the bakery. 'If it's all the same I think I'll go and lie down at home. I am, as you rightly say, very hungover.'

'Don't go,' Jasmine called as Millie headed for the back door.

Millie shook her head, tears starting to burn her eyes as she yanked at the handle. 'Damn…'

'Wait!' Dylan said, leaping up from his chair. 'Millie's jacket is still in the other room.' He disappeared down the hallway.

Millie was desperate to get out. Jasmine's timing couldn't have been worse. Jasmine crossed over to the door and placed a hand on Millie's arm. 'I didn't mean to offend you.'

'I didn't sleep with your brother,' Millie stuttered through the tears she was failing to hold back.

'I know. And even if you had it wouldn't make you a bad person. It's just… I know him so well. He has a sort of track record with women.'

Millie turned and stared at her. 'We're two of a kind then. I have sort of a track record with men. Maybe we're better suited than you think.'

'I bet it's not quite the same as his,' Jasmine smiled. She pulled Millie into a tentative embrace. Sensing no resistance, she hugged tighter. 'I don't know what is in your past and I don't want you to tell me until you're ready. If that's never then it's fine by me. If you want to tell me tomorrow that's fine too. I will never judge you and I'll always be ready to listen.'

'I know,' Millie sniffed. 'Thank you.'

Dylan returned waving Millie's jacket at her. He stopped in his tracks at the sight of the two women locked in their hug.

'Whoa… Do you want me to come back later or something? I don't do all that hormonal touchy-feely stuff.'

'Oh, shut up, Dylan, you twat,' Jasmine groaned as she pulled away from Millie and straightened her blouse. 'Just shut right up.'

Millie had barely let the door slam behind her when Jasmine launched at her brother. 'What the hell are you playing at?'

'I'm not. I like her.'

'That's what worries me.'

'I really like her, Jas.'

Jasmine stared at him, the beginnings of a new sentence dying on her lips.

'I really like her,' Dylan repeated. 'A lot. She's… different from the other women I meet.' His expression was earnest now, not the cocksure grin he usually wore.

Jasmine offered a silent stare as she mulled over his words.

'Say something then,' he insisted.

'I have no idea what to say.'

'That I have your blessing to try and get her to like me?'

'I don't think getting her to like you is the issue.' Jasmine sat on a chair and blew a stray ringlet away from her face. 'I can see that she already does. But I can't say I'm entirely comfortable with the idea of you two being together.'

'Jasmine… We're both adults and, with respect, it's actually none of your business. If she likes me and I like her, I don't see what it has to do with you.' He held his hand up to silence the protest. 'And before you start shouting again, I understand that you're trying to look out for me, but I really don't need you to.'

'It's not you I'm looking out for,' Jasmine replied darkly.

Dylan laughed. 'Probably not. Just live your life and, for once, let me live mine the way I want to. Is that so much to ask?'

Jasmine looked at him thoughtfully. Perhaps he had a point. She couldn't help it, but sometimes even she realised that she treated her brother like her fourth child. 'Promise me you won't screw her around?'

'I won't. But she's never going to give me the tiniest chance if you keep telling her that I'm a waster, is she?'

'You really do like her? Properly? Not just another conquest?'

'Hand on heart. You know me better than anyone, Jas, surely you can see it.'

'It isn't just me you have to convince.'

'I know that. But I'm ready to do what it takes to convince Millie too.'

Jasmine didn't know what to make of this new development. She had thought that she knew Dylan completely, and then he went and did this. Perhaps he really was growing up after all.

Millie had spent far too long dwelling on her mortified exit from Dylan's house that morning. At first she had wanted to scream and cry with frustration at how her bad decisions always seemed to complicate every situation, but then she had calmed down a little. She had even begun to see Jasmine's interference as smothering. Who made her guardian of Millie's personal life? How on earth did Dylan put up with the constant nagging? Even if Millie had chosen to sleep with him, what business was it of Jasmine's? After all, they were two consenting adults, with no one to answer to but their own consciences. All these thoughts had hurtled through her head as she scrubbed viciously at the front windows, trying to work it all out. Her mood swung wildly between affection for Jasmine, the friend who was only trying to look out for her, and resentment for a bunch of village busy-bodies who seemed to think she was incapable of making her own decisions.

Finally, exhausted from her cleaning, her late night, her hangover, and her unreliable mood, she tipped the bucket of black water out into the street drains and wiped a hand across her forehead. The sun was high, a fierce orb again. It had been so long since the weather had been anything but sweltering that it was hard to remember what a cool day felt like.

Millie had just decided to head back to bed when there was a knock at the front door.

'Hi… Peggy, isn't it?' Millie asked as she opened up, a look of faint surprise on her features. She had seen the woman around the village – in a place that small you had usually seen everyone around – but they had not exchanged more than vague pleasantries before. The only reason Millie knew her name was that Ruth had pointed her out once and whispered something about a scandalous affair with another woman, back in 1977, which had sent the village gossip chain wild. According to Jasmine, whom Millie had quizzed for a more reliable and less dramatic version than Ruth's, the woman in question had been forced to leave the village and Peggy's husband had followed shortly afterwards, too ashamed to stay. Peggy had never remarried or taken a new partner – male or female – but she had stayed in Honeybourne and the scandal had died down, as all scandals eventually do.

Peggy nodded, and then glanced up and down the deserted street before speaking. 'I'm sorry to bother you but I wondered if you had a moment.'

'Of course…' Millie opened the door wider, her curiosity now piqued. 'What can I do for you?'

Peggy stepped over the threshold. She fell silent as Millie closed the door, gazing about her at the dusty skeleton of the old building.

'Wow, I haven't been inside here for years. I remember when this was a thriving business.'

'What happened to the owners?'

'Clarissa and Joe Williams? They ran it for a good few years. But their children… Well, there's not so much for young ones in Honeybourne, and a lot don't stay. Sadly, the old bakery wasn't enough to tempt them, and when Clarissa died, followed a year later by Joe, who keeled over pretty much where you're standing now, they still weren't persuaded to come back and take over the business. The lad is in Australia, as far as I know, and their daughter married a doctor in the French Alps. I suppose you wouldn't come back to Honeybourne if you could live there, would you? The old place was run down, to be honest, long before Joe died, but folks still brought their trade in here out of loyalty to him and his wife. They were as loving a couple as you could meet.'

Millie gave a small smile. It explained a lot about the feeling of loyalty she had for the place. Walls that had soaked up so much love and happiness over the years were bound to retain some of that and beg for happy days again, and Millie was more attuned to the phenomenon than most – at least, she knew how to recognise it where others didn't. It was just a shame that it was starting to look like it may be someone other than Millie to bring that love and happiness back. 'So nobody has owned it since they died? How long ago was that?'

'I'm not sure, but a good while. I think there was some trouble over the will, and it sat for a few years, then it took a few more to sell it… Somebody did buy it but I don't recall what happened to them and they certainly didn't ever live here. Don't you know anything about the vendor from when you bought it?'

Millie shook her head. 'It was all done through the agent. I didn't have any contact with the seller at all.'

Peggy took another swift glance around the old walls. 'It makes me so sad to see it now.' She turned to Millie with a slight smile. 'Are you really going to get it up and running again?'

'I'm going to try,' Millie replied.

'I think people around here would like that. It's all very well having the supermarket just outside the village but somewhere like this could be just what we need to put the heart back into our home – somewhere for people to meet and relax.'

'There's the Dog and Hare, isn't there?'

Peggy smiled. 'Not everyone drinks alcohol, though. Are you planning to open the café up again as well as the bakery?'

'I was going to try it, see how much demand there is. I just have to work out the practicalities. Like staffing; I don't think I'll be able to do it all and I'm not sure if I'll be able to afford help at first.'

'I think there'll be a lot of demand for a café though. And in the summer you might get passing trade from people travelling through to holiday destinations on the coast.'

'I certainly haven't planned that far ahead!' Millie laughed.

'You must be wondering why I've come,' Peggy said.

'A little bit.'

'I… well… I got chatting to Ruth Evans yesterday evening…'

Millie stiffened. Why hadn't she seen this coming? Of course it was about Ruth. 'So I was wondering if you could help me,' Peggy said, desperate hope in her expression as she watched Millie carefully.

'I know Ruth said you didn't want everyone knowing and I won't tell a soul, but I'd be ever so grateful if you could give me something.'

Millie sighed. 'I want to help, but it really isn't that straightforward.'

'So you can't?' Peggy's bottom lip actually wobbled. Millie didn't think she had ever seen anything quite so pitiful but if Peggy's act had been premeditated, it got the desired effect. Millie's heart went out to her. She let out another, even heavier sigh. Because when people said they wouldn't tell a soul, that usually meant they would probably only tell three or four souls, who would in turn tell another three or four souls, so that the soul count rose exponentially until the entire county of Hampshire knew about her cures. Knowing all this didn't change the fact that Millie would end up helping Peggy, because, despite wanting to keep people at arms' length, her conscience simply wouldn't allow her to do anything else.

'What is it I can help with?' she asked wearily.

'I have the most terrible migraines,' Peggy said, a grateful smile lighting her face. 'They began when I was a teenager. I can't tell you how I've suffered over the last forty years.'

'Don't you have medication for them?'

'Oh yes, but it doesn't often work. It dulls the pain, but it's still there.'

'What causes them?'

'The doctors say it's idiopathic. I've lost count of the number of consultants who have fired that word at me.'

'They can't find a reason and they don't want to sound stupid so they give you a lovely Greek medical word that essentially means nothing,' Millie clarified.

'Exactly.'

She was thoughtful for a moment. 'What you need is something to treat them at the root, to eradicate them for good.'

'You could do that?'

'There are never any promises. But I can try.' Millie glanced across at the pile of boxes containing her equipment and books. 'I'll need some time to put something together. Can you come back later today?'

Peggy nodded like an eager child. 'What time?'

Millie considered what she would need. Without consulting her books, there were herbs she knew would have to be scavenged from the nearby hedgerows and woodlands. 'After six should do it.'

'Thank you so much,' Peggy said as Millie subtly herded her towards the door. 'Thank you so, so much…'

'Honestly, it's nothing. I just hope I can help you. Remember, I can only try and it may not work.'

'I know, but it's the trying that matters. It's so kind of you. Ruth said you were lovely and she's right.'

Millie felt the blush rise to her cheeks. 'Please, don't mention it. I'll see you this evening, alright?'

Peggy beamed at her before turning for the street; somehow, her step a little lighter in leaving than when she had first arrived. Millie watched her go. She sincerely hoped that she could help; she didn't think she could stand the look of disappointment on Peggy's face if she failed.

Chapter Nine

Peggy had duly returned at one minute past six, her eyes bright with hope. It turned Millie's stomach to see it. What she did was not an exact science and not always reliable, and although the ingredients she used were entirely natural, there was always the possibility – however remote – of side effects; though she tried not to dwell on the consequences of that.

During the afternoon, as she had been scouring the local hedgerows for plants, Millie had been accosted no less than three times by people who had heard Ruth's story. One of these was the local GP, wanting to know what she had given Ruth and issuing a veiled warning that she should not be meddling in matters that modern medicine was more equipped to deal with. Whilst the rebuke left Millie smarting, she couldn't help but see his point. The other two were villagers who had their own ailments and problems and expressed hope that Millie would be able to help.

What could she do? The fear of becoming too involved in people's lives – of being a danger if they came to rely on her and she was unable to help – was still as real here as it had been back in Millrise. But she needed an even better reason to refuse to help. She was beginning to learn that Michael's death would haunt her for ever, but perhaps the best she could hope for was that she'd be able to keep the ghost locked away so that it didn't invade every moment of her life. So she told each hopeful villager that she would research a remedy and see what she could come up with. In return, they had pledged assistance with the bakery in whatever small way they could. Millie suspected that their help would be more reliable than hers, no matter how small, but when people asked her for aid she found it hard to say no.

Another scorching week had passed in which Millie had become the proud owner of new curtains for every window of her home, skirting boards and a new counter for the shop, courtesy of her neighbours. They weren't exactly going to get the bakery running but they were a start. Millie had no idea whether the remedies she had given them were working, but they reassured her that they felt one hundred per cent better and she was happy to see them believe it. Her mother had often said that believing was half the battle and Millie was inclined to agree.

Millie was watering the begonia-filled hanging baskets when she heard a nervous cough. She turned to see Spencer regarding her with a hesitant smile.

'Spencer! Aren't you meant to be filling the youngsters of Honeybourne full of wisdom?' Millie glanced at her watch, surprised to see that the day had somehow slipped away from her and it was just after five.

His smile broadened. 'I decided that was a thankless task long ago. Now it's just about crowd control… If I can stop one boy a day from picking his nose and flicking the contents at the girl in front then I count that as a success.'

'Can you stay for a bit?'

'That sounds nice. Here…' Spencer took the rusted watering can from her. 'Let me finish this for you.'

She gave a grateful smile. 'I've got soft drinks – though they're not very cold, I'm afraid. I'm trying not to run too many appliances at a time until the place is rewired, in case I blow it up, so the fridge is on a strictly need-to-cool basis, enough to stop my food going off and that's it. Or I could make you a cup of tea.'

'A soft drink is just fine,' he replied, reaching up to the next basket. He leapt back with a sharp cry as the stream of water ran down the side of the can, down his arm, and soaked the front of his shirt.

Millie giggled. 'I should have warned you that the can is a bit temperamental. I think there's a leak somewhere.'

'How come it hasn't soaked you?'

She shrugged. 'I've worked out the knack.'

'At least it's cooled me down.' He gave her a sheepish grin as he wiped a hand down the dark stain on his shirt. 'It'll soon dry.'

As she pulled glasses from a cupboard, Spencer followed her in with the watering can.

'They're all done,' he said. 'Where do you want this?'

'It can go out the back.' She pointed to a small, paved yard beyond the back window. It was deep in shade, bordered on all four high walls by lush, rambling clematis and honeysuckle, all the more beautiful for growing wild over the years. Millie had considered cutting them right back when she moved in, but soon decided that she rather liked their unruly freedom and so left them as they were. 'We could sit out there too, if you like. It's a lot cooler than out the front and, if you'll excuse the obvious pun, it's like a bloody oven in here.'

Spencer laughed. 'Sounds great.'

'You'll find a couple of folding chairs stacked against the shed,' she called after him as he made his way through the back door.

'No problem,' he called back.

She couldn't say why, but Millie felt a certain rush of pleasure that Spencer had sought her out. He never turned up without Dylan or Jasmine – he always seemed a little too shy for that – and when he did come along with them, although he was pleasant and charming company, he always let the others lead the conversation. She followed him outside with their drinks.

'I had no idea this little garden existed,' Spencer said as Millie found him already settled on a floral canvas chair. 'It's amazing. Fancy living here all my life and not realising that the bakery had more than just a boarded-up front.'

Millie smiled as she handed him a glass. 'It's hard to see beyond all the grim work that needs doing to the place.'

'I suppose it takes someone of vision,' Spencer agreed. 'And that does seem to be you. Lucky for Honeybourne that you arrived, eh?'

'I'm not so sure about that. I'm going to do my best to make it home, but sometimes it seems like I've set myself an impossible task.'

'Dylan's helping you, isn't he?'

Millie nodded. 'I can't say that I'm comfortable with the idea but he's insisting.'

'You should snap his hand off. It's not often Dylan offers anyone favours.' Spencer paused and took a sip of his drink. He glanced over the top of his glass at Millie, then lowered it, opened his mouth to speak before closing it again and regarding her in silence, his expression slightly less assured than it had been a moment before. There was history with Spencer and Dylan; Millie sensed it. In fact, anyone who spent more than ten minutes in their company could see it. Perhaps now wasn't the time to ask, though.

'I do realise that there may be an ulterior motive,' she replied instead with a wry smile. 'That's partly why I'm uncomfortable with the whole situation. So you needn't worry about saying it.'

'I know Dylan. He means well and I don't think even he realises that everything he does seems to come with a condition attached.'

Millie sighed. 'That said, I do need all the help I can get here.'

'He'll do a good job too. It takes a long time to galvanise him into action but once he sets his mind on something he does it properly and he doesn't give up.'

'I'm not sure if that makes me feel better or worse,' she replied, her mind flitting back to the drunken night where Dylan had made his interest in her very obvious. And she hadn't exactly put him off. But his lips had been so wonderfully soft and warm, and his arms safe and strong, and his torso lean and muscular… and she had been so lonely for so long…

'He's a jack-the-lad but he'd never do anything to hurt you,' Spencer said, interrupting her thoughts, 'at least, not intentionally. He's a good kid really.'

'You make it sound like you're about ninety.'

Spencer laughed. 'I do feel like that sometimes after a day at work. And there are times when our little age gap feels very big.'

'Like he's having all the fun?'

'Something like that.'

'But what you do matters. If he disappeared tomorrow who would even notice? I mean, Jasmine would, obviously, but would the world be a vastly different place without him?'

'You'd miss him…' Spencer said carefully.

'Only as a neighbour,' she replied with equal care.

'I bet you're wondering why I've come over,' he said brightly. A little too brightly, Millie reflected. She had seen that glossing over of an inner sadness a thousand times. Spencer, she realised with a jolt, was lost and lonely, just like she was.

'Enlighten me,' she said.

'The kids are doing a citizenship project this term about respecting others with different religions and beliefs. We've looked at all the usual stuff – Christianity, Hinduism, Islam… but I thought it might be interesting to study some more obscure beliefs too. I know…' He paused. 'When we went to Stonehenge that day I got the feeling that you knew rather a lot about that sort of thing…'

'You are allowed to say it.'

'I was reading about Wicca. I wondered if that was something that you knew about.'

'A little. I've read a lot of mythology and books about alternative beliefs.' Millie's admission surprised even her. But there was something about Spencer that invited trust. She felt a kindred spirit in him, someone who would respect her beliefs and her views on the world.

'Do you think the kids would benefit from hearing about it?'

'It's a fairly complex bunch of ideas to explain to them at their age and I'm no expert. I suppose I could gen up and give them a brief insight, but it's only as much as you could do yourself.'

'I still think you'd know more than me.'

Millie smiled. 'Do you mind very much if I don't? It's not that I'm trying to be unhelpful, it's…' Her sentence trailed off. She didn't have an excuse good enough apart from one that she didn't want to share.

Spencer was thoughtful for a moment as he took a long draught of his lemonade. 'It's ok.'

'Sorry.'

'Millie… I hope you don't mind me saying but sometimes I feel as though you need a friendly ear to offload things. I'd like to listen if you wanted to share.'

Listen to what? Millie wondered. Did he mean he wanted to know more about her immediate problems, or could he sense something more, and simply want to help shoulder the burden of her past? Once it was out, there was no taking it back. It was tempting, because never being able to talk about it was eating her from the inside out, but every time the words formed in her mouth something stopped her. What if he thought badly of her once he knew the truth? What if he told everyone else what she had done, the awful, fatal mistake that had sent her running from her old life to a tiny village in Hampshire? Would they drive her away again if they knew?

From beyond the open back door, Millie suddenly thought she heard a faint knock. She cocked her head to listen and it sounded again almost immediately.

'I should probably go and see who it is,' Millie said, her stomach dropping. The queue of villagers wanting a remedy was growing longer by the day.

Spencer nodded and she got up.

A few moments later she returned with Dylan. He stopped, a half-frown on his face, a beat of silence as he clocked Spencer.

'I just came around to ask for Millie's help,' Spencer said uncertainly.

Millie looked between them in some confusion. She could detect that undercurrent again, and now it was impossible to ignore. On the surface their friendship seemed to be old and solid, but something wasn't right. Millie reached for the answer as she watched them both exchange some kind of subliminal dialogue, but she couldn't put her finger on it.

'Struggling to get the top off your jam?' Dylan said with a grin.

'Are you?' Spencer fired back, 'as you seem to be here too.'

'I, my friend, am not here for Millie's help. I have come to offer mine.'

'Dylan,' Millie interrupted, 'we were just having a drink. Can I offer you one?'

'What have you got?' Dylan dragged an extra chair from against the wall and opened it out to take a seat.

'No alcohol I'm afraid, but I can do cloudy lemonade.'

Dylan shrugged. 'I suppose I'll have to be a good boy this afternoon then. Lemonade is fine by me.'

When she returned, they were laughing and joking and she wondered whether she had imagined the moment of awkwardness and distrust between them.

'I saw Ruth Evans today,' Dylan said, taking his glass with a nod.

'Oh?' Millie replied.

'She said that Peggy Nicholls had been to see you too and that you gave her another one of your hippy potions.'

'It was nothing,' Millie excused. 'She said she suffered from migraines and all I gave her was a simple herbal painkiller.'

'According to Ruth, Peggy is completely cured. I wouldn't call that nothing.'

Millie forced a laugh. 'She can't know that after a few days. Migraines come and go – everyone knows that.'

'I'm telling you,' Dylan insisted, 'you should think about selling them. You'd make a lot more money than you do on soap and cakes.'

'And you'd also get sued by the first unscrupulous customer who decided they could prove you were a charlatan,' Spencer cut in.

Both Millie and Dylan turned sharply towards him.

'You know I'm right,' Spencer continued. 'Either that or someone will say that your potion has done more harm than good. People are out to get what they can in this world and I'm afraid someone as nice as you would be a prime target, Millie.'

'As nice as me…' Millie said with a half-laugh. 'You mean someone as gullible and soft?'

'You know that's not what I mean. But I think you should keep this stuff to yourself. Keep it small, amongst friends.'

Millie sipped her drink. Spencer had a point. She'd already known it but hearing it from someone else only reinforced her fears. Already things were getting out of hand.

'I think Spencer is right,' she said.

'Seriously?' Dylan spluttered.

'So what's your take on it?' Spencer said, smiling, but his tone a little less forgiving.

'I think she's missing a golden business opportunity.'

'Yeah,' Spencer said, 'because you know so much about business.'

'I just think you're being overcautious. I don't see the point in throwing away a chance like this. It could make you way more money than slaving over hot ovens all day and it wouldn't be nearly as much work.'

'It could also lose you a lot if things go badly,' Spencer said.

'Jeez, have you ever taken a chance in your whole life?' Dylan cried. 'Always mister careful, mister goody-two-shoes schoolteacher, mister bloody voice of reason. Would you listen to yourself?'

'I took a chance, remember. It didn't work out all that well, did it?' Spencer said quietly, his jaw muscles tight.

Dylan started a reply but Spencer stood.

'Thanks for the drink, Millie, but I'd better get back. I have marking to do.'

'I'll see you to the door,' Millie said, glancing at Dylan uncertainly. 'And I'll think about what you asked me for the school project.'

'Thanks. I appreciate that.'

Spencer turned briefly towards Dylan, but he was gazing down into his glass. 'See you around.'

'Yeah,' Dylan said without looking up.

Millie frowned, annoyed on Spencer's behalf. She looked at him, his shoulders hunched in defeat as she followed him through to the front door. His obvious distress pained her. Whatever had happened in the past between these two, feelings still ran deep. Jasmine had told her briefly that they'd had a falling out, but she had never known what over. It seemed that, despite their efforts, the rift wasn't quite mended yet. Millie wanted nothing more than to throw her arms around Spencer right now and give him a hug.

'For what it's worth,' she said, keeping her voice low, 'I think you're right.'

Spencer gave her a tight smile. 'I appreciate that. How about I come over one night during the week? I'm still interested in what we were talking about.'

'That sounds lovely. Thanks for popping by.'

Millie waved him from the step and closed the door with a sigh. Then her expression hardened as she made her way back out to the yard.

'I thought you two were friends.'

'We are.'

'So what was all that about? Why go out of your way to make him feel small? That's not how friends treat each other.'

'I happen to think he's wrong, that's all.'

'No…' Millie narrowed her eyes, hands on hips. 'There's more to it than that.'

'Spencer knows me well enough by now. He won't take offence.'

'I think he very much took offence. You were mean and dismissive.'

'You think?'

'Yes.'

He folded his arms. 'Poor Spencer. That's what everyone always thinks. He's so sweet, so harmless, so vulnerable. You want to wrap him up and keep him safe.'

Millie raised her eyebrows in a silent question.

'He's not what everyone thinks he is,' Dylan continued.

'So?' Millie shrugged, feeling vexed on Spencer's behalf. She had never liked to hear someone bad-mouthed when they weren't present to defend themselves and she especially didn't like it now. 'I speak as I find and I happen to think he's a kind and sensitive soul. Besides… We all have our dark secrets. We're entitled to keep them too if they don't harm anyone.'

'Oh? So what's yours?'

Millie couldn't help but smile at the flirtation that was now in his voice and the danger in his question. His mood changed direction as quickly as leaves on an autumn wind. 'Never mind mine, what are yours?'

'I don't have any. Scratch the surface and you get more of the same.'

'Which is?'

'I don't know. You should ask Jasmine that.'

Millie watched him, waiting for more, but his attention seemed to flit elsewhere as quickly as the statement was made. He glanced around the tiny walled yard.

'Are you keeping all this?'

'What do you mean?'

'When I start the building work.'

Millie took in the space and then looked back at him. 'Why would I get rid of this? It's lovely.'

'But you could get an extension here, something to make more space for the business. It makes sense.'

'No…' Millie took a seat. 'I need somewhere quiet, away from the business, somewhere to collect my thoughts. I like it out here.'

'It's your call.' He stretched his legs out and yawned. 'How do you feel about having me around a lot in the next few weeks?'

'You can start the building work?'

'Why not? Haven't got much else to do.'

Millie smiled. Despite her misgivings about involving Dylan, about the debt she would owe him and how he might want repaying, her stomach was now aflutter at the news. 'I'll help you,' she said breathlessly. 'I won't be much good but I'll do what I can.'

'Any good with a cement mixer?'

She laughed. 'No, but point me in the direction of the on switch and I'm sure I can have a go.'

'I'll bring some things over on Monday. Bony will get me started and then he'll have to go off to Salisbury for a job there, but he says he'll call in from time to time.'

'What about money?' Millie asked doubtfully, the first flush of excitement now tempered by more practical and worrying consider-ations. 'What if I don't have enough to finish the work?'

'If you sold those potions you would have, no problem…' Millie frowned and opened her mouth to argue but he laughed. 'I know, I know. We'll come to some arrangement. And a respectable one at that. Give me what you can at the moment to get started and then we'll follow the plan with Jasmine to start raising the rest.'

'It's a lot to raise in a short time.'

'I'm in no rush and Bony is already loaded, he can wait for his money. Don't sweat it.'

'You've been so kind to me. Everyone has. I don't know how I can repay it.'

'Stick around for a while,' he said with a smile. 'Promise you won't move away any time soon and that will be payment enough.'

'That's easy to promise. I've done enough moving to last me a lifetime.'

Chapter Ten

Over the next week, Dylan was in and out of her home so often that Millie became thoroughly used to his presence. Without even realising it, she was starting to feel comfortable with him. Their chats in between working became longer, more intimate, more revealing. And any worries Millie might have had that he would be a sloppy worker, or easily distracted from his task, were so far unfounded. To her delight he had made short work of removing the old and crumbling plaster from the walls of the kitchen, ready for an electrician to come in and fix the wiring. Millie had hardly been able to tear her gaze from the flexing of his glistening muscles as he worked; a desire building inside her that she hadn't felt in a long time.

'You need a break,' she said on the Friday afternoon as she watched him, shirtless, sanding down the old ceiling beams.

At her voice, he span round and slipped on the ladder, almost tumbling off it. 'How long have you been there? I thought you'd gone out.'

'About ten minutes,' Millie said with a sly smile. 'I was admiring the view.'

'Oh yeah?' Dylan made his way down. He leapt from the bottom rung and flexed his muscles. 'A bit dusty, but still the goods, eh?'

'I meant the beams… They look great now all that muck is off them.'

Dylan grinned and took a seat on a rough bench fashioned from old wooden crates. He had put it together to take breaks on during the first day, so he didn't dirty Millie's other furniture, and she had been struck by how sweet the gesture was. As the week had progressed, she had been struck by more than that too. From behind her back, Millie produced a can of beer and offered it to him.

He took the can and turned it around to look at the label. 'The good stuff.'

'I figured you deserved a treat for working so hard.'

'You've worked pretty hard too. You're not having one?'

Millie shook her head. 'Not just yet, it's still a bit early for me.'

Dylan smacked his lips as he took a swig from the can. 'It's never too early for a good beer.' He patted the dusty old bench next to him. 'Care to sit and watch me drink your beer instead?'

'Why not?' She took a seat. The air between them seemed supercharged and Millie was suddenly, painfully, aware of the need to speak, to break the frisson that fizzed and crackled and stole all rational thought.

Eventually, Dylan said, 'Weirdly, I've quite enjoyed working this week.' He let out a low chuckle. 'I never thought I'd hear myself say that.'

'Weirdly, I've quite enjoyed it too.'

He turned to her. 'You actually like me being around?'

'I wouldn't go that far,' she laughed. 'But it hasn't been *too* much of a chore.'

'That's good to hear.' He took another gulp of his beer and wiped a hand across his forehead.

Millie tried not to make it obvious as she watched him, but there was no hiding the gaze that lingered just a little too long on his lips, the parting of her own, the quickening of her pulse. Could she trust this man with her heart? Could he be the one to transform her, to banish the sadness that haunted her? It had seemed such an unlikely prospect when they first met, but she had seen a different side to him these last couple of weeks; the kindness and consideration for others that his sister displayed so openly was buried just a little deeper in him, but it was there all the same.

'I feel I need to repay you somehow,' Millie said, firing him a coy glance.

'I could think of a few ways,' he laughed.

'Why don't you try me?'

Dylan turned to her, eyebrows raised in disbelief as he set his beer down on the floor. 'I don't know what you mean…'

'Oh, I think you do. You were keen enough that night I slept at your house—'

'But I didn't—'

'No, you were the perfect gentleman in the end. I was drunk and you didn't take advantage of me. I'm beginning to think that you really aren't the man you pretend to be to everyone.'

'Don't let that get out. My reputation will be ruined.'

And then Millie leaned over and kissed him.

Almost immediately his hands were all over her, hunger in every caress as he kissed her in return. He was sweaty, covered in dust, but she didn't care. He fiddled desperately at the top buttons of her shirt, but then he suddenly stopped, and yanked himself away.

'This isn't right…'

Millie regarded him with a quizzical look. 'You're refusing me?' she asked, but she wore a half-smile.

'I know. The world has gone upside down, right?' The smile he returned was one of bewilderment. He ran a hand through his hair and shrugged. 'I consider my reputation well and truly knackered now.'

'I don't think so…'

'It's just… I really like you, Millie. I mean, *properly* like you, in a way I've never felt for anyone before. And I want to do this, more than anything. But the reasons have to be right… I want you to like me too.'

Millie had hoped that this would be his reaction. A few weeks ago she knew he would have jumped at an offer to sleep with him as repayment for working on her home, but here he was, telling her how wrong it was. Her heart was fragile, and she needed to be certain of the man who took on the job of strengthening it. Dylan Smith had seemed like the most unlikely of candidates, but his actions today showed her that perhaps he was the man after all.

As he gazed at her, Millie was suddenly struck by how vulnerable, how young he looked. All he wanted was love. Jasmine had often talked about how their parents' death had affected her, but Dylan never talked about it. She could see now that it had rocked him to the core, had damaged something so deep that even he couldn't reach that place to mend it. Millie needed healing, and so did he. Perhaps it was a good match after all. Perhaps they could heal each other. She reached over, gently took his chin in her fingertips, tracing the line of fine stubble beneath her touch. He stared at her uncertainly. Millie was filled with a new courage. She had spent so long waiting for the universe to put her life back on track, but she could do that herself. This was where she took that step into the void, and she would fly or fall. She leaned over and kissed him again.

'Wow…' he whispered as her lips left his. He had let her take complete control this time, and she knew that it was his way of making her feel safe. 'I could get some more of that.'

'You can have a lot more of that,' Millie smiled.

She reached for him again. His fingers went back to her blouse, fumbling at the buttons, his hands slipping inside the first gap to caress her breasts and she gasped as a wave of desire crashed through her, the sheer force of it taking her by surprise.

Then he pulled away again, breathless, his expression pained. 'You're sure?'

'I've never been more sure of anything.' Millie straddled him this time, plunging her hands into his hair as she pressed her mouth to his, dominating every move they now made. She heard him groan beneath her, and knew that she now owned him completely. She was hot, desperate for him, but not as desperate as he was for her and the idea was thrilling.

And then a knock at the front door boomed through the old building.

'You need to get that?' Dylan panted.

'No. They can come back.' Millie kissed him again, her tongue dancing with his.

The knock came again, more forceful and insistent this time. Millie pulled away with a frown.

'They sound like they really want you,' Dylan said. 'Nobody is more pissed off with their timing than me but perhaps you ought to get it.'

'What if it's your sister?'

'We'll just have to pretend we're playing Scrabble.'

Millie giggled as she buttoned up her blouse. 'Try to remain hot while I'm getting rid of whoever it is.'

'I'll be waiting. You've no idea how long I've been waiting.' The look in his eyes was warm and genuine, enough to leave Millie in no doubt of his need for her.

She smiled as she went through to the main shop to answer the door. Smoothing a hand over her hair, she opened it, expecting to see Jasmine or Ruth, a polite excuse already formed and waiting on her lips.

She stopped dead, losing all colour as the door swung open to reveal a face that she hadn't seen for a long time, one she had hoped never to see again.

'Hello, Millicent,' the woman said coldly. 'I was beginning to think I'd never track down your hiding place.'

Chapter Eleven

Millie stumbled back against the doorframe. 'Rowena,' she said in a weak voice.

'Surprised to see me?'

'Where…'

'Aren't you going to ask me in?' Rowena stepped back and swept the front of the building with a critical gaze. 'I never had you down as a hovel sort of girl.'

'What are you doing here?' Millie hissed, her faculties returning. 'How did you find me?'

'It's not that hard really. A few well-placed questions up in Millrise, a newspaper report down here about your plans to breathe life back into the…' she crooked her fingers into speech marks, 'heart of the sleepy village of Honeybourne, a chat with the village gossip… and *voila.*'

'You have to go.'

'But I only just got here.'

'And you're not welcome.'

'Oh…' Rowena stepped forward, forcing Millie back from the threshold and into the building, 'I think I am.'

'Why do you have to keep tormenting me? Haven't you had enough? I'm truly sorry for what happened to Michael but don't you think I've paid for that now?' Millie cried, emotions overwhelming her. She'd worked so hard, finally got to the place where she could start to move on and it was all about to be snatched from her.

'There is no price you can pay that will atone for what you made him do.'

'Rowena… please…'

And then Millie's legs almost buckled beneath her as another voice came from beyond the room. She clung to the shop counter and tried to calm her breathing.

'Millie… Is everything ok?' Dylan appeared at the doorway.

'Of course,' Millie replied stiffly.

'Only I heard you…' he began, confusion in his expression as he looked between the two women. 'I wondered if you were alright.'

'I'm an old friend of Millie's,' Rowena said, sidling past Millie before she could do anything. 'And you are?'

'A neighbour,' Dylan said carefully, glancing at Millie for guidance. But she simply looked down at her feet, desperately trying to control the emotion that squeezed her throat. 'I'm helping out, with the renovations.'

'How noble of you. And I bet you're just fabulous at it too.'

'I try,' he replied.

'And so handsome… You know,' Rowena said, eyeing him up and down, 'you remind me a lot of my brother.'

'Do I?' Dylan asked hesitantly.

'You're about the same age as he would have been, too, at a guess.'

'Dylan…' Millie found her voice and looked up at him, her eyes silently trying to communicate what she dared not speak in front of the newcomer. 'I think Rowena and I need to talk some things over. I don't suppose you'd mind popping back later?'

He looked from one to the other again, clearly trying to weigh up the situation. Then he nodded. 'Sure. You know where I am if you need me… It was nice to meet you, Rowena.'

Rowena nodded carelessly and took herself to sit in the window seat. Millie walked with Dylan to the door.

He stepped out into the street, and then turned to face her. 'You're sure you don't need me to stick around?' he said in a low voice.

Millie shook her head. 'It's something I have to sort myself. I wish I could tell you about it, but I can't… Not yet.'

'Don't shut me out, Millie. We're past that now… Alright?'

'I won't.'

He hovered for a moment, uncertain of the etiquette of the strange moment in which he found himself. And then he turned with a barely audible sigh and left for his own house. Millie watched him go, regret scoring her guts. Already she knew that all she had hoped for, only an hour ago, could never be. She would never be free of the guilt that plagued her, of the mistake that Rowena had brought back to her doorstep. The sooner she accepted that, the less it would hurt.

'You can't stay here,' Millie said as she closed the door behind her and turned to Rowena. 'I don't have any room.'

'Don't you worry. I've rented a cottage in the neighbouring village.'

'For how long?'

Rowena was silent for a moment as she held Millie in a penetrating gaze. 'For as long as it takes to ruin your life.'

'It won't bring him back.'

'It will bring him justice and it makes me feel good.'

'Michael would hate to see you become this, you know that.'

'As he isn't here to express an opinion either way we'll never know if that's true, will we?' She glanced around the dusty room, arching a pencilled brow. 'It's a bit of a tip, isn't it? But I see you have some facilities...' Her eyes fell on a pack of beers, one missing from the corner. 'And you are geared up to entertain. Do you always ply your builders with beer while they work? You must be popular.'

'He was taking a break and he was hot.'

'Oh, he's that alright. Lining him up as your next victim, are you?'

'What else can you get from me, Rowena? I mean, really, what else? Are you going to spend your entire life following me around so that you can drive me out of wherever I go? Are you really so twisted by vengeance? We used to be friends. I loved Michael as much as you. When he died... I was angry and hurt too. And I know it's my fault but I can't change it. If you don't stop this destructive path you're on, then...'

'Then it will be your fault. You'll have that on your conscience too and I'll love every minute of your suffering.' Rowena stood up and brushed down her long black skirt with a sneer. 'God, it's filthy in this place. And it stinks.'

'Rowena—'

Rowena held up a hand to silence Millie. 'Don't think this is over,' she snarled as she headed for the door. 'It's only just begun.'

Jasmine watched with a huge grin as the triplets squealed and laughed, willing their swings higher and higher in the best kind of sibling rivalry. She turned to Dylan as they sat on a garden bench together, the sun skimming the distant treetops as it began its fiery descent for another roasting evening.

'Thanks so much for putting those up. I've been asking Rich for weeks but he's in his creative bubble so expecting him to do practical things is hopeless.'

'Ah... And how is the Oscar-winning film score coming along?'

'I don't think it's going very well...' Jasmine lowered her voice, despite the fact that her husband was locked in a soundproof studio in the house, the smile fading from her lips. 'It's making him snappy too. Not good for the kids to be around right now...'

'Is it bad?'

'Nothing I can't handle.' She let out a sigh. 'I just wish he'd talk to me about it. This is Rich all over – brilliant company when things are good, but unable to let anyone in when he's feeling low.'

'I suppose he wants to spare you.'

Jasmine let out a mirthless laugh. 'I don't call this sparing me. You can't say two words to him at the moment without a look that could fry you on the spot. I'd take half his problems any day to avoid that. We're supposed to be in this together, that's what marriage is about.'

'He'll snap out of it once he gets his mojo back.'

'God, I hope so. I just hope composer's block is all that's bothering him and it's nothing more serious.'

'Don't you take any shit from that man.' Dylan sipped his glass of beer. 'You're far too good for him and he knows it.'

Jasmine fired a sideways look at her brother, but his expression betrayed not a hint of irony. 'I think that's the first time you've ever actually paid me a compliment,' she said.

'Don't get used to it.' He flashed a quick grin.

'How are the renovations going?' Jasmine asked. She was more tired from Rich's recent frustrated moods than she cared to admit and suddenly felt the need to talk about something completely unconnected.

'Really well. This time next week I reckon Millie will be able to make her next batch of pies for Doug in her own ovens.'

'Seriously? That's amazing!'

'I mean, she won't be anywhere near ready for business, but the kitchen should be plastered and the mains gas and electricity for it should be good to go. She keeps harping on about food standards inspectors and stuff, saying she can't bake in there until she's got her certificate, but the way I see it, she's not actually trading yet, she's just donating the food in return for favours, so I don't see how she can get into trouble.'

'She wants to do everything right,' Jasmine replied sagely. 'I can't say that's a bad thing. And she has put up with you for an entire week without throwing anything at your head… Things must be going well.'

Dylan laughed. 'We've got on better than I could have imagined.'

They were quiet for a minute or two, only the sounds of squealing from the swings and birds in the outlying woods punctuating the silence. Jasmine waited for him to say something else, but his look had become distant as he gazed across the garden and out to the fields that bordered it.

Jasmine finally broke the hush. 'You *do* like her, don't you?'

'It's crazy, but…' He shook himself and grinned. 'She's a good laugh. Pretty fit too.'

Jasmine sighed. It was as close to an admission of love as she was going to get from him. And it was more than she had ever heard from him about any woman before. 'Pretty fit? She's absolutely beautiful.'

'Yeah,' he said with obvious longing in his voice. 'Out of my league.'

'Not if you're deserving of her. It's what's inside that counts.'

'Cliché alert…' Dylan turned to her with a mocking grin.

'Shut up. You know what I mean. If you like her, don't mess it up by being a dick.'

'How could you say that about your baby brother?'

'Because I know him very well, that's how.'

'You adore me really.'

'Sadly, that's true. But it doesn't mean that you're not a dick sometimes.'

'Aren't all men?'

Jasmine's gaze travelled to the house, where she imagined her husband working feverishly in a dim, locked room. 'Sometimes. These days quite a lot.' She turned her attention back to Dylan. 'I wondered if Millie would call tonight. We were supposed to be making plans for a craft fair in Lymington next week.' She glanced at her watch. 'It's getting a bit late for her now though.'

'It's only just gone nine,' Dylan said, checking his own. 'There's still time. Unless she's still with that woman who turned up today.'

'What woman?'

He shrugged. 'Someone named Rowena. Said she was a friend of Millie's from way back.'

'Millie's never mentioned her to me.'

'Millie never mentions anything from her past,' Dylan reminded her.

'True… So what was this Rowena like? Let's see if we can figure out whether Millie is an ex-KGB spy.'

'To be honest, if I turned up on someone's doorstep and made them look that pissed off I wouldn't bother going back.'

'Millie didn't seem pleased to see her?'

'Quite the opposite. And Rowena… Well, I can't say I cared that much for her. She was creepy.'

'Really?' Jasmine's expression was thoughtful as she watched the triplets, who were now playing some elaborate, made-up game of what looked like swing tag. 'No wonder Millie hasn't mentioned her before. I wonder what she wanted.'

'I don't know but her timing was lousy.'

Jasmine shot him a sideways look. 'I bet you were even less pleased to see her then.'

'I can't say I was that chuffed about it. I had to take a very cold shower when I got home.'

'So, you really might be an item, you two?'

'I think we could be getting there.'

'And you mean what you say about not messing her around?'

'Scout's honour.'

Jasmine smiled. 'She'd make a fabulous sister-in-law.'

'Bloody hell!' Dylan spluttered. 'Steady on!'

Jasmine erupted into a fit of giggles. 'Oh my God, you're so easy to wind up!'

'Well bloody stop it. You want me to have a heart attack?'

'Oh, don't be so melodramatic. I'm glad if you like her and she likes you and you're getting it together. I like her a lot myself and it would be great for us all to be able to spend time together. Just make sure this one lasts longer than a week, eh?'

Millie paced the stone floor of the front shop. Her gaze went to the window for the fourth time that minute. Every time she expected to see Rowena's mocking face at the window. The shadows on the bakery floor told her that the sun was setting. She had promised to see

Jasmine this evening, but somehow she couldn't seem to make herself venture out.

What was Rowena planning? Millie had spent the rest of the day obsessing over it, all thoughts of her glorious moments with Dylan banished to make way for unease and fear. Rowena hadn't tracked her all this way to leave her alone now that she had found her. Millie had run from her once and she wasn't sure she had the strength to do it again – let alone the finances, now that she had sunk everything she had into the pile of dust and bricks that currently surrounded her. She could draw all the protective circles she wanted around herself, but she couldn't stop Rowena's acid tongue working its way through her friends and neighbours. The idea was terrifying. Rowena had the cunning, the vindictive streak and the power to destroy Millie's life and it seemed like she had every intention to do just that. Even when they were friends, Millie had been a little afraid of Michael's sister; she always had a slightly unhinged side to her that made Millie wonder about how far she would go for revenge if someone crossed her. It looked as though Millie was about to find out.

There was a gentle knock and Millie's heart raced before Dylan's voice came through the letterbox. 'Millie, are you there?'

Heaving a sigh of relief, Millie opened the door a crack. Dylan seemed to do a double take. She guessed she looked as pale and strained as she felt, but couldn't bring herself to care.

'We were worried…' Dylan said. 'I mean, Jasmine was worried. You told her you would go over.'

'I'm sorry. I don't feel well. Would you apologise to her for me?'

'I don't think she needs an apology. She just wanted to know you were ok.'

'I'm fine, just a little under the weather. I'll text her to apologise.'

'Anything I can do?'

'No, thank you.'

There was a pause. 'Want me to come in?'

'No.'

Another pause. Dylan looked at his boot as he scuffed it on the old brickwork like a child being told off. 'Shall I come over tomorrow? I can finish work on the beams and maybe we can get the rest of that beer?'

Millie shook her head. It was taking all her strength not to cry. She knew what she had to do. Rowena would stamp out any relationship that showed the tiniest promise of love, and her methods would be cruel. Millie had to stop anything with Dylan before Rowena got wind of it. In the end, it was the kindest thing to do, for Dylan's sake, at least.

'I think we should keep things on a professional level from now on. I don't think you should do any more work for me until I can pay you properly.'

Dylan's mouth fell open. 'I don't understand…'

'I'm sorry. But I think it's for the best.'

He looked hurt and it was a knife to Millie's heart. She had to stay strong, though. 'But today… I thought we had something… I really like you. I thought—'

'It was a silly mistake,' Millie cut in. 'I'm sorry if I gave you the wrong idea.'

His expression darkened. 'It did that alright. I'm sorry I thought otherwise.'

And before she had a chance to reply, he had stalked off. Millie watched him go through his garden gate and disappear behind the hedge, her throat tightening. But there was no point in crying. It had to be this way.

Chapter Twelve

Night had turned into day and Millie had been awake to witness it all. She had turned over every possibility, every solution to her problem, but short of hiring a hitman to take out Rowena (and that would use up valuable plastering money) she couldn't seem to make anything fit. One thing was certain: when Rowena came knocking again, which she would, Millie didn't want to be around to answer it. She dressed early and took a walk through the fields that bordered the village as the first light of dawn skimmed the treetops, savouring the dewy chill in the air that would soon burn away and trying to clear her head and calm her thoughts. She couldn't be away from home all the time, but she could make it as difficult as possible for Rowena to find her. She wondered if she ought to go and apologise to Jasmine for not showing up the night before, and not even texting as she had promised Dylan she would. But she needed to keep Rowena away from the people she cared about, and if that meant cutting herself off from Jasmine for a while then that was what she would have to do. At least until she'd figured out a way to make Rowena see sense and forget whatever insane plan she was cooking up.

Feeling fresher after her morning walk, Millie returned to the old bakery and collected some of the equipment she'd need to work at the pub. The plan had been to bake pies there for the lunchtime trade. The rest of what she needed she hoped they would have, otherwise it meant a trip into a larger town to buy it before she could start any cooking. She didn't really mind that either, any excuse to be missing for a while was fine with her, but the landlord might not be so happy with the delay. She had left the ingredients in Doug's large fridges the previous afternoon.

When Millie arrived at the Dog and Hare she found that Doug had gone to a farmer's market in a neighbouring village. His wife, Colleen, was already busy in the kitchen preparing vegetables, but she assured Millie that the kitchen was plenty big enough for them both and she was more than happy to have the company. As Millie gratefully dragged her own equipment in, feeling a frisson of excitement as she gazed around at the vast steel landscape of top equipment at her disposal instead of the dismal excuse for a kitchen that she had at the bakery, she couldn't help but note that Colleen didn't quite look herself. Whenever they'd bumped into each other before, Millie had thought that for a woman she guessed to be in her early fifties, Colleen looked youthful and glamorous. She was more reserved and thoughtful than her gregarious husband, but had a more genuine warmth to her that made Millie like her all the more. Today, Colleen's make-up looked hastily applied over swollen eyes. Her clothes were obviously designer and as tasteful as always, but something about the way they had been thrown on didn't seem quite right, as though Colleen hadn't cared which top she teamed with which skirt. As they worked, mostly in silence apart from the humming of a radio in the background and the odd comment about the weather, or the state of the pub trade, Millie began to find these incongruous details about Colleen more and more distracting. She had troubles of her own, more than enough to go around, but Millie hated to see anyone else suffer. Other people's troubles had a way of making hers melt into the background.

Eventually, Millie could stand it no more. Even though she knew she might open up a whole Pandora's Box of problems, she had to ask. 'Is everything alright with you?'

Colleen stopped dicing a carrot and looked up. Her bottom lip trembled.

'Ignore me,' Millie said, immediately regretting her question. 'I'm always putting my foot in it and sticking my nose in where I shouldn't.' She had clearly tipped Colleen over the edge by asking and wondered now whether she had done more harm than good.

'No…' Colleen said, taking a deep breath and running a delicate finger beneath each eye. 'I've always thought you seem a kind soul, and I know it now. Please don't feel bad.'

Millie nodded silently, waiting for more. But Colleen went back to chopping her vegetables. After a moment, Millie returned to poring over a dog-eared recipe book.

'People used to say I was good looking,' Colleen started to explain, hesitantly.

Millie gave an encouraging smile. 'You are. You always look lovely when I see you.'

Colleen waved a dismissive hand in front of her face. 'It's all make-up now. The foundation gets thicker every year, the figure that bit harder to maintain. I'm not good looking anymore, just well preserved.'

'Beauty is about more than looks. You're beautiful on the inside and that shines through. And every new line is merely a record of each wonderful experience you've had in your life.'

'That's easy for you to say. You're still young and gorgeous.' She sniffed. 'I've seen the way all the men around here look at you, including my Doug... Like slobbering dogs watching their dinner put out.'

Millie's eyes widened.

'Sorry, sorry,' Colleen said quickly. 'I didn't mean to offend you. I'm not surprised they stare at you and I didn't mean anything by it. I'm not myself today, ignore anything I say.'

'Do you want to talk about it?'

'No...' Colleen sighed. 'Yes. I suppose I do.'

Millie closed the recipe book and leaned against the worktop. 'I'm all ears.'

'I'm going to get a brandy and lemonade first. Doug can moan about his precious stock because I'm going to drink it dry this afternoon. Care to join me?'

Millie nodded. A bit of brain-cell obliteration seemed like an appealing prospect for her too; it would certainly take her mind off her own woes. She watched, deep in thought, as Colleen disappeared to the bar to get their drinks.

So, it seemed Doug was at the heart of Colleen's distress. It was obvious, when she thought about it. Part of her wondered whether it was wise to get involved in a marital spat, but the other part of her knew that she couldn't stand by whilst someone as lovely as Colleen was so upset. The least she could do was listen while she got it all off her chest.

Colleen returned with two tall glasses, topped up with ice. 'Doubles,' she smiled, handing one to Millie. 'Cheers.'

Millie took a sip. It was still early but she was surprised how good a tall brandy and lemonade tasted at this time of the morning. Perhaps in her own fragile state she needed the warming, friendly alcohol as much as Colleen obviously did. Whatever the reason, it didn't seem half as wrong as it ought to.

'Doug told me last night that he didn't love me. Just said it out of the blue after we'd locked up.' Colleen's lip quivered again and she knocked back another swig of brandy to quell it. 'He said he didn't find me attractive anymore. We're old, you know, but I thought married couples were supposed to accept that they'd grow old together and love one another for what's in their hearts, not what their skin looks like.'

'You're right,' Millie said. 'That's how I think it should be too. Does he think time has stood still for him while it's marched on for you?'

Colleen let out a mirthless laugh. 'That's a very good point. I don't know. I asked him if he was having an affair and he said no. I asked if he wanted to have an affair and he said no to that too. He just doesn't love me and that's that.'

'Maybe he's in a rut and he's mistaking that for something else. Maybe he just can't see that he still loves you because you're always here, running the pub, and you never get time for each other.'

Colleen nodded. 'Maybe.'

'So, what's going to happen now?'

'He wants to put the pub on the market. We'll sell it and go our separate ways.'

Millie's eyes widened. 'Bloody hell.'

'He must have been feeling it for months and never said a word...' Colleen sniffed. 'I feel like such an idiot. Did it look obvious to everyone else that he wasn't happy?'

'Not one bit. You're not an idiot. How could you know if he doesn't tell you what's in his heart? If he had said something at the beginning then perhaps you could both have worked on the marriage.'

'Do you think it's too late for that now?'

'Do you? You know him better than me.'

'I only know I love him dearly. I can't let him go, not without a fight.'

Millie paused, staring into the depths of her drink. A flashback came to her, like a slap in the face, of a moment in her own past. Hours later Michael was dead. She paled at the memory, the ice in her glass clinking against the sides as the tremors hit. Placing the glass on the worktop, she took a deep breath and looked up at Colleen, who seemed not to have noticed that anything was amiss.

'I have to do something to make him love me again,' Colleen continued. 'What can I do?'

Millie gripped the worktop, her head beginning to spin. 'I don't know. Perhaps you could talk to him,' she said weakly.

'He wouldn't listen. Once he's made his mind up about something he doesn't change it.'

'But this isn't choosing where to go on holiday or how many barrels of beer to order in… This is your marriage. He has to listen. How long have you been together?'

'Thirty years.'

'See… there you go. Who would throw thirty years away without talking about it first?'

'But you could give me a love potion!' Colleen blurted out, before clapping a hand to her mouth.

Millie tried to speak but nothing would come out. Was this some sort of cruel karma?

'You could, right?' Colleen said quietly. 'I mean, you've been giving everyone else things to help them.'

'Colleen… I don't know what you mean.'

'The potions.'

'They're not potions, they're just simple herbal remedies.'

'Ruth told me you do magic.'

Millie stared at her. She had certainly misjudged Ruth.

'There is nothing magical in what I do. I can't make people fall in love or stay in love. I'm interested in old remedies and the uses for plants and herbs that our ancestors used on a daily basis, that's all,' Millie said, fighting to keep the bitterness from her tone. If she'd had that sort of power, she wouldn't have hesitated to use it; Michael would still be alive and she'd still be blissfully happy in Millrise in the house they had once shared.

'Then why does everyone say your potions are magic? Is it a lie – don't they work?'

All Millie needed to do was confirm Colleen's doubts and it would all be forgotten. She could get on with her cooking while she lent a sympathetic ear and Colleen could cry all the pain from her system. It would be that easy. But Millie could not deny the help she might be able to give someone when they asked so desperately for it, even if her life depended on it.

'I'm not saying it's a lie; but there is no potion I know of that can change the path of love. Love won't be ruled, not by me or anyone else. It doesn't answer just because you call it. Love will do only what love wants to do.'

Colleen thought for a moment. 'But you could make him see me in a different light. Perhaps if he fancied me again he might fall in love later?'

'You can do that just as well yourself.'

'How? I'm already made up to the nines every day and I always dress as well as I can. I get my hair done every week, have facials… I can't do any more than I do already to look good.'

'Perhaps you two could spend some quality time together; he might fancy you again if he remembers what it was he liked about you at the start... I'm talking about more than clothes and hair; I mean the way you made him feel when you laughed at his jokes, your kindness and sweet nature.'

Well...' Colleen said, clearly becoming exasperated. 'Could you give me something just to smooth the wrinkles a little? Anything would be a start.'

Millie sighed. She would get more sense from a brick wall at the moment. Perhaps she could fob Colleen off with a harmless herbal brew. If half the battle was believing, then perhaps if she thought Millie's placebo was doing the trick, the confidence it gave her might actually make her more attractive to Doug. It was probably the only way she was going to get Colleen off her back.

'I'll see what I can do.'

Colleen beamed. 'Thank you! I always said you were a lovely girl.'

'But,' Millie added, 'please don't tell anyone about this...' She had visions of villagers queuing up to satisfy their every heart's desire and was beginning to feel rather sick. 'I'll bring something over for you later.' She suppressed a huge, frustrated sigh.

'No... I'll come to you. I wouldn't want Doug getting wind of it.'

Millie wondered whether Colleen had inadvertently stumbled on the real problem with their marriage, in that one duplicitous sentence. But she had a feeling Colleen wouldn't see that even if she tried to explain it to her. 'Alright,' she agreed. 'Just remember, you can't tell anyone else.'

'I won't,' Colleen said, her tears all dried up now and a spring back in her step. 'It'll be our little secret.'

Millie was almost certain that was exactly what Ruth had said.

Chapter Thirteen

A note lay on the floor as Millie pushed open the front door of the old bakery and tumbled over the threshold. A day of baking, listening to Colleen, then later helping out with the lunchtime rush in the pub and having to pretend to Doug that she knew nothing about their problems when he returned from the market, had taken its toll on her already frayed nerves. She was exhausted, both physically and emotionally. And she still had Colleen's fake potion to prepare. It wouldn't take a great deal of skill but it had to be convincing.

She eyed the note anxiously for a moment as she closed the door behind her. It could be from anyone – she left her mobile phone behind all the time (not that she was particularly fond of it anyway) and Michael had often joked that he would have to send her messages by owl whenever he wanted something.

After a long moment of indecision, she bent to retrieve the carefully folded piece of paper and opened it up.

I called your phone but I think you were out of charge or it was off so I popped round hoping to see you. I just want to know that you're alright. Dylan says he's worried too.
Call me
Jasmine. x

Millie let the paper fall onto the front counter and began searching through boxes to find what she needed for Colleen. Dried herbs would do, she decided; some sort of chamomile infusion would be good to calm her down as well as giving her a bit of Dutch courage.

By eight thirty a grateful Colleen had been to collect her concoction and all Millie wanted to do, as she saw her out of the door, was fall into bed. It had been a long day, on virtually no sleep, and she was exhausted. There were things to do – there were always things to do these days – but they would have to wait. She was just about to lock up when there was a knock at the door. Millie froze, her key halfway to the keyhole. She waited. It could be Rowena. Of course, it could also be Jasmine. The idea of that pained Millie almost as much, but she knew it would still be a bad idea to answer the door. She needed to keep some distance for now, to keep Jasmine safe.

Just as the silence allowed her to think she had got away with it, a face appeared at the bay window. Millie's hand flew to her chest.

'Ruth…' she said as she yanked the door open and called her in. 'You gave me a heart attack.' Glancing quickly up and down the street she shut the door again and turned to face her neighbour. 'What can I do for you?' she asked, trying to keep her tone civil. Her patience was fast waning with Ruth, who, in one way or another, had caused her quite a bit of trouble these last few weeks.

'I haven't seen you much this week,' Ruth said. 'You're always so busy… and Dylan is always here.'

'He's been helping me with the renovations, as you know. And we invited you in for tea and cake on Thursday afternoon, remember?'

Ruth squinted, as if it took all her brainpower to recall the event. And then she smiled. 'So you did. It was that lovely coconut sponge you make.'

It had been carrot cake, but some things were easier left uncorrected. 'Was there something in particular you needed me for now?' Millie asked. 'Only I was planning to get an early night.'

'Ooh, with Dylan?'

'No!' Millie squeaked. 'What on earth would make you think that?'

'He's been here so much I thought you two were a couple now.'

'He's working for me, remember?'

'And the way he looks at you...' Ruth pursed her lips and gave the most disturbing wink Millie had ever seen.

'He can look all he wants,' Millie replied primly. 'Now, is that all you came to see me about?'

Ruth looked blank for a moment. 'I think it might be... No, wait... I've just seen Colleen come away from here. She looked very happy. Did you sort her little problem with Doug?'

Were there no secrets in this village? More importantly, how did the woman with the biggest mouth always get to unearth them?

'She was a little upset earlier, and I sent her away with a chamomile brew, that's all.'

'I've brought some whisky,' Ruth continued.

Millie began to herd her subtly towards the door. 'I really am shattered tonight, Ruth... Do you mind terribly if I take a rain check on that? Tomorrow night, eh?'

Ruth was still talking when Millie shut the front door, her neighbour on the other side. Ruth didn't mean any harm and she was a lovely lady. Millie knew all this but it didn't make it any easier to listen to her, especially tonight. She thought about Dylan, that niggling doubt returning, the stab of regret, the realisation that she had been falling for him, that he might have been the one to save her and she him… It was all too much to bear. After hastily turning the great iron key in the door, Millie ran upstairs and fell, weeping, onto her bed.

'I'm going to see if Millie is ok.' Jasmine grabbed her keys from the kitchen counter. 'It's been bothering me all night.'

Rich swallowed a mouthful of buttered toast. He glanced down at Jasmine's plate, where her breakfast lay virtually untouched, and then back at her again. 'Now? She might not even be up yet.'

'Yes, Rich, now. What if something bad has happened to her?'

'What is going to happen to her in Honeybourne? Is she going to get attacked by one of the ducks from the pond?'

Jasmine pursed her lips. 'Very funny.'

'She doesn't need you poking your head in every ten minutes. Maybe she wants to be alone so she's politely ignoring you. Not everyone wants to be part of your social circle all the time.'

'I don't poke my head in every ten minutes. And I'm not stupid, I realise people need their space. I just get the feeling something has happened. You heard Dylan the other night – he said she was fine until that Rowena woman arrived and then suddenly she was all cagey.'

'Maybe she's her girlfriend.'

Jasmine's frown deepened. 'If you're not going to say anything constructive then you can shut up.'

'I just think you're getting yourself worried about nothing. Millie is a grown woman and if she needs help she'll come to you for it.'

'That's just it, I don't think she would. She's too proud for that.'

'Not too proud to have your brother working for nothing.'

'Dylan offered. And he is not working for nothing.'

Rich let out an impatient sigh. 'Whatever... Go and do your Good Samaritan stint. But don't come running to me when it all blows up in your face.'

Jasmine glared at him, arms folded tight across her chest. 'Just because your composing isn't going well, it doesn't give you the right to be vile to everyone. I married a man who would have been as worried as me once upon a time. What happened to him?'

'Nothing happened to him. And stop blaming everything on my work. It's alright for you to prat about with your little bits of silver in that workshop but one of us has to bring in proper money...' As soon as he had stopped speaking, Rich's face twisted into a mortified grimace.

'Sometimes,' Jasmine said in a cold voice, 'I actually hate you, Richard Green.'

'Jas... I'm sorry...'

His apology went unheard as Jasmine slammed the kitchen door behind her.

Millie opened the heavy front door a crack and peered out from behind it. Her expression was strained and lacking any of her usual warmth. It looked to Jasmine as though Dylan had been right when he reported something was amiss.

'I'm a bit busy today...' Millie said, without waiting for Jasmine to speak. 'Sorry.'

'I just wanted to see if you were ok... You didn't come over.'

'Yes... I'll call you later...' The door began to close but then another voice called out and it swung back open.

'You shouldn't keep your new friends away on my account.' A woman appeared and smiled sweetly. She stuck her hand out to Jasmine, Millie moving aside with an air of resignation. 'I'm Rowena, an old friend of Millie's from up north. And you must be Jasmine, unless lots of the ladies in Honeybourne have pink hair, of course…'

'Yes…' Jasmine replied, trying to get a handle on the situation. What was going on here? Why did Millie look so distressed? This was the woman Dylan had warned her about. Her brother wasn't usually the most astute man when it came to reading emotional situations but in this instance Jasmine had to agree.

Rowena turned to Millie. 'Aren't you going to ask Jasmine in?'

'It's fine; I have somewhere I need to be,' Jasmine said, glancing at Millie for some direction. 'I just called to make sure everything was ok.'

'Nonsense… I'm sure Millie would love you to pop in.'

'If Jasmine is busy I'm sure she can come back later.'

'But I won't be here then and I do so want to know all about your new life with your new friends,' Rowena insisted, taking a forceful hold of Jasmine's arm and almost yanking her over the threshold.

Millie watched helplessly, and it worried Jasmine. She had always seemed so strong, so collected, but this was a very different woman to the positive and energetic one who had taken on the massive task of the bakery and never once flinched in the face of it – at least, not in public. Jasmine saw this Millie and knew something was very wrong.

'Maybe I could stay for a little while,' she said brightly. 'It's always nice to make new friends.'

'I couldn't agree more,' Rowena said, closing the door behind Jasmine. She wandered over to the window seat and perched there, a benign smile lighting her features as she watched Jasmine sit on an old wooden bench. 'Well, isn't this nice?'

'How long have you known each other?' Jasmine asked. She glanced from one to the other – Rowena on her seat looking like the cat that got the canary, Millie hovering by the counter as though her legs might give way.

'Ooh,' Rowena said, 'it seems like for ever. How long would you say it is, Millie?'

Millie shrugged.

Rowena looked thoughtful for a minute. 'You were seeing Michael for about four years… and we knew each other before that…' She smiled, but to Jasmine it reminded her of a shark – not so much a smile as a showing of teeth before the fatal snap. 'After all,' Rowena continued to Jasmine, 'I was the one to introduce Michael to her… and we all know how that ended…'

'Oh,' Jasmine replied, wondering what else she was expected to say. She found it strange that Millie had never mentioned this Michael before but figured she had her reasons, and that was enough for her until her friend was ready to share more. And if she never did, that was her business too. Jasmine wasn't there to judge, only to be a comfort or confidante should Millie ever need it.

'So,' Rowena said, cutting into her thoughts, 'you're in business too? And I hear you have triplets and an adorable husband.'

Jasmine glanced at Millie who seemed to be trying to convey in a single look that the information had not come from her. 'I…'

'Honeybourne is such a friendly and open place,' Rowena continued. 'It doesn't take much to get its residents to share what they know about people. You and your husband seem to be minor celebrities here. Must be all that fertility zinging out of you.'

'Something like that,' Jasmine replied. The idea of this woman already knowing so much about her after being in the village for about five minutes was unnerving. 'We did get quite a bit of coverage in the local paper, and I suppose an event like the birth of triplets is quite memorable in a small place like this.'

'Particularly when the parents are such larger-than-life characters themselves.'

'I'm not sure what you mean…'

'A film-score composer, his pink-haired wife and a house with a giant metal statue of Poseidon in the front garden? Not exactly Mr and Mrs Ordinary, are you?'

'I never thought of it like that. And I don't actually think the other villagers really think of us like that. I mean, we've lived here our whole lives so we're just an unremarkable part of the furniture now.' Jasmine held back a frown. She had stayed with the intention of finding out more about this woman, but instead she seemed to be the one under interrogation and was struggling to find a way of turning the conversation around to her advantage. She turned to Millie instead. 'How did you two meet?'

Rowena jumped in with her reply before Millie's mouth had even opened. 'We sort of fell into the same circle of friends. We had a mutual… *interest* and it brought quite a few of us together.' She winked at Millie. 'Isn't that right?'

'I was going to show Rowena around,' Millie replied, as if she hadn't heard the leading question. 'I thought we should go soon. And I'm sure you have lots to be getting on with today,' she added, throwing Jasmine a desperate look that begged for her agreement.

'Oh yes,' Jasmine said. 'I did only pop over for a short visit. But now I see you're ok, I'll make myself scarce. I have a lot to do.'

Millie smiled gratefully as Jasmine made for the front door.

As it was closed behind her, Jasmine couldn't get Rowena out of her head. Dylan had been right, something was off about her, even though she had been perfectly pleasant and friendly. Or maybe *unnervingly over-friendly* was the phrase more suited to her behaviour. She looked to the cloudless sky for divine inspiration. When no bolt came from the blue, she gave a sigh and headed for Dylan's house to drag him out of bed. She needed a second opinion from someone close, someone she trusted, and right now, Rich was not the man to offer it.

It took five knocks at the front door and a handful of stones at Dylan's bedroom window to finally rouse him.

'What the hell?' Dylan stood at the front door in his boxer shorts, hair sticking up at odd angles and his eyes gummed with sleep. 'It's still the middle of the night.'

'Don't be such an arse,' Jasmine said as she pushed past him. 'And get the kettle on.'

Dylan closed the door and padded after her, yawning and scratching his belly. 'I don't know how Rich puts up with you. Tyrannical, that's what you are. Genghis Khan would have quivered in his furry boots at one look from you.'

'It's a beautiful day and you should be up,' Jasmine admonished. 'Life's passing you by as you lie rotting in that pit.'

'Jeez…' Dylan went to the sink and filled the kettle. 'Something's rattled you this morning. Have you and Rich had a row?'

Jasmine thought about their parting words that morning. Perhaps her current agitation did have something to do with that, and not just what she had witnessed between Millie and Rowena. The arguments at home had been more frequent; the loaded comments, skirmishes at the sink, disapproving looks and bitten-back insults. Something was off-kilter in their marriage these days, and Jasmine wished she could get a handle on what it was, but it was like smoke, and as fast as her hand closed around the answer, it was gone again. The stubborn part of her brain refused to acknowledge it and she could do nothing but push the thoughts aside and hope things would work themselves out.

'Millie's *friend*...' Jasmine uttered the word with sarcastic emphasis as she took a seat at Dylan's dining table. 'You didn't like her?'

'Dislike is maybe a bit strong.'

'I know. But I've just been over and she's there now. I have to say that I completely agree now I've met her. And Millie doesn't seem to be very comfortable with her around.'

'Yeah... What's even weirder is that she came over here last night.'

'Rowena?' Jasmine asked, leaning forward.

Dylan nodded. 'Just came over, stood at the door asking me loads of questions, and then handed me that...' He angled his head at a bottle of wine sitting on the kitchen worktop.

'Why would she do that?'

'I don't know – to be friendly? Some people are like that. Perhaps she's been enchanted by the wonder that is Honeybourne and wants to relocate.'

Jasmine's gaze was drawn to the bottle again. 'I don't think you should drink it.'

'Why on earth not? You sound mental.'

'I know...' Jasmine replied, her tone defensive. 'I can't help it.'

'I nearly downed it last night, actually. I was going to ask her in, just to be friendly, you understand, but then...'

'What?' Jasmine prompted.

'I don't know. Millie was at the window of her place and I just felt like... like I shouldn't. I can't explain it.'

'Aha! So you do think there's something up with Rowena!'

'I thought it might look like I was into her,' Dylan said. He suddenly looked deadly serious. 'I mean, Rowena is attractive and I didn't want Millie to think I fancied her… or that anything was going to happen between us…'

'You really do like Millie, don't you?' Jasmine's voice was softer now. She gazed at her brother and her heart went out to him. She could nag him to keep his house and finances in order, she could do his washing when he was too lazy, she could clean his cupboards out when the bacteria reached plague proportions, she could cook him the odd meal… but there were some things that were entirely beyond her power to do anything about. More than ever, she wanted him to find the right woman to finally settle down with. Since their parents' death he had been rudderless, anchorless and cast adrift on life's unpredictable seas. She had been lucky to find Rich but Dylan… He had gone so hopelessly off course that he couldn't stay still long enough to get close to forming those sorts of ties with a woman.

Without reply, he pushed himself from his chair and reached into the cupboard for two mugs.

'Dylan? Sit down.'

He turned to her. 'It doesn't matter now, anyway. She told me that there was no future in a relationship. I don't know why I was bothered about what she thought. In fact, I probably ought to shag Rowena.'

'You're too good for that,' Jasmine said. 'And deep down, you know that version of Dylan Smith is not who you are. Maybe if you let the real you come to the surface occasionally your princess might be able to find you.'

'The real me? You mean that monumental loser who can't even hold down a job?'

'You choose not to hold down a job. That's exactly what I'm talking about. If you know your faults, why do you continually play to them?'

'I don't even know the answer to that myself. I wish I did. It's like I'm programmed for self-destruct or something and there's nothing I can do about it. I had thought… Millie, working on the bakery… It was something to focus on…' He rubbed a hand through his hair and glanced at the worktop. 'Maybe I'll open that wine now. Fancy a drink?'

Jasmine got up and put the bottle on the floor by the back door. 'Don't you dare! When you clean up – next millennium or whenever it is – you have to throw this wine out. And if you want Millie then you'll need to work a bit harder, quit this defeatist attitude.'

'She doesn't want me.'

'She does. I've seen the way she looks at you. Something is holding her back and I'll bet that something is Rowena. You said yourself that Millie suddenly went cold when she arrived.'

'Yeah, but—'

'No buts.'

Dylan was silent for a moment as he appraised his sister with a thoughtful expression. 'You've changed your tune,' he said finally. 'I thought you were dead against me and Millie. If I recall correctly, you more or less threatened to disown me if I so much as breathed in her direction.'

'That was before I realised that you were actually serious about her.'

He gave a lopsided smile. 'So, now that she doesn't want me I finally get your blessing? A bit ironic, that.'

'More than a bit,' Jasmine agreed with a rueful smile of her own. 'Isn't it funny how life can turn on a sixpence?'

'So it is…' Dylan replied. He stretched and yawned again. 'Now, I do believe you were making me a cup of tea.'

Rowena had taken some getting rid of but had finally gone, leaving Millie a nervous, emotional wreck. That was a couple of hours ago. Millie had no idea where she was heading next, and the idea terrified her. She had watched her head across to Dylan's the previous evening, exchange words and hand him a bottle (relieved beyond measure that he hadn't invited her in), but there wasn't a lot she could do about that, despite the urge to race across screaming for him not to get involved. She wasn't going to give credence to Rowena's lies by presenting herself as a dangerous loon. The best she could hope for was that Rowena would head back to her own accommodation, if only for a short while, so that Millie could get a brief respite from the emotional bombardment.

Rowena was sneaky and she was smart. Even when they had been friends, Millie had been a little afraid of her. There was no end of mischief she could cause should she choose to and Millie knew she hadn't even started yet. It was becoming increasingly and depressingly obvious that she couldn't stay in Honeybourne. But in order to leave, she had to at least try to salvage something from the financial mess she had landed herself in. The bakery was in no fit state to sell on as it was. Rowena would be well aware of Millie's options, and would go out of her way to make things as difficult as possible, but it was up to Millie to try and do what she could before the axe fell.

All these thoughts ran through her mind as she hauled the ingredients for a batch of beef and ale pies to the Dog and Hare for the day's supper trade. The last thing she wanted was to be locked up in a kitchen with Colleen, but it was just another torture she would have to bear if she wasn't going to go under completely. Rowena was trying to ruin her life, and it seemed as though the world was conspiring to help her, and maybe Millie even deserved it… but that didn't mean she had to accept it just yet.

Millie knocked at the back door of the pub. A few seconds later a beaming Colleen greeted her and waved her inside.

'Oh, Millie, I'm so happy to see you!'

'Really?' Millie replied, slightly bemused.

'Yes, yes! Doug and I…' Colleen hesitated, blushing slightly. 'Well, let's just say that, whatever you gave to me, it worked.' She lowered her voice and continued in a breathy giggle. 'He couldn't keep his hands off me last night.'

'He couldn't?'

Colleen grabbed Millie's bag and dumped it on the table. Pulling her arm, she led her into the bar area. 'This calls for a celebratory drink.'

'It's a bit early for me…' Millie began, but Colleen waved away her excuse.

'You have to join me. It's all down to you. Ruth was right, you are remarkable!'

'I'm really not.' Millie's mind was racing. She had given Colleen what amounted to nothing more than a herbal tonic. Whatever had changed between her and Doug was down to them, not her. She had to admit to being a little confused. 'I'm amazed myself how quickly and how emphatically it seems to have taken effect.'

'Oh, don't be so modest.'

'I'm not. I do believe that you and Doug have worked this out for yourselves, which is wonderful and I'm really happy for you both.'

Colleen tapped the side of her nose. 'I see. You don't want people to know what you can do. Your friend said as much.'

Millie stared at her, the blood draining from her face. 'My friend?'

'She left not long before you arrived. She said she'd be seeing you later and didn't want to bother you while you were working.'

'What did she say her name was?'

'I don't actually recall… She was tall, lovely hair, dark skinned…'

Rowena. Millie should have known that she wouldn't be able to resist raking up some more trouble. But how was she getting people to tell her so much about Millie's new life in Honeybourne? Was she systematically going through every villager until she had quizzed them all?

'She came here today?' Millie asked in a dazed voice.

'Early doors. I was outside on the front watering the hanging baskets when we struck up a conversation. I noticed straightaway that her accent is like yours. When I mentioned it she said she was from your old town and was visiting you.'

'What else did she say?'

'That she knew you very well, practically sisters she said. Naturally I asked her in for a cup of coffee. She could tell that something good had happened to me, said it was in my aura.' Colleen grinned and Millie suppressed a groan of dismay. 'So I told her that it had. Doug said a quick hello before he went off to the cash and carry and she could tell by his face that something good had happened to him too.'

'What did you tell her?'

'You mean, the problems between me and Doug?' Colleen looked a little offended for a moment. But then her smile returned. 'I wouldn't share that sort of thing with a stranger.'

Millie mused on the fact that Colleen had been happy to share her marital troubles with her and she was little more than a stranger herself, but thought better of pointing this out. What worried her more and more were Rowena's plans, and how she seemed to be one step ahead of Millie all the time.

Colleen carried on: 'I said that you were a remarkable person and that you had made a real impact on the lives of people here and that everyone had really taken to you... I think she was very pleased for you. She said that she was sure Dylan Smith had a thing for you and I said that he almost certainly had and that it was about time he settled with a nice girl and I hoped it would be you because he seems very keen on you – if you don't mind me saying – and that you get on very well with his sister already. And she said that she hoped you would get everything you deserved.'

Millie felt herself go stone cold, even in the heat of the sun-warmed pub. She was certain that Rowena would see to that. The trouble was, Rowena had a very different idea of what Millie deserved than everyone else did.

Chapter Fourteen

Millie had made up her mind. She had to go and see Dylan, warn him somehow. She had no idea what Rowena was planning and even less idea what Dylan's reaction would be to such a conversation, but she would never forgive herself if he came to harm and she had done nothing to prevent it. All she knew was that Rowena had issued a warning. She had known that Millie would be calling at the Dog and Hare to make pies – which was why she had deliberately got there early to catch Colleen before Millie arrived. Rowena was one step ahead – no, five steps ahead – all the time. And playing this game was her twisted way of telling Millie that it was only a matter of time before she ripped the heart out of her.

Without arousing suspicion and causing a lot of ill feeling into the bargain, there had been no way Millie could leave Colleen in the lurch, so she'd had to make the evening's batch of pies before she could get away. Now she was marching towards home, frantic about what the lost hours might mean for her mission. Had Rowena already beaten her to it?

As she turned the corner her gaze settled on the gate of Dylan's garden, and then travelled up the path. All seemed to be quiet. She started making a beeline for the tiny cottage.

'Yoohoo! Millie!'

Millie groaned, and turned round, forcing a smile on her face. 'Hello, Ruth, how are you?'

'Slow down!' Ruth panted as she waddled over the road, trying to match Millie's leggy strides. 'You'll give me a heart attack.'

'Sorry...' Millie glanced back at the cottage and then at Ruth again, biting her lip. 'What can I do for you?'

'It's more what I can do for you. I've got some help for you. Diana at the WI knows a carpenter in the next village. Actually I think she knows him a little too well... must be all that HRT... and she was never the same after Derek left her... Anyway, she says that Russ... that's his name... can do you a very good deal for any woodwork...'

Millie listened to her ramble on, feeling more desperate with every passing second.

'Ruth,' she interrupted when she could stand no more, 'maybe we can have a cup of tea later and you can tell me all about this then. I'm sort of in a hurry now...'

Ruth glanced across at Dylan's cottage and then gave Millie a cheeky wink. 'Oh yes. I'm not surprised you're in a rush to see that bit of rumpy pumpy.'

On any other occasion, Millie might have laughed at Ruth's choice of phrase. But she simply nodded. 'Just about the renovations.'

'Of course...' Ruth said in a very deliberate voice. 'The renovations...' But then she looked back at the cottage again and smiled and waved at someone. Millie turned to see who it was and froze.

Rowena gave a mocking wave to Millie before heading up Dylan's path.

'Isn't that your friend?' Ruth asked.

Millie nodded vaguely as she watched Dylan answer the door. He glanced up at her with a puzzled expression, before Rowena spoke to him. Millie wished desperately that she could hear what they were saying, and that she could get rid of Ruth and race over there to put a stop to whatever Rowena was planning. But it all seemed such a mess now and she didn't know what to do next without looking like a loon or a psycho to Dylan, which wouldn't do much for her cause at all. Ruth, prize town gossip that she was, would take great delight in spreading the rumour of any strange behaviour too.

'Looks like she's a bit sweet on Dylan Smith too. Ooh, he does like the ladies, that one,' Ruth cooed.

Millie watched as Rowena sidled up to Dylan and whispered something to him; a moment later he stepped aside to let her in and the door shut behind them. She hoped it wasn't what it looked like and she wished she didn't feel quite so wretched about it. A woman who was the ultimate seductress and a man with a reputation as a major player – as far as Millie could see, there was only one way that was going to end. But the thought of Dylan's betrayal wasn't the thing that cut the most; it was that Rowena was using him as a puppet to exact her revenge on the woman she believed had killed her brother that really plunged the knife into Millie's heart.

'Didn't you want to go over and see him?' Ruth asked as Millie turned to the bakery.

'Not now,' Millie said in a dull voice. 'It can wait.'

'I'm sick of your moods!' Jasmine yelled.

'And I'm sick of your bloody hormones!' Rich snarled back.

'Don't you dare bring hormones into this!'

'You seem to think that having a bad day is exclusively your territory. I can have bad days too, you know.'

'Bad days are all you've had since you landed that stupid contract. If I'd known what it would do to you I would have nailed the front door shut so you couldn't go to the meeting!'

'Maybe if my wife was a bit more supportive instead of running around fussing about every waif and stray that happens into our village I wouldn't have quite so many bad days. It's nothing to do with my contract!'

'You twat, Richard Green!'

'You're a bitch, Jasmine Green, so we're well suited.'

An anxious little face appeared at the kitchen door. 'Reuben says he can't sleep,' Rebecca whispered as they turned to her.

'I'll be there shortly,' Jasmine said, trying to level her voice. 'Tell him to try and settle and I'll come to tuck you all in when I can.'

'That's if she isn't out doing her agony aunt bit to complete strangers,' Rich cut in.

'Millie is not a complete stranger!' Jasmine fired back as Rebecca raced back down the hallway to the stairs. 'I don't understand why you have such a problem with her.'

'Because she's all you seem to talk about since she arrived.'

'So what?'

'It's pissing me off.'

Jasmine planted her hands on her hips. 'You're *jealous*?'

'Of course I'm not! It's not just that anyway. But you're always busy doing something else. Me and the kids come a poor second place behind every bugger else in the village, maybe even third if you count your precious workshop.'

'You never had a problem with the workshop before. We have to earn a living, you know.'

'But you seem to think that your work is more important than mine. I don't have a purpose built workshop—'

'You have a studio,' Jasmine cut in.

'I have a studio that is in the house. I can't get away from the family when I work like you can.'

'What... So you're saying you want the workshop? How am I supposed to use blow torches in the house?'

'That's not what I'm saying. You're not bloody listening, as usual.'

'You're saying that you don't like being around the family?'

'When I'm trying to work, no!'

'Well, I have news for you, buster. You are responsible for the fact that you have three children and they live here whether you like it or not.'

'And sometimes I wish I didn't know that quite so well!'

Jasmine ground her teeth and stared at him. 'You want us to leave?' she said in a low voice. 'Is that what you want?'

'I don't honestly know.' Rich ran a hand through his hair and stared at his feet. 'I really don't, Jas. But sometimes, I feel like a spare part here. Your business is more successful than mine, you're a better parent, you actually belong to this village in a way I will never do...'

'I can't believe you're saying any of this!' Jasmine gasped, fighting back tears. They weren't tears of sadness, but of frustration. 'Do you have any idea how selfish this sounds?'

'Maybe it does. But I feel it.'

'And now I know. So I'll just make up a bed on the sofa right after I've tucked the kids in. Or perhaps you'd like to sleep in the workshop since you like it so much. Can I also remind you that I tuck the kids in every night… not because I'm better at it but because you just can't be arsed. You have to work at being a parent, Rich, and sometimes you have to work at being a decent human being.' Jasmine turned and walked towards the stairs. Rich called after her, but she kept on walking.

This argument had been brewing for some time, and Jasmine had watched it blow in from the horizon, not knowing how to stop it. What she hadn't seen was how it would end. She had always been so certain of Rich's love for her that she never even questioned the way she lived her life with him. Perhaps she did ask too much of him, perhaps she did take him for granted. But then, why should she give up on her dreams, on the things she wanted out of life just because she was a wife and mother? Would he give up his music? She doubted it.

She needed to talk, someone to help her work through this. And as she tucked her wide-eyed triplets into bed and reassured them that everything was fine and that Mummy and Daddy shouting didn't mean divorce, she knew she wasn't even certain of that much herself any more. A life without Rich was unthinkable, but for the first time in their marriage the possibility had been raised.

She decided to go and see Dylan. He wasn't much use when it came to advice, but in the absence of anyone else, at least he would be a friendly face with a fridge full of beer. Maybe it would be good to get another man's perspective on the situation too.

But when she arrived back downstairs, Rich was nowhere to be seen. She found a note on the mantelpiece that informed her he had gone to the Dog and Hare. A little selfish and very clichéd, she thought with a newly growing rage. But it looked as though her evening was going to have to be here, in the silent house.

Picking up her phone, she dialled Dylan, but there was no reply. She couldn't think what message to leave, so she simply cut the call. Her finger hovered over Millie's number. But her friend had seemed so reluctant to have her around that morning. Whether it had been down to Rowena being there or not she had no clue but it didn't seem such a good idea right now to call her either. With a sigh, Jasmine went to fetch the spare bedding, which she dumped on the sofa for Rich before heading up for a sleepless night alone in their bed.

Jasmine prodded a snoring Rich awake the next morning to discover that his mood had been made no better by the hangover he had acquired at the pub. Following this a terse exchange had resulted in a reluctant and irritated agreement that Rich would get the kids up and take them to school, while Jasmine went to Dylan's (under the pretence that she needed to reclaim some borrowed tools). So Jasmine found herself walking to her brother's house, her mood low and confused at best. It was early by Dylan's standards, and he would hate her for getting him out of bed yet again, but she needed him.

The morning air was stifling, still hot, but heavy with a building storm. Jasmine raised her eyes to the clouds massing on the horizon and wished that it would just rain and get it over with. It was a little like the feeling she had about her spat with Rich right now. If he was going to swing the axe on their marriage, she wished he would just get on and do it. At least she wouldn't be left in this terrible limbo and she could decide what to do next. Although she still couldn't quite believe that he had even contemplated such a notion, now that he had aired it she wasn't going to be held to ransom. She knew couples whose miserable marriages were characterised by the constant threat of divorce with neither party ever daring to take that plunge, and she had decided very early on that she and Rich were never going to be one of them.

Dylan's cottage was silent, the curtains drawn as Jasmine trudged up the path to the front door. She hadn't expected anything else but somehow the fact irritated her. She raised her hand to knock at the door…

Millie couldn't remember what time she had finally drifted off, but when daylight filled her room and prodded her awake, she didn't feel as if she had been asleep for long. Her first coherent thought was what Rowena would have in store for her today. She didn't want to know what might or might not have happened at Dylan's house the previous night but could think of little else. Millie didn't want to believe that Dylan would be so weak, but how could she protest? She had relinquished any claim on him and had no right to ask Rowena to spare her any pain. It was only a fraction of the pain she herself had inflicted on Rowena, no matter how much of a mistake it had been, and she knew that Rowena wouldn't be happy until she had crushed Millie completely.

She thought about going to see Jasmine. She could phone, of course, but the conversation she needed to have could only really be face to face. If she had already lost Dylan, then she needed to try to save his sister. It was too early yet, though – Jasmine would be getting the children ready for school and she definitely didn't want the triplets within earshot. Because Millie had decided that it was time to come clean about her past. Rowena was going to destroy life for her in Honeybourne anyway; there was nothing left to lose.

She'd give it an hour and then go and visit Jasmine in her workshop.

After the third unanswered knock, Jasmine was about to go around to the back and try the old pebbles-at-the-window trick when the front door swung open. Standing on the step, perfectly made-up, hair poker straight and glossy, and dressed in nothing but one of Dylan's shirts, was Rowena.

Jasmine couldn't help the gasp that escaped her lips.

'Good morning,' Rowena said glibly, with that smile that reminded Jasmine of a shark. 'Are you looking for your brother? I'm afraid he's sleeping right now.'

'What…' Jasmine felt the heat rise to her face. What the hell had Dylan done now? Jasmine was quite sure she was going to kill him. At the very least she would never believe a word that came from his lying mouth again.

'I can go and wake him if you really want me to,' Rowena said. 'But he's sooo very tired that it might take dynamite.'

Jasmine opened her mouth to reply, when there was a scuffling sound and Dylan staggered to the door, clumsily shoving Rowena aside.

'Jas—'

'Save it, Dylan. I don't want to hear it.' Jasmine glared at him. She turned to leave, taking long and purposeful strides down the path.

'Jasmine!' Dylan repeated.

He sounded as though he was still steaming drunk and the thought made Jasmine's blood boil. Whatever she had considered confiding in him in her hour of need, it was obvious to her now that she would get no support from that quarter. Her brother was still as immature and irresponsible as ever. It was like having a fourth child, but one that she couldn't control no matter how much chastisement she meted out. She turned to see him pause at the front door, glance down at himself in nothing but his boxer shorts, and then seem to come to a decision. Rowena looked on in mild amusement, arms folded as she leaned nonchalantly against the doorframe.

Lumbering down the path, he called after her again. Jasmine emerged onto the road, determined to get as far away from the whole hideous situation as possible.

'Jas…' Dylan grabbed her arm and spun her around. 'It's not what you think…'

'Shut up, Dylan. I know you better than that so spare me the barefaced and, frankly, insulting lies.'

'I'm not…' He looked confused and glanced back at Rowena who was still watching them with a half-bored, half-amused expression. 'Just let me…' He clutched at his head. 'I don't know…'

Jasmine shook her arm free. She looked up in time to see Millie emerge from her front door and freeze as she took in the scene.

Jasmine turned and stood, staring at Millie. Then Dylan stumbled past her towards the old bakery.

'Millie…'

Millie took one look at him, and the colour drained from her face. Rowena began walking towards them, a smile playing at the corners of her mouth. Millie turned to her.

'What have you done?' she gasped.

'Oh, you know what I've done,' Rowena said sweetly, 'and you know why.'

Millie looked at Dylan again. His eyes were unfocused and his expression vague, as though he didn't quite know where he was. She turned to Rowena once more. 'I didn't mean to hurt Michael, you know that! I loved him! I tried my hardest not to hurt him, but we were living a lie...' She waved a hand at Dylan, 'I didn't do *this* to him.'

'It hurts, doesn't it?'

Millie flew at her with a scream. Before she knew what was happening, Jasmine had caught her by both arms and was struggling to hold her back. Dylan was sitting in the middle of the street staring dumbly at the fracas.

'He didn't want you,' Millie spat. 'It's just sex.'

'I think you'll find he did. All men want me.'

'You bitch!'

'Millie!' Jasmine shouted, still holding tight. 'Stop it, please! Tell me what the hell is going on!'

'Yes, Millicent,' Rowena crowed, 'why don't you tell her what is going on? Why don't you tell her all about my brother—'

'No!' Millie yelled, tears springing to her eyes.

'And how you broke his heart into a thousand pieces...'

'Please,' Millie begged, her struggles against Jasmine's grip weakening.

'Tell Jasmine how you drove him to kill himself.' Rowena came closer and dropped her voice. 'And as if nothing happened, you've moved onto another unsuspecting victim... Will this end the same way?'

Millie glanced at Dylan who stared up at her, his eyes empty. 'I just wanted...'

'You killed Michael.'

'No...' Millie's voice was barely a whisper now.

'You killed him, Millicent Hopkin, as certainly as if you had put a gun to his head. You destroyed his hopes and dreams for the future,

and you made him believe there was nothing left worth living for.'
Rowena addressed Jasmine, who was still standing behind Millie, a
slack grip on her arm. 'You should think yourself lucky that all Dylan
got out of this little adventure is a good shag. If she had got her claws
in him, your brother could have ended up as dead as mine.'

Without another word, Rowena turned on her heel and walked
calmly back to Dylan's cottage. Millie stared after her. She felt her
arms released and turned to face Jasmine.

'Jasmine, I'm so sorry!' Millie sobbed. 'I didn't want any of
this to happen, I didn't mean to hurt Michael – you have to
believe me!'

'I don't know what to think,' Jasmine said in a dull voice.

'Rowena's crazy,' Millie pleaded, 'she'll stop at nothing to get her
revenge. She's punishing me for what she sees as murder but I didn't
mean for Michael to die, I swear!'

'I believe that. I don't think you're capable of inflicting that sort
of pain deliberately. What I don't believe is that you didn't warn us.
You let that woman into our lives and you didn't warn us what she
was capable of.'

Millie glanced at the cottage to see that Rowena was already back
in her own clothes and leaving. She threw a smile at Ruth Evans, who,
it appeared, had been standing on the side of the road the whole time
watching events unfold. She turned back to see that Jasmine was pulling Dylan up to stand.

'What the hell is wrong with you, Dylan?' She stared at him but
he didn't reply. Instead, his eyes simply rolled in his head and he
stared back.

'I think it's something Rowena has done—' Millie began, but Jasmine cut her off.

'You should have warned us,' Jasmine repeated. 'You could have stopped all this.'

'I didn't mean it, Millie…' Dylan slurred as Jasmine pulled him back towards the house. 'I love you!' he called behind him. 'I mean it, I really do. I don't know why I slept with her; I don't even fancy her…'

Millie's tears fell faster still. Amidst all the chaos of the morning, Dylan's sudden admission was the cruellest cut. Was that how he really felt? She realised with a jolt, as she watched Jasmine drag him stumbling back to his house, that she had fallen for him too. But he would never want anything to do with her again after hearing what she had done to Michael, and Jasmine hated her so much now that even if he did, a relationship between them would never be accepted. She had lost them both. Rowena had ruined everything, just as she had promised.

Chapter Fifteen

Jasmine left Dylan sleeping and closed the bedroom door. It was distressing to see him looking so vulnerable again after all this time. She was reminded of times when he had arrived back from school and cried himself to sleep over some bullying incident as Jasmine tried desperately to comfort him; and of the day they had learned of their parents' deaths, when he had collapsed from grief and she had had to be the strong one, tucking him into bed and forcing herself to carry on household chores as if nothing had happened. She had always been his big sister, and she would never be able to stop now.

Sitting at the kitchen table, she stared at the wall. Maybe Rich had been right not to trust Millie after all. Rowena was obviously a certified bunny boiler, but if her accusations were true, what did that say about Millie? Not only did she have to get her head around what Dylan had done after he had more or less proclaimed his love for Millie, but she also had to confront the fact that the friend she knew as a sweet, considerate person could wreak the sort of havoc that would drive a man to suicide. What sort of woman was that? Not one who Jasmine wanted anywhere near her family. And she brought people like Rowena in her wake. Even if Millie hadn't intended any of this, even if she had not been instrumental in her ex-boyfriend's death, she

still could have done something about the mess they found themselves in now if she had just been honest about it all.

Even knowing Dylan as she did and what kind of mischief he
was capable of, something about this situation wasn't right. His
current malady was like no hangover she'd ever seen before. Her
gaze swept along the evidence of the previous evening. Two wine
glasses sat on the worktop, alongside an open wine bottle. Jasmine
let out a groan as she recognised the wine she had warned Dylan
not to drink. She pushed herself up from the table and sniffed
cautiously at the bottle. It smelt fairly normal. But as she thought
about it some more, she couldn't understand why Dylan had let
Rowena in to drink with him in the first place. He wasn't a fan,
from what he had told Jasmine, and it hardly seemed likely that
he would have wanted to socialise with her. Unless he had already
started drinking the wine before Rowena arrived and had been
pleasantly sozzled with his guard down. Or maybe he had let her
in for another reason.

She sighed and put the bottle down before running the tap and
squeezing some washing-up liquid into a bowl. Rich was probably
locked in his studio right now and she wasn't in the mood to talk to
him, despite what had happened here and what needed to be said
there. She wanted to stay with Dylan until he woke up to see if he was
ok, perhaps even get some answers from him. If it was going to be a
long wait, she might as well make herself useful.

Sometime around noon, Jasmine inched open the bedroom door to
check on Dylan. There had been some neurotic moments through
the morning, where she had convinced herself that he had somehow

fallen into a coma or choked on his own vomit, and she had looked in on him more often than was really necessary. Each time he had been sleeping soundly with no signs of distress. This time, he flipped himself over as the door creaked and opened his eyes.

'You look better,' she said as he rubbed his eyes and sat up.

'I feel better… I think. Although I'm not entirely sure what I feel better from.'

'You can't remember anything?'

'I have a vague recollection of being out on the street in my boxers. And falling down quite a lot. It's weird, like I remember stuff but it feels as though I was watching someone else do those things and not really participating myself.'

Jasmine went over and moved his legs so she could sit on the edge of the bed. The room smelt fusty, and she made a mental note to air it as soon as he was up and about. 'You were pissed as a fart so I'm not surprised.'

His eyes widened. 'I was pissed, I know that much. But I don't know if it's just that. I've never felt like that on booze before. It's like I was drugged; like Rohypnol or something?'

Jasmine stared at him.

'That sounds mental, I know,' Dylan said, scratching his head vigorously. 'But then a lot of stuff has sounded mental since Millie arrived.'

'Don't mention her,' Jasmine pouted.

'But it was Rowena's fault, not hers. I can't even remember… God, Jas, it's bloody awful. I can't even remember what made me do it.'

'Did you sleep with her?' Jasmine asked in a quiet voice. It was a question she didn't want the answer to but she felt compelled to ask. Though she often teased him and chastised him about his love life, when it came down to it, she didn't want the sordid details of what her baby brother got up to in his bedroom, especially with a woman like Rowena.

He nodded slowly. 'I think so. I didn't want to, though. Do you believe that?'

'I do.'

'It was like… I knew what I was doing was bad but I couldn't stop doing it. I didn't want to sleep with her but something drove me to it. I couldn't stop thinking about Millie's face if she could see us but Rowena kept telling me to love her and it was like I had to obey. But at the same time, I can't actually recall any details. I want to think that means I didn't sleep with her. Maybe I only think I did?' he said hopefully.

'God knows,' Jasmine replied. 'I certainly don't want to. Whether you did or didn't, the damage is done now.'

He let out a huge sigh. 'I feel like a total shit and I don't think it makes a difference whether I slept with her or not. What matters is that Millie thinks I did.' He smiled ruefully. 'There was a time when I'd have found the idea of mad, drugged-up sex quite exciting.'

'Perhaps you're getting old,' Jasmine smiled.

'Millie saw us this morning, didn't she? And I guess it looked pretty damning.'

'She was out on the street when you came running out in your boxer shorts. She and Rowena had a massive bust up. Did you know about Millie's ex? Or the reasons she came to Honeybourne in the first place?'

'No. Should I?'

'He killed himself. Rowena said that it was because of something Millie did, that she made him do it.'

'That doesn't sound right. She wouldn't be capable of something like that, not deliberately.'

'We've seen otherwise the last couple of days. Look at what happened to you last night.'

'That wasn't her fault.'

'As good as.'

He held her in a thoughtful gaze. 'What do you really think?' he asked after a silent moment. 'Deep down, do you believe Millie is a bad person?'

'I don't want to believe that she is. But I don't want her being around those I love. I don't think she's a bad person but I think she brings bad things with her. She's got a past that's not ready to let go of her yet. If you're around her you risk getting caught up in it.'

Dylan let himself fall back on the pillows and lay staring at the ceiling. 'Maybe you're right.'

'Why on earth did you let Rowena in? It's not as if you like her.'

'She wanted to talk to me about Millie. I suppose I should have told her to get lost but I couldn't help myself; I wanted to know what it was.'

'And what did she tell you?'

He scrunched his nose. 'I'm not entirely sure. She said we should open the wine before we got onto it… and you know I don't need telling twice where booze is concerned… and then it's all a bit random after that.'

'I'm sorry.'

He flipped onto his side. 'What for?'

'You really liked Millie.'

'Yeah. That'll teach me to think about fidelity.'

'You said… In the street this morning, you told her you loved her. Did you mean that?'

'Bloody hell, did I?'

Jasmine nodded, a smile playing about her lips. 'You didn't mean it?'

'Now I know I must have been stoned, but… I don't know. Maybe I did.'

There was a faint tap at the front door. Millie had lost count of the times she had hidden from Ruth as the old lady peered in through the front window. She couldn't face anyone today, least of all Ruth Evans. The events of the morning had been humiliating, mortifying, shaming, hurtful… and just about any other adjective you could use to describe your heart being torn from your chest. She had spent the morning still dressed, but huddled beneath the bedclothes despite the damp heat blowing through the upper floors of the bakery. Anything to shut the world out. From there she had heard people call through the letterbox: Ruth, Colleen, Peggy… How fast did news travel in this place? But no Jasmine and no Dylan. No Rowena for that matter, and she didn't know whether that fact was cause for relief or concern.

She doubted there was any reason for Rowena to stick around now that she had achieved what she had come to do. But as the day drew on, she realised that a decision would have to be made. It was time to cut her losses and pack. Nobody in Honeybourne would want her around now and she didn't blame them. Financially, it would pretty much ruin her. Emotionally, it was the only decision that would save her now. She had to leave Honeybourne and find somewhere new to settle. It seemed extreme, but if she changed her name maybe Rowena wouldn't track her down again. She would keep to herself, build a quiet life somewhere small, some tucked away backwater hardly on the map at all. Most importantly, no more men, not ever. She couldn't be trusted not to hurt them, especially the ones she really cared about.

She was just dumping a pile of books into a box when there was another tap at the door. As she had with all the others, she swiftly took herself into the back room and waited for them to go. There was a second knock, and then a third. A pause. And then, when Millie thought they had finally gone, a voice through the letterbox.

'I know you're in there, Millie… I just want to see if you're ok and I'm not going anywhere so you'll have to open the door eventually.'

There was a part of her that desperately wanted some comfort, someone to talk to, to explain her side of the story. But she had convinced herself that she didn't deserve it, and that the rest of the village believed she didn't deserve it either, and so she hesitated.

'Come on… please.' He lowered his voice. 'Ruth is stalking the streets and if you don't let me in soon she'll see me and then you won't be able to escape her gossip radar.'

Millie couldn't help a small smile as she walked to the front door. She opened it to find Spencer staring anxiously back at her.

'I heard what happened this morning… Well, the version that has probably undergone the Chinese-whisper treatment around the village. It sounded nasty.' He stepped in and Millie quickly closed the door again. 'You want to tell me what *actually* happened?'

'Come into the back room,' Millie said. 'Do you have time for a drink?'

'I've got marking, but as long as I head back at around eight-ish I should get that done ok.'

'Who told you?' Millie asked as she led him away from the front door.

'Terri…'

Millie turned to him and raised her eyebrows in a question.

'The newsagent,' he clarified.

'I've never even met him…'

'*Her*,' Spencer smiled. 'I don't know where she had it from. I just called in after work to pay the newspaper bill. You're a murderer who should be run out of town, apparently.'

'I'll be sure not to pop in any time soon then; she might have a pitchfork behind the counter. What else did she say?'

'A lot of stuff I knew wasn't true. That's why I came round to see you. I know what people can be like around here. There are a lot of good souls and for the most part they're welcoming, but news travels fast and people close ranks against outsiders pretty quickly if they think they're bringing trouble to the village.'

'I guessed as much. That's why I'm packing.'

Spencer shoved his hands deep in his pockets and scanned the room. Boxes lay open alongside hastily collected piles of belongings ready to fill them. 'That seems a bit extreme. Surely when people hear what really happened it'll all blow over?'

'That's just it. What really happened is pretty much as bad as people believe.'

'I don't think for a minute—'

Millie raised a hand to silence him. 'You don't think that I could kill someone? I didn't raise a gun to his head or cut his throat – but it was my fault.'

Spencer stared at her.

'You can leave now if you want to. I wouldn't blame you.'

There was a heartbeat's pause before he answered her. 'I think I'm a good judge of character. I don't think there's any reason for me to leave and if you want to talk, I'm good at listening too. Maybe I can make my own mind up about whether you're really a cold-blooded killer or not.'

Millie shifted a box from a bench seat and gestured for him to sit, settling herself alongside him. 'You're sure you want to hear this?'

'Of course.'

Millie took a deep breath. 'Michael was my soulmate. We shared no interests, had almost completely opposing views on the world, even hated each other's music and films... but there was something that connected us. I can't describe it, but it was like I couldn't breathe unless he was breathing with me...'

Spencer nodded again. But this time there was sadness in his expression. 'I know that feeling,' he said quietly. When he said no more, Millie continued.

'But one day everything changed. I don't know why or how, but I felt different. It happens, I suppose the differences between us became too much and I realised I'd fallen out of love with him. We limped on for a few months, and all the while I lived this lie, letting him think that I still saw a future for us because I was too afraid to cause the pain I knew would come from telling him the truth. I still loved him dearly as a friend, and I desperately wanted to spare his feelings. It was awful, every day smiling and telling him that everything was good, and I was terrified of what it would do to him if I told him the truth. I suppose part of me wanted to fall back in love, to get back what we once had. It felt like my fault, like there was something wrong with me that I couldn't love this amazing, kind, gentle man who any woman would be lucky to have and who I didn't deserve, and I kept convincing myself that if I just gave it time things would be right again. Deep down I knew it wouldn't happen, but anything was better than breaking his heart.' Her eyes filled with tears and she sniffed them back.

Spencer shifted his weight slightly, moving imperceptibly towards her, as if uncertain whether to offer some physical comfort. Millie mirrored the move to distance herself, certain that she didn't deserve his sympathy and the relief that a hug would bring.

'It was ok for a while,' Millie continued. 'I knew it was wrong, but I never thought any actual harm could come from the pretence – well, apart from the emotional harm. I needed to find the right moment to break it to him with the least pain. But then he went and asked me to marry him...' She looked up with a pained expression, trying to gauge his reaction. 'You still want to hear this?'

He nodded.

'There was no way I could pretend anymore, and I certainly couldn't marry a man I didn't love, no matter how much I wanted to spare his feelings. I had to refuse him, and when he demanded an explanation, all my good intentions meant nothing. I had to tell him the truth. I think it was the straw that broke the camel's back and I felt like the world's most evil woman. Maybe I was. Not only had I shattered his dreams of an idyllic future as a married man, but he learned that the previous few months had all been a hollow sham. He never said a word about where he was going, but he walked out of the house we'd shared as a couple, went to the woods and hanged himself.'

Spencer's mouth dropped open. Instinctively, he drew back from her. She tried not to flinch as it registered.

'I knew you'd think badly of me once you'd heard,' she said. 'I tried so hard to do the right thing that I got it all very, very wrong. But I don't suppose it matters now as you'll probably never see me again.'

'No! I mean... you wouldn't do anything stupid, would you?'

'Like hang myself?' She gave him a rueful half-smile. 'I'm too cowardly for that.'

Spencer seemed satisfied with her response and relaxed. He was thoughtful for a moment. 'I don't understand what made him do that. Was he prone to depression?'

'I made him do that.'

'I don't buy it.' Spencer sat back and held her in a steady gaze. 'Have you ever considered that Michael might have had some instability in his own personality that drove him to do what he did?'

'If he did, I certainly made it worse.'

'What if all you did was highlight a latent flaw, some suicidal tendency that would have shown itself eventually anyway, no matter what you did or what happened in your relationship? Maybe ten years down the line some random life event would have sent him off into the woods in the same way. An action of that magnitude, Millie… He took his own life; that's huge. It had to have come from inside him in the first place. I don't believe for a second that you could have made that happen.'

Millie shrugged. 'I know what you're trying to do and it's very sweet but not necessary. I have suffered for what happened and it's what I deserve.'

'Where does this woman fit in?'

'Rowena is Michael's sister. At the funeral, I was distraught. People were asking me what happened and I didn't know what to say. The police had his note, of course, so the official version was the one they pieced together from that. But people in our circle, they knew there was more to it than that. One of my friends asked me and it all came out. Next thing I knew, she had told Rowena everything. My life in Millrise was hell after that. I stuck it out for a few months, but then it all got too much. I saw the bakery here for sale, and I kidded myself that I came to start a business but really I packed up and ran away.'

'So now she's found you she wants to pick up where she left off?'

'Something like that. When she went to see Dylan… Well, it was her way of taking something away from me in the way she felt I'd done to her. It was her way of ensuring that I never have love from a man again.'

'So that bit is true?' Spencer gave a low whistle. 'He's always kept his brains in his dick but I didn't think he would stoop that low.'

Millie shrugged. 'I don't suppose I blame him, she's persuasive and she's gorgeous. I'm just glad he didn't come to any harm.'

'You care about Dylan?'

Millie looked up from the fingernails she had been picking and saw an expression she couldn't read on Spencer's face.

'I don't know… There was something, yes.'

'You should be careful.'

'That's what everyone's been telling me. I don't suppose it matters now.' She forced a smile.

'So you're really leaving?'

'I don't have a choice.'

'You always have a choice. If you run won't she just keep on running after you?'

'Maybe. I'll just have to stay one step ahead.'

Spencer blew out a breath and ran a hand through his hair. 'This is crazy. Stay and talk to people here. Explain it how you did to me and they'll support you. She'll get short shrift for what amounts to victimisation. Can you get the police involved?'

'What do I tell them? That I made someone kill himself and now his sister is out for revenge. I'm not sure that's a great idea.'

'Nobody should have to live as you are now.'

'I'm still living, though. That's all Rowena is concerned with.'

'Then why hasn't she tried to murder you and have done with it?'

'Because that would be too easy and too kind. I have to leave.'

'It's not the answer.'

'Spencer… you're sweet and generous, and I appreciate your sympathetic ear, but you wouldn't know. How could you? Home is Honeybourne, you fit in; everyone knows and loves you…'

'It hasn't always been like that. I left once.'

'To go to university.'

'That wasn't the only reason.'

'What happened?'

'Love being as unpredictable and unruly for me as it was for you… that's what happened.'

'I don't—'

'I was in love with someone, had been for years. She was never interested in me as more than a nerdy friend. But I got close to the family and I was fond of them all. I liked to believe that they were all fond of me too. One day I decided that I couldn't stand it anymore. She had started to see someone and they seemed to be getting serious. I could love her from afar while I thought that some time in the future there might be a chance that she would develop those feelings for me too, but this new man threatened to take her away from me for good.'

'What did you do?'

'I confided in my best friend. I told him that I had always loved this girl and that I was going to tell her how I felt before it was too late. He was all for it, said that life was too short and that I should go for it. So I did.'

'What happened?'

'It earned me a beating from my best friend after she turned me down. Perhaps I should have told him who the girl was before I went off declaring my love.'

'Was it his girlfriend?'

Spencer shook his head. 'His sister.'

Millie frowned. 'So you had to leave?'

'I thought it was best. But while I was away I came to terms with everything that had happened, and I missed the village. I heard she had got married and was deliriously happy. She's been cool about the whole thing really, and we're sort of friends again.'

'Does her husband know?'

'Rich? No, I—'

'Hang on! Did you say Rich? As in Richard Green?'

'I thought you knew...'

'God no! So it was Jasmine?'

He gave a rueful smile.

'And Dylan beat you up?'

'To be fair, he probably had a point. She was happy and everyone loved Rich. Me putting my tuppence in really did put the cat among the pigeons.'

'But you loved her. Falling in love with the wrong person isn't a crime.'

'No, it's not. But it causes problems... Perhaps you and I are not as different as you might think.'

'Maybe we should be miserable and perplexed by love together. We'll make a stand against it: *Down with love!*'

'There's an idea.' He raised his eyebrows and Millie couldn't help but erupt into laughter. Spencer always had this calming effect on her. She wished that she could feel something more for him than friendship. He was a much better match than Dylan Smith, and yet she couldn't get Dylan's face out of her head.

'I'm so glad you came to see me,' she said.

'And I'm glad you let me in. Are we going to get these boxes unpacked again?'

Millie cast her eyes over her half-packed belongings and shook her head. 'Your situation is very different from mine. I have no ties here in the first place.'

'What about the bakery?'

'You mean the one I'll never be able to afford to get up and running? Someone else can worry about it.' She fished in the pocket of her jeans and drew out a key. 'Want it?' she asked, dangling it in front of him.

'No, thanks,' he laughed. 'I think I'll stick to teaching.' His expression became serious again. 'Where will you go?'

She shrugged. 'I have no idea. I hear Scotland is nice at this time of year.'

'Couldn't you pick somewhere warmer? If I'm coming to visit you I don't want to haul a load of thermal undies with me.'

'You'd come to visit?' Millie smiled.

'Of course I would. Nobody should be friendless in this world. Maybe, before you decide, though, you should go and talk to the people you think you've wronged. You might find that they're not as upset as you imagine.'

'No, I don't think so. It's best all round if I go.'

Chapter Sixteen

Not in the mood for a conversation, Jasmine had waited at the far corner of the schoolyard and collected the triplets without so much as an exchange of pleasantries even with Spencer. Her mind was still full of the things she had seen and heard that morning, and the conversations she'd had with Dylan. He pretended to be ok, but behind that bravado he was still a vulnerable boy. If he had fallen for Millie then perhaps she owed it to him to speak to her, get Millie's version of what really happened with Rowena's brother and see where they could all go from there.

Walking home, the triplets had been full of their school day, squealing and laughing, hopping along kerbs, climbing fences, bickering and hugging alternately. It was white noise and Jasmine zoned it out, still lost in her thoughts, until Rebecca's question jolted her back to reality.

'Will Daddy still be at home?'

Jasmine turned sharply to her. 'Of course. What makes you say that?'

'I just thought… we thought…' Her reply tailed off and she looked hopelessly at her siblings.

'All families argue,' Jasmine said in the most reassuring voice she could muster. 'You three do it all the time.'

'But we can't get divorced,' Rebecca said.

'Neither can we,' Jasmine smiled. 'How would your daddy be able to find his socks in the morning if I wasn't there to show him where they were?'

Rebecca looked distinctly relieved. 'What are we having for supper?'

'I don't know. How do you fancy big greasy burgers?'

'Yay!' all three children chorused at once.

She smiled as she pushed open the gate, the children skirting the giant statue in the front garden, each one patting it affectionately as they passed. Jasmine had always made it her number-one priority to give them the best, most fulfilled and interesting childhood she could, and she harboured a hope that the little things, like patting Poseidon on the backside whenever they passed him, would give them wonderful memories of their childhood to cherish when she and Rich had long gone.

The door to the conservatory was open and they filed in, shedding school bags along the way, Jasmine collecting them up with a sigh. It didn't matter how many times she told them to put things away, it never made a difference, and today she wasn't in the mood to worry about it. She heard Rich's voice drift through from the hallway as he greeted the triplets, and her heart seemed to beat out of time. She hoped she was wrong, that he had been full of bluster and hadn't really meant any of the things he'd said the previous night. She hoped that he would take her in his arms and kiss her and tell her that he was sorry and that everything was alright. Because it was, wasn't it? No matter how angry she had been with him she had never contemplated separation. Surely he felt the same? The oppressive, sultry heat that lingered throughout the house, warnings of the storm to come, seemed to mirror her mood and fears.

'Why don't you get changed out of your uniforms and then you can tell me all about it?' Rich said to the kids as Jasmine appeared in the hallway door. She watched them nod eagerly and skip off up the stairs.

As soon as they were out of earshot, Rich turned on Jasmine, his voice urgent with barely contained irritation. 'How is Dylan?'

'He's fine. Almost his normal self by the time I left.'

'Did you take him to the emergency department? To see Dr Wood, at least?'

'He's fine. He slept whatever it was off.'

'We should call the police. That woman is a danger to society.'

'You're overreacting,' Jasmine replied tetchily. She had been just as angry herself that morning, but somehow Rich's sense of drama seemed too exaggerated for what she had explained to him on the phone earlier. And now she was beginning to wish that she hadn't told him quite so much. There was almost righteous glee in his voice. 'Rowena has gone now, as far as I can tell. She did what she came to do.'

'I'm not talking about Rowena. It's all over the village…'

'What is?'

'That Millie got someone killed.'

'You know how people gossip here. That's a half-baked truth.'

'Half-truth is still some truth.'

'Don't you think Millie's been through enough? Don't you think it's bad enough that some nutter is stalking her across the country, spreading rumours about her so that idiots like you can spread them a bit more?'

'You didn't say that earlier—'

'I was angry earlier! I was worried about Dylan. I wasn't thinking straight. But you've had it in for Millie since she arrived. I can't see what she's ever done to you.'

'You can't see the evidence in front of your eyes? We're having another blazing row about her! That's what my problem is!'

'And you started the row. I can't believe you're being so petty about this. You're bigger than that, Rich. Or at least the man I married was.'

'So you're choosing a woman you barely know over me?'

'Don't be ridiculous! I'm just saying that we should give her a chance to tell her side of the story, not believe someone who has just turned up in the village, drugged and taken sexual advantage of someone, and then shouted a lot of very serious accusations around in the streets. I know who my money is on to be more reliable.'

Rich paused for a moment and then his voice dropped. 'Why *did* Dylan let Rowena in?'

'Because she said she wanted to talk to him about Millie.'

His look was triumphant. 'There! It always comes back to her.'

'Oh, grow up, Rich!'

'I'm right about her and you can't stand it.'

'You're wrong. And you can't stand *that*.'

'I don't need this on top of everything else.' Rich pushed past her into the kitchen. She watched him march through the conservatory and out through the back door.

Silence echoed through the house. Jasmine was aware that the triplets had probably listened to the whole row. She would have to explain it to them later, but right now she was having a hard time even explaining it to herself. What had happened to their relationship? Rich was angry, and he was hurting, but the reasons he was giving didn't seem enough on their own. And she couldn't help but get defensive every time he pointed the finger of blame at Millie. He was right that they hardly knew her, but that didn't make it ok to distrust her like that. The more she had thought about Millie through the day, and the more she and Dylan had talked about her and the things that had happened, the more she began to see that Millie was a victim. Whatever she had done, it didn't justify the treatment she was getting. There was Dylan to think of too, who seemed to have genuine feelings for Millie, and must be hurting just as much right now for a relationship that appeared to be doomed before it had begun.

Wearily taking herself to the kitchen to start preparing their evening meal, she discovered that Rich had left his mobile phone behind. She let out a curse under her breath. Now she couldn't contact him even if she wanted to, which was just another thing to feel aggrieved about. He had probably done it on purpose.

Pulling a pack of mince from the fridge, she set about making the homemade burgers she had promised the triplets, chopping and mixing like a robot, while her thoughts raced and swooped from one track to the next. Everyone seemed to be hurting in one way or another, and Jasmine hated to see it; she always wanted to fix everyone, and usually found a way, but not this time, it seemed.

Reuben sidled up to Jasmine. 'Has Daddy gone out?' She was dragged from her thoughts with a start.

'I didn't see you come in,' she smiled. 'Were you being extra sneaky?'

He smiled uncertainly. 'Is Daddy having supper with us?'

'I expect so. He went out to do something.'

'What?'

'A little errand. He won't be long.'

Reuben was silent for a moment, and then nodded his head sombrely.

'Go and play for a while.' Jasmine broke an egg into a bowl.

'Can we go outside?'

The sky was a leaden grey, low, like it was trying to smother the earth. 'It looks like thunder is coming,' she said, thinking about Rich and wondering whether he was indoors or not. 'You should probably play upstairs. Do you have homework?'

Reuben shook his head. 'Not tonight. I think Mr Johns was in a hurry because he said he was going to give us some but then he didn't and he told us we could just go.'

'Hmm. Ok then. Go and play, or you can watch TV. I'll call you when your food is ready.'

'What about Daddy? Are we going to wait for him?'

Jasmine looked through the windows again. 'No. I think we're on our own for a while.'

Supper was a subdued affair. The tension in the air was as palpable as the electricity building in the billowing clouds outside. Jasmine's mood grew ever more anxious and irritable the longer Rich was absent, and the children instinctively picked up on it.

At seven thirty, Jasmine ran the first of three baths, one for each of the children, who now refused to share. Bath nights were a notorious drain on their evening time because of this and usually she and Rich did the chore between them. Tonight, it looked as though she was on her own. As she sat on the side of the tub, watching the water grow into a sea of bubbles, she thought about Rich's phone, sitting on the kitchen worktop. She hated snooping… It was distasteful and made her feel like one of those women she had always sworn she wouldn't be: suspicious, unreasonable, perpetually paranoid. Her trust in Rich had always been unshakeable, and yet, for the first time, the word *affair* began to sneak into her consciousness.

With the bathtub full of fragrant foam, made from one of Millie's natural recipes, Jasmine called Reuben in first, leaving the two girls playing in the bedroom. Then she went back downstairs. There was no sign of Rich. She went to the windows, where the skies over the horizon were now so dark they were almost slate, and scanned the fields beyond the garden. Rich sometimes took himself for a walk when he wanted to think. But there was no familiar figure anywhere to be seen. She opened the front door and walked through the garden, shielding her eyes to better see down the path and into the distance, but it was still and quiet; that special hush before a storm where even the birds seemed to have gone into hiding to escape it.

Back in the house, she dried Reuben and put him into his pyjamas, repeating the whole process with the two girls until, at around nine, all three were in bed. But there was still no Rich.

Jasmine flopped onto the sofa and flicked on the TV. But she was tense and hyper-alert for any sign of Rich's return and took nothing in. Finally, with an impatient sigh, she got up and fetched Rich's phone.

The first thing she noticed was a missed call. *OLLIE*. Rich's agent. Jasmine noted the time of the call with a frown. It had come in way after Ollie's usual working hours. This could only be very good or very bad news. She thought about calling him back, but she didn't often speak to Ollie and anyway, whatever the news, Rich deserved to hear it first.

Instead she went into his call history and was relieved to see that there didn't seem to be any incongruous numbers listed there. She chided herself for being so silly, and was just about to put the phone back when something stopped her.

She had often complained to him that he didn't use a pin code for his phone but right now, as she logged into his email account and scrolled through, she had never been more relieved that he'd ignored her advice.

At just after two that afternoon there had been an email from Ollie. Jasmine could see that it had been opened already and so Rich must have read it. Her finger hovered over it. She knew what she was about to do was probably unforgiveable, but she was beginning to feel as though her world was imploding. Rich was hiding something and she needed to know what it was. Without another thought, she opened it up and scanned the message.

Hi Rich,

I need to speak to you urgently. As you know, there has been some less than favourable feedback from the film people at World's End Pictures and I'm afraid that they're pushing for another composer. I've done my best to persuade them this is a bad idea, but I need to give them something from you to keep them on board. How is the project progressing? I'm afraid we're going to lose this contract if I can't give them something soon.

Give me a call when you get this.

Ollie

Jasmine read the email again. She checked to see if there were others but this was the one she kept coming back to. Rich had seemed agitated for weeks. She was used to him being tetchy whenever he was working on a new composition but it always settled once the job was done. Although he had been worse than usual this time, she put it down to the fact that this was the biggest contract of his career. He had never once confided in her that he was struggling to write, and although she had seen the signs, she hadn't really understood the extent of the problem, believing that he would work through it eventually, as he had always done before.

Her gaze was drawn yet again to the skies outside and the knot of worry swelled into a boulder that lodged in her throat. From the call history it didn't look as though Rich had called Ollie back. Was he too afraid to? If he had lost the contract it would tear him up. He had seen this as the turning point for the family's fortunes and Jasmine knew that he would feel like an utter failure if it all went wrong. In that sort of mood, there was no telling what he might do. And she had driven him out; absorbed in her own problems she had not seen the signs, had not given him time to talk it through. If anything happened to him... Oh God, if anything happened it would be all her fault.

Chapter Seventeen

Spencer had stalled the packing process, but Millie had been grateful for his presence. She had opened a bottle of brandy and, pleasantly warmed by its effects, thoughts of belongings and boxes had almost disappeared from her mind, while thoughts of school marking had faded from his.

When the knock at the door boomed through the old bakery like a clap of thunder, Millie almost leapt from her seat. She shot Spencer an alarmed look. Rosy cheeked and a little the worse for wear, he gave her a benign smile.

'It'll just be Ruth,' he said in a sleepy voice.

'It's a bit late for her.' Millie glanced at her watch.

'Yes, but you've presented her with a conundrum that she won't be able to resist. If you don't answer the door to her she'll be up all night going mad with curiosity.'

'I can't talk to her now.'

Spencer shrugged. There was a second knock. Millie held her breath and placed a finger to her lips.

For a moment they sat in silence, staring at each other. She was just about to express her relief when a third knock was accompanied by a shout through the letterbox.

'Millie!'

Spencer bolted upright, all signs of tipsiness suddenly vanished. 'Dylan,' he whispered.

'What do you think he wants?' Millie replied in equally hushed tones.

'You, by the sounds of it.'

She shook her head. 'I don't know… I can't face him now.'

'I don't think he'd be too pleased to see me here either.'

'It's got nothing to do with him,' Millie fired back, suddenly feeling defensive on Spencer's behalf. 'I decide who I'm friends with.'

Spencer stared at her for a moment, and then burst out laughing. 'He's met his match in you, hasn't he?'

'It's not funny.'

'Yes, it is. We're being ridiculous and paranoid. You should answer the door.'

Millie let out a sigh. 'I suppose so.'

She flung it open to find Dylan on the doorstep. The moment she set eyes on him she found herself studying his face intently for signs of sickness or injury.

'Are you going to let me in?' Dylan asked. He hooked a thumb at the darkening skies. 'I think I'm about to get rained on.'

Millie stepped back and he closed the door behind him.

'I wanted to explain—'

Millie held up a hand to silence him. 'It should be me explaining to you.'

'But this morning… I mean the thing with Rowena…' He pushed a hand through his hair, his distress evident in the faltering tone of his voice. It was a Dylan that Millie was unfamiliar with, the sight of it twisting that knife of guilt again. 'I wish you hadn't had to see that.'

'So do I. But I can't blame you for something you had no control over. If it's anyone's fault it's mine. I'm just glad you're ok.'

'Is it true?'

'I don't—'

'The things you and Rowena said. Is any of it true?'

'Would it make matters better or worse if I said yes?'

Dylan gave her a tight smile. 'I really don't know. It's hard to get my head around.'

'I get that. I'm sorry you had to get dragged into it... you know, with the wine and everything. That was unforgivable.'

'I've had worse trips than that after cooking up mushrooms from the fields, so I'm pretty sure there was something more than wine in that bottle, because I recognise the effects.' Millie raised her eyebrows and he laughed lightly. 'Don't look so shocked. I haven't always been this angelic.'

'You don't hate me?'

'No, I don't hate you.'

'You ought to.'

'Don't be silly. It wasn't your fault.'

'But it was. And everyone will see it that way.' There was a pause. Dylan stuck his hands deep in his pockets, and then Spencer emerged and stood at the doorway, giving Dylan a curt nod of acknowledgement.

'Oh,' Dylan began, 'if I'm interrupting something—'

'You're not,' Millie said quickly. 'He's helping me to pack.'

Dylan's vexed frown gave way to a look of shock. 'You're leaving?'

'I don't see what else I can do.'

Dylan looked at Spencer, who held his hands up. 'I've tried to talk some sense into her but she's determined she's going.'

Millie frowned at him. 'We've been over it and you agreed.'

'No, I didn't. I said I would help you if you were adamant that you wanted to go. The two things are very different. I don't think you should. I think you should stand your ground and show Rowena that you won't be victimised any more and that you're settling in Honeybourne whether she likes it or not.'

'What about the residents of Honeybourne? They might not be so keen on that idea.'

'We're two of them and we are.' Spencer looked at Dylan, who nodded agreement.

'I think you'll be the only two.' Millie let out a sigh. 'I saw the look on Jasmine's face this morning. I don't think she's ever going to speak to me again. That on its own is enough to make me want to go.'

'Look, I think you guys need some privacy,' said Spencer, 'so I'm going to wash up our glasses and then skedaddle.'

Dylan took Millie gently by the shoulders. 'Is this why you told me we couldn't be together?'

Millie opened her mouth to argue. But what was the point? She had wanted to protect all the people she had come to care about over the last few weeks and she had failed miserably. She nodded.

'I don't want you to go,' Dylan said quietly, holding her gaze. 'And I think you might be the first woman I've ever said that to and meant it.'

'I have to.'

'Is this about me sleeping with her, because I don't think—'

Millie shook her head. 'I know what she's like, and what's done is done now. But what if she's not finished yet? I can't put you in any more danger and I don't want her manipulating any more of my friends to get back at me; it's not fair to drag anyone through it.'

'I can handle her. Once bitten twice shy.'

Millie shook her head. 'Even I underestimated the lengths she was prepared to go to. I worry that she might be willing to go even further and I can't take that risk.'

'Because you like me?' Dylan gave her an impish grin and Millie couldn't help a small smile in return.

'Nothing is ever that simple. It's not just you I'm worried about either. Anyone who is anything to me is a target.'

'Half the village knows what happened,' he said with a rueful smile, 'or at least a version of it. But they all know that she's trouble. So anyone she comes across is going to be on their guard. She won't fool people again.'

'She doesn't need to fool them and she doesn't need to be in contact with them to cause mischief.'

'We can give as good as we get. Ever seen the film *The Wicker Man*?'

Millie's smile returned. 'I know that you're trying to make light of this, but you can't deny what happened to you last night. Whatever you think it was, she got to you and you were at her mercy. She's capable of doing it again.' She pulled herself gently from his grip. 'I'm sorry, but leaving is the only way I can be certain.'

'And what if she follows you to the next village?' Dylan said as she walked to the front door to see him out. 'And the next one and the next one? Are you supposed to spend the rest of your life as a hermit, just in case?'

'Yes,' Millie replied.

'No way!' He strode across and took her hand from the door. 'You're too funny, too clever, too beautiful for that. How can you deny the world the gift of all that you are? Without you in it, life is a darker place and I'm not going to stand by and watch this happen.'

'You don't know what you're messing with,' Millie fired back. Why couldn't he accept her decision? Why couldn't he see it was for the best? And why did he have to choose this moment to show the real Dylan Smith – a considerate, sensitive, eloquent man, the man she had always known was inside him. Why did he have to make it so damn hard to leave him now?

He took her by the shoulders and gazed down at her. She was mesmerised, knowing that he was about to kiss her and undo all her stoic resolution and there was nothing she could do to stop him. In her heart, she didn't want to. But as the moment came, it was shattered by a frantic hammering at the door that made them both leap apart. Spencer ran through from the back room. If it was Rowena, at least Millie had the two best allies that she could hope for. Emboldened by this, she undid the lock with a shaking hand and opened the door.

Jasmine stood on the doorstep, hair wild around her shoulders, trainers on beneath her linen trousers and a raincoat pulled around her. She had the triplets in tow and Ruth bringing up the rear. She glared at Dylan.

'I've been calling you for hours! Don't you ever answer your phone?'

'What the hell?'

'I told you he was here,' Ruth cut in, but nobody took any notice of her.

'Is Rich with you?' Jasmine asked sharply.

'No…'

'Have you seen him?'

'Not today. What's going on?'

Jasmine looked at Millie. 'Have you seen him tonight?'

Millie shook her head.

'Me neither,' Spencer said as he came to the door.

'I can't find him,' Jasmine said.

'Maybe he can't get a signal on his phone,' said Dylan. 'There are some dodgy spots around the Dog and Hare—'

'No!' she fired back in a strangled voice. 'He doesn't have his phone with him.'

'But he'll turn up. Have you been to the pub?'

'I've been everywhere. Nobody has seen him. I don't know what to do.'

Millie stared helplessly at her friend. She wanted to reach out, to comfort and help in any way she could. But she wasn't sure it would be welcome.

'What do you want us to do?' Spencer asked. 'We can go and search if you like.'

'How long has he been missing?' Dylan asked.

Jasmine shrugged. 'Four, maybe five hours.'

Dylan looked at the triplets, wide-eyed and fearful. Clearly their mother's anxiety was rubbing off on them. 'Hey, kids, how's it going? Do you fancy a night in the pub?'

Jasmine opened her mouth but Dylan silenced her. 'It'll be cool. I'll run them down and they can sit with Colleen in the back room while we sort this. If we're out late they can sleep over in one of the guest bedrooms. She won't mind.'

'That's a good idea,' Spencer agreed. 'I'll call ahead.' He ran to get his phone. Dylan looked at Jasmine. 'Come in and sit down.'

'I'll come to the pub with you,' she began, but Dylan stopped her.

'I can do it. I need you to think about where Rich might be.'

'I don't know. I've tried everywhere I can think of. He's not at any of his friends' or at the pub or any of his other haunts. We—'

'Not now,' Dylan said, glancing at the kids who were listening intently. 'Tell me later. Or tell Millie and Spencer while I'm gone. Ruth…' He turned to the old lady who had sidled in with the children. 'Would you care to accompany me to the Dog and Hare? I could do with an extra pair of hands to keep these rascals in order.' He gave her a cheeky wink and Ruth almost squealed her reply.

'Ooh, yes!'

'Well, we'd better get a move on; it's ten thirty now and we don't want to keep everyone up.'

'Quite,' Jasmine said, trying to appear cheerful. 'It's not the school holidays yet so you definitely can't stay up all night.'

Millie smiled. She was impressed by Dylan's ability to siphon Ruth off without it seeming to Ruth that she was being got out of the way. And it was reassuring to see that some of the flirting, charming rogue was still in evidence; the new Dylan she was coming to know was both attractive and oddly disconcerting in equal measures. But her smile faded as she realised in that same moment that she was expected to take care of Jasmine. And now that she knew about Jasmine and Spencer's past, she wondered whether his presence would make things better or worse.

Spencer returned, phone in hand. 'Colleen says she'd love to see them and she's getting ice cream out right now. I didn't tell her exactly what the situation was, just that we had a bit of an emergency on our hands.'

'Good man.' Dylan nodded his approval. He turned to the children. 'Glad to see that you've got your raincoats on over those PJs, I think you might need them.'

By now, night was almost upon them. More worryingly, so was the storm.

'Jas…' Dylan said gently. As she turned to him, he nodded his head towards the triplets.

She bent to kiss each of them on the head. 'Be good for Colleen, won't you?'

They all nodded.

'Will you find Daddy?' Rachel asked.

'Of course. He's probably just gone somewhere I haven't thought of and he'll think I've been very silly when he turns up.'

Rachel didn't look convinced, but she followed without another word as Dylan offered Ruth his arm and then whistled for them to follow him out into the night. Spencer, Jasmine and Millie were left staring at each other as the room fell eerily quiet.

'Is there anything I can get you?' Millie asked Jasmine awkwardly as the tension became unbearable.

Jasmine shifted from one foot to the other. She wrapped her raincoat tighter, despite the warmth of the room.

'No… thank you.'

Spencer draped a comforting arm around Jasmine 'He'll turn up. Everything will be fine.'

'I know. I'm trying to be sensible about it but…'

'But what?' Spencer asked. 'What's happened?'

Jasmine sighed. 'We had the hugest row. And we both said things… There was talk of divorce. And there was…'

Jasmine faltered. Millie glanced at Spencer, trying to read his expression. Whatever his feelings might have been about the prospect of Jasmine and Rich splitting up, he didn't show them. Millie's admiration of him grew, but so did her pity. He was everyone's rock: kind, selfless, principled to the last, and yet he was so obviously lonely. A man like him didn't deserve to be lonely. Millie didn't know whether he still carried any sort of torch for Jasmine, but if he did, this situation would be hard for him.

'Millie,' Spencer said, 'have we got some of that brandy to spare?'

'Sure.' She turned to fetch the bottle and a glass but was stopped by Jasmine.

'I'm alright. I need to keep my head clear.'

'Just a drop will calm you down,' Spencer insisted.

'How can I sit here drinking brandy when I don't know where he is? He could be anywhere, lying in a ditch, hanging from a tree...'

Millie gasped. Even Spencer looked at Jasmine in shock.

'He wouldn't do anything like that, would he?' he asked, his face seeming to drain of all colour.

'I honestly don't know.'

Spencer raced through to the back room and emerged after a second, pulling a thin jacket on. 'Let's go and look now. I've got my phone; Dylan can join us when he's dropped the kids off.'

'I'll come with you,' Millie began, but Spencer cut her off.

'I need you to stay here.'

'I want to help!'

'And you can, by waiting for Dylan. Tell him we've gone to look for Rich and we're going to start where the old rope swing is. He'll know where that is.'

'Rope swing?' Millie repeated.

'Not as random as it sounds,' Spencer replied briskly, before ushering Jasmine out and slamming the front door behind them.

Millie spent the next ten minutes pacing the room. It felt vast and far too quiet in the aftermath of the drama that had unfolded there and she felt increasingly useless. Millie had almost come to the decision that she would leave a note on the door for Dylan and go to join Spencer and Jasmine, when Dylan arrived back on the doorstep, dripping wet and shaking the rain from his hair as she let him in.

His gaze swept the room.

'Where's Jas?'

'She went out with Spencer. They seemed really worried about Rich. They said to tell you that they were going to start looking in the place where the old rope swing is.'

Dylan's expression darkened. 'What the hell happened today?'

'What do you mean?'

'That's a notorious spot… It's…' He turned for the door again. 'I've got to go and find them.'

'Notorious for what?' Millie cried as he yanked open the door again. He spun to face her.

'Let's just say there are plenty of sturdy branches on the trees there, and tyres aren't always the only things found swinging from them.'

A wave of nausea swept through Millie, and the floor seemed to drop away from her. 'Oh my God,' she whispered.

'Wait here,' Dylan said, turning again for the door.

'No!' Millie grabbed his arm. 'I need to come!'

'You need to stay here. The storm is going to get bad.'

'I don't care. Please… I can't just wait here…'

Dylan turned to her again and paused. His expression was unreadable and he seemed to be weighing up his options. Millie searched his face as she waited for his answer. She was terrified that Rowena was somehow involved, as irrational as it sounded, and even more terrified that her arrival in Honeybourne had somehow played a part in the current events, as if she was some walking jinx. If anything happened to Rich, to any of them, Millie didn't think she could ever forgive herself. She had to do something to help, however small. Being part of the search was the only thing she could think of.

After a moment Dylan nodded. 'Have you got some good boots? It gets pretty boggy out there. You'll need a waterproof jacket too… and a torch if you have one.'

Millie raced around collecting what she needed and returned to find Dylan stamping his feet at the door.

'Ok?' he asked. With a brisk nod, Millie followed as he led them into the storm.

There was a tense silence for the first fifteen minutes, broken only by the howling of the wind and patter of rain against Millie's hood as she desperately held it in place on her head. The streets of Honeybourne were lit, albeit sparsely, but when the village gave way to wild countryside, holding the torch Millie had brought made the going much harder. The rough terrain forced them to slow their pace, and allowed them to finally exchange words.

'How much further is it?' Millie asked, wiping rain from her eyes.

'Ten minutes or so. But that's on a good day. Maybe fifteen, twenty tonight.'

'What if Rich isn't there?'

'We look somewhere else. You should be more worried about what we'll do if he *is* there.'

'You're fond of him, aren't you?'

'Of course. He's like a brother.'

Millie paused for breath. And the next question was out as if it had a will of its own. 'Is that why you warned Spencer off?'

Dylan turned sharply, his expression hidden by shadow. 'What does that mean?'

'I know… about Spencer and Jasmine.'

'Nothing happened between Spencer and Jasmine.'

'I didn't mean that. But I know how Spencer felt about her.'

'He had no right to blab.'

'He couldn't help it. And look… Tonight he was the first one out looking for Rich. So it's all water under the bridge now, isn't it?'

'I wouldn't say that. Spencer keeps his secrets close. I think, given half a chance, he'd still be in there.'

'But he seems such good friends with them.'

'Rich doesn't know anything about it and Jas is too forgiving. Besides, it's a small village; you have to get along with people if you're going to live here.'

'He still thinks a lot of you, too.'

'Like I said, you have to get along around here.'

'It's more than that, I can tell.'

'When we were kids he was always hanging around our house,' Dylan said. 'I thought it was because we were mates and I was flattered. He was older than me and when you're teenagers a tiny age gap is massive. I never realised that it was all for Jasmine's benefit, even back then.'

'It must have been more than that. He thinks you're amazing now.'

'Maybe now, but back then I was an annoying little twerp. A useful one, but annoying just the same. He quickly realised that if he was nice to me it made Jasmine happy. It was nothing to do with us having anything in common, he was just using me.'

'That's a bit harsh.'

'I don't suppose he knew he was doing it. But that doesn't change anything.'

'Is that why you're frosty with him now?'

'Do we have to do this?'

'No… but I just thought it would be less tense if we talked about something.'

'I'd be less tense if we talked about Man United's defence last season.'

'Why do you still hate him after all this time?'

Dylan stopped. 'What makes you think I hate him?'

'It just seems that way sometimes.'

'That's because you don't know the facts.'

'So, fill me in.'

Dylan began to walk again, Millie keeping pace alongside him. 'I just don't always trust him.'

'It's funny, because I think he feels the same way about you.'

'What makes you say that?'

'Nothing in particular…'

'He's warned you away from me. I'm the original Casanova, right?' Millie smiled wanly.

'I've had a few girlfriends, there's nothing wrong with that. He ought to try it. That's why I don't trust him. What's he waiting for?'

'The right woman?'

'Or the woman he's wanted all along.'

'And there was me, flattering myself that you were jealous there might be something going on between me and Spencer.'

'Nah… Although Ruth told me she was convinced there was, especially as he'd been with you all afternoon and you wouldn't answer the door. I think she was hoping for a tale of debauchery and large amounts of rubber. I put her straight when we took the kids to the Dog and Hare.'

'How can you be so sure my afternoon didn't feature large amounts of rubber?'

'I know Spencer.'

'So you say. But he can't pine for one woman for the rest of his life. He's not Greyfriars Bobby.'

Dylan was silent for a moment. When he spoke again, Millie wished he hadn't. 'Love makes us do strange and silly things. Surely you know that better than anyone.'

She had no answer for that, so Millie concentrated on keeping the torch trained on the ground and watching where she put her feet.

After another five silent minutes, Dylan held up a hand to halt their progress.

'D'you hear that?'

'Sounds like Jasmine… and Rich!'

Relief flooded through Millie. They began their trek again, following the voices. And then a scream split the night air.

Chapter Eighteen

Spencer and Jasmine had sprinted through the village and over the fields in their haste to get to the old rope swing. They were both soaked through, ankles were twisted and curses were muttered, but they kept going, calling Rich's name as they went. Jasmine was so grateful to have Spencer's lean outline marching alongside her. After all that had happened in the past, she wouldn't have blamed him if he never wanted to speak to her again, but not once during the year he had been back in Honeybourne had he shown any sign of bitterness. He had endured the knowledge that she was married to another man and had three children with him; he taught her children and showed them nothing but kindness and fairness, as he did to everyone he knew. She loved that they could still be friends. If she couldn't have Dylan or Rich beside her now, there was no better substitute than Spencer Johns.

Having left in a hurry with no flashlight, Spencer was using the torch on his phone. The light was feeble and he had to use it sparingly to avoid it getting soaked in the rain, but it was the best they had. He fished it from his pocket now and swept the landscape with the meagre beam. Then he stopped and caught his breath.

'Good news... The rope swing is up ahead.'

'Is there bad news?' Jasmine asked, fear hollowing her out.

'I'm not sure. I thought I saw something but I can't be certain.'

Taking great care, they picked their way, almost blind, up an incline before scrambling and sliding down the bank on the other side to where a rope swing hung from a platform over the river. Usually the river was shallow in this part and fairly tame. In all the years that kids had been playing up here nobody had ever been seriously hurt… at least not in the river. But back in the seventies two suicide victims had been found hanging from the trees nearby within six months of each other. There had been nothing since then, but there were tales of hauntings and spirits, embellished by teenagers, and the place had come to be known as Hangman's Hill.

Tonight, the sheer volume of rain had inundated the riverbed, and they could hear the rush of water below them, a dangerous and invisible force.

Spencer dug his phone out of a sodden pocket and flashed the light around again. And suddenly it lit up a pale and eerie face. Jasmine screamed. Until she saw that it was Rich, sitting under the swing platform, caked in mud and distinctly bleary eyed, clinging onto a bottle. He turned to face them, but said nothing as he struggled to focus.

'Pissed as a newt,' Spencer said, the relief evident in his voice. 'Nice one, Rich.'

'What the hell!' Jasmine shouted, trying to hold back the tears that had been threatening to overwhelm her all night. 'We've been looking everywhere for you!'

'Why?' Rich slurred.

'Why the hell do you think? Nobody had any idea where you'd gone!' She waved a hand at the river. 'For all we knew you could have been face down in there!'

'Probably the best place for me,' Rich said. 'I thought about it...' His eyes rolled as he looked up into the dark canopy of trees. 'I thought about swinging from one of them... but I was too scared in the end. Pathetic, eh?'

'Richard Green... If I ever hear you say anything like that again I'll push you in the river myself!'

'Yeah, but you'd be better off without me. Let's face it, I'm crap.'

'Stop it!' Jasmine shouted. She dragged in a deep, calming breath and bent down to sit next to him under the platform, her voice softer now. 'I don't know what I would do without you. I've never been as scared as I was tonight.'

He waved the almost empty bottle around as he spoke. 'I don't know why you put up with me. You could have any man... *any* man... and you stick with me... argghhh, Jas, I can't offer you anything. I don't have a proper job and the one I have I can't—'

'Shush!' Jasmine said, taking the bottle from him and placing it to one side. 'You have no idea, do you? It doesn't matter what job you do, whether we're poor or rich, whether you get fat and bald and fart in bed... I just want you, whatever you are or do. You mean the world to me, and my life would be pointless without you in it. I will never, ever stop loving you. The sooner you get that into your fat head, the sooner we can get out of this rain and go home.'

'You can't mean that...'

'Of course I do.' She reached over to kiss him lightly before pulling away with a grimace. 'You stink. What the hell have you been drinking?'

'It doesn't matter. Go... Leave me here to rot...' He looked up, trying to focus on Spencer who had bent down to join them in the now cramped space under the wooden platform. It was damp and dirty, but at least there was some respite from the rain. 'Spencer, for instance…' Rich slurred, 'would be much more deserving of your affections. I bet you fancy her a bit, don't you, Spence?'

'Stop it,' Jasmine said again.

'Come on, Spencer… Take her home, look after her like I can't…'

'Rich!' Jasmine looked hopelessly at Spencer, her heart sinking with every word her inebriated spouse uttered.

'Jasmine Johns… It has a ring to it!' Rich laughed. 'A good honest day's work from Mr Johns, regular pay packet coming in and someone who can actually help the kids with their homework.'

'Right, that's enough,' Spencer cut in. He sounded close to breaking point and Jasmine was suddenly more afraid of what he might do than Rich. 'You really want me to take her off your hands? I'd be more than happy to. She doesn't deserve a self-absorbed loser like you.'

'Spencer… don't…' Jasmine pleaded, but he continued.

'How about this? I love Jasmine, and I've always loved her. I'll fetch you a rope and I'll help you fix it to a sturdy tree, you narcissistic cretin, and then when you've done twitching I'll take her home and have the life with her that you stole from me.'

'Spencer!' Jasmine squealed. 'Stop it!'

'Stop what? Stop telling your husband that he should quit feeling sorry for himself and be thankful that he has a beautiful wife and three beautiful children? That he should be thankful he doesn't sit alone night after night wondering about what could have been when the only woman he ever wanted runs around after an egotistical pig trying to make him happy? But of course, he'll never be happy because he's Richard Green and the world owes Richard Green. He's just listened to you pour your heart out and that's still not proof enough of your love for him. If you want me to stop then I will, but only because you've asked me to.'

Rich stared at Spencer, his mouth hanging open stupidly in the shadows cast by the feeble glow from Spencer's phone. 'I should punch your lights out.'

'Do it!' Spencer goaded. 'I'd take great pleasure in the excuse to throw you off this ledge right now.'

'Please…' Jasmine began to sob. 'Please, Spencer, don't.'

'Then…' Spencer paused, heaving breaths, 'tell your husband to stop being a dick and get on with making his marriage work. Because he's right, there's a queue of men waiting to take his place.' Without another word, he started the climb back to the top of the riverbank.

'I'm sorry,' Rich said in a small voice.

'I just want to go home,' Jasmine replied.

Rich nodded. With Jasmine's help he emerged from the shelter of the wooden platform and they stood, surveying the steep incline, Spencer's shadow clambering up it.

'Can you make it up there?' Jasmine asked.

'I'm sorry I'm pissed. You must hate me right now.'

Jasmine pressed her lips together in a hard line. She was angry as hell and irritated with both men, but she couldn't imagine what Spencer must be feeling right now. She wished there was something she could do for him. She guessed that part of his speech to Rich had been to galvanise him into action, but in doing so, he had opened a rift between them for ever. How could they go back to being friends now that Rich knew the truth? It was another selfless act in a history of selfless acts on her behalf. She could never love him like she loved Rich, but she loved him nonetheless, and his words were still ringing in her ears and breaking her heart a little more every time she thought of them. She tried to shake the melancholy that had replaced the blind panic of the previous hour and think about how to get Rich back to safety. The bank was far more treacherous on the way up than it had been going down just ten minutes earlier.

'It's dangerous and the rain has loosened the soil. We're going to have to take it steady and check every bit of ground before we put our weight on it.' She turned to Rich. 'You understand? I can't have you being a drunken idiot now; save it until we get home.'

He nodded slowly. She wondered whether to call Spencer back to help her but she couldn't bring herself to do it. Instead, she resolved to get Rich up there herself, whatever it took.

Even as these thoughts ran through her mind, a whip-crack of lightning tore across the sky, followed closely by a deafening roar of thunder. The flash lit the whole river bank so that each nook and cranny was clearly illuminated. Jasmine thought quickly, making a mental note of as much as she could from that brief glimpse.

'Come on, we'd better get up there.' Jasmine guided Rich by the elbow towards the simplest looking path, the proximity of the storm filling her with a new sense of urgency.

Rich scrambled and slipped, using clumsy handholds in the rock-strewn mud. They slid down almost as many times as they made steps of progress up. But after what seemed like hours, they had almost caught up with Spencer, who hadn't got much further despite his head start.

He turned and waited for them on a narrow ledge. 'It's desperate up here. God knows how we're going to make it.'

Jasmine grimaced. Even though she was now genuinely afraid that they might have to spend the night there, waiting to be rescued, she was glad to hear that all the rage from Spencer's voice had subsided and he sounded more like the old, reliable Spencer she knew and loved.

'Do you think I should call Millie, see if she can get the emergency services out to us?' he suggested

'That seems a bit extreme,' Jasmine said doubtfully. 'Surely we'll be able to scramble up there eventually.'

'This bank's been baked hard all summer and it's now been flooded with a month's worth of rain. It's coming away in chunks up here, Jas. If we miss our footing, the river is raging below.'

'We won't fall,' Rich shouted back. 'And the river isn't that deep anyway… A Munchkin could wade down and be in the Dog and Hare, barely wet, in half an hour.'

Spencer clenched his jaw shut. There was still tension between the two men and Rich's comment had obviously been a dig at Spencer.

'Rich…' Jasmine hissed, 'he's just trying to be sensible. One of us has to be and you're certainly not capable. Take a look…' She glanced back at the river. In the dark it was hard to make out at all, but the water gurgled and rushed, the crack of waterborne debris hitting the banks every now and again telling her that it was much deeper than normal.

'I'll call Dylan,' Spencer announced, 'get him to bring a rope or something to help us up.'

Even as he spoke, Jasmine heard a sort of sucking, squelching sound. Loose stones and twigs skittered down the riverbank towards her, followed quickly by larger clumps of soil.

'JAS—'

Spencer's cry was cut off. There was another blaze of light across the sky, and as it lit up the landscape she saw a shadow, hurtling towards her. Shoving Rich aside, she grabbed desperately for a flailing arm but missed. Spencer disappeared below them as the sky went black again and a rumble of thunder filled the stunned silence.

When they heard the ominous splash, Jasmine's hand flew to her mouth. 'SPENCER!'

There was no reply.

'Spencer!' Rich yelled. 'Spencer, mate, are you alright?'

Still nothing.

'Spencer… Please!' Jasmine shouted into the inky void. She turned to Rich. 'We've got to get down there.'

They began to make their way down at a speed entirely dictated by the unstable riverbank beneath them, and suddenly heard a shout that filled Jasmine with unutterable relief.

'Hey! Is that you, Jas?'

At the top of the bank, Dylan stood silhouetted over the drop as he called down. He was joined by a second shadow.

'Yes! Thank God you're here!'

'We heard a scream,' Millie said, 'is everything ok?'

'I think Spencer is hurt. We can't see him but I heard him go into the river and he's not responding.'

'Shit… I'm coming down,' Dylan shouted.

'It's too dangerous!' Jasmine shifted her weight to get a firm foothold as another section of riverbank began to move.

There was another flash of lightning. In the brief moment that the scene was lit up Jasmine saw that someone was already making their way down much faster than was safe. But it wasn't Dylan, it was Millie.

'What the hell are you doing?' Jasmine shouted.

'I can help here,' Millie said.

'If she's coming down then so am I.' Dylan began to follow her, skidding down so quick that he had caught up in seconds.

Moments later they were level with Jasmine and Rich. Millie didn't stop, but continued to shuffle and slide down on her backside, leaving the other three to follow in her wake.

At the river, Jasmine grabbed a nearby tree root to halt her progress and prayed that everyone else would be able to do the same. She squinted against the beam of torchlight that Millie was sweeping across the bank to search the river. They had to find Spencer, but the state he might be in filled Jasmine with a cold fear. If anything had happened to him, on this night, in these circumstances, she would never forgive herself and she didn't know if she'd ever be able to forgive Rich either. The river looked clear, apart from twigs and leaves racing over its bubbling surface. They were silent as they followed the beam wider to search further down the river, and then along both banks.

That was when they saw it. The shapeless mass of clothes and limbs sprawled at the base of the incline not far from where they were. He was motionless, face down, leaves in his dark hair, water churning around him, though thankfully he was on the bank and away from the torrents that would carry him further downstream. Jasmine's breath caught in her throat.

'SPENCER!' she cried as she waded towards him.

Rich and Dylan dragged Spencer clear of the water. Jasmine barged past and bent to him, turning him over, her heart beating wildly and a cold sickness creeping over her. He had a gash on the side of his head that was bleeding badly and the unforgiving torch beam lent him a grey pallor. It looked bad.

Millie handed Dylan the torch and gently guided Jasmine out of the way. 'Let me see.' She bent to Spencer and listened. 'He's not breathing. He must have water in his lungs.'

Jasmine watched, half fearful, half in awe as Millie worked to save him. She had never seen anything like it and neither had she seen this new Millie: calm, knowledgeable and confident, calling out orders for help with Spencer's positioning and the torchlight, until, after an anxious few minutes, he began to cough.

'That was amazing!' Rich said in hushed tones, echoing Jasmine's thoughts.

Millie shrugged. 'I picked up some first aid tips, it's no big deal.' Her expression was still tense as she scanned the steep incline now stretching above them in its entirety. Then her gaze went back to Spencer, still not moving, despite the fact he was now breathing. 'There's no way we can get him up there. Someone is going to have to phone the emergency services.'

Dylan nodded. 'I'll do it.'

Jasmine sat down next to Spencer. She stroked his hair and took off her raincoat to cover him. She knew he was already soaking wet but she had to offer him something. He had saved her marriage, possibly Rich's life, and had almost lost his own for his pains. She glanced up at Rich as another fork of lightning jagged across the sky. His gaze slid over the two of them, and then away to the river. His expression was unreadable. Maybe he was jealous. Maybe he was still stinging from the revelations Spencer had finally laid bare so ferociously after years of bottling them up. Right now, although she was glad to see Rich safe, she didn't much care. She would forgive him eventually, but not tonight.

'They're on their way,' Dylan said, interrupting her thoughts. 'What the hell has been going on here?'

'It's a long story,' Jasmine said.

'I'm sure the rescue team can't wait to hear it,' he replied drily, 'especially when we've dragged them out on a night like this.'

Jasmine and Rich looked at each other.

'How's Spencer?' Dylan asked.

Millie turned her attention to the patient again. 'I think he's breathing normally now… but that head will need stitching. It's hard to see if there are other injuries in this light. And he's still unconscious.'

'Let's hope the paramedics get here soon then.' Dylan picked his way over to where Millie knelt next to Spencer, handed the torch to Jasmine, and then pulled Millie to stand. She gave a little gasp of surprise as he pressed his lips forcefully to hers.

Jasmine looked at Rich, who raised his eyebrows slightly. She couldn't help a small smile in return.

Dylan was grinning as he let Millie go. 'It's a weird, dangerous night, and that makes you do weird and dangerous things.' He hugged her. 'You are incredible.'

'I don't know if this is the time…' Millie replied uncertainly.

'Oh yeah,' Dylan said, the steel returning to his voice, 'thanks for reminding me. I owe Rich a beating for being a dickhead.'

'I'm sorry,' Rich said quietly.

'You need to sort things out. You've got three kids going out of their minds right now because they don't know where their dad is. Don't you think about this stuff at all?' Dylan asked. 'They hear how their grandparents died and it makes the possibility real. They make connections and they know that if it happened to me and Jasmine it can happen to anyone.'

'I know,' Rich said. 'You're right. I owe everyone an apology.' His gaze went to Spencer. 'Even him.'

Dylan frowned as he looked from one to the other. A shadow crossed his features but then seemed to clear. 'You two are ok, though?' he asked Jasmine.

She nodded and shot a questioning look at Rich. 'I think so…'

Rich squirmed slightly as he looked at Spencer again. 'You don't want… You know, after what you've heard tonight…'

Jasmine shook her head. 'Don't be an arse. I told you before that I love you and I meant it.'

Spencer groaned softly. Jasmine turned back to him and stroked the hair away from his forehead. 'I hope you're going to be ok,' she murmured.

Chapter Nineteen

Millie opened her eyes. Dylan's sleeping face swam into view. His breath tickled her cheek and she smiled. Turning her head slightly, she glanced at the clock on her bedside table. It was gone midday, but considering what they had all been through the night before, she was amazed to be awake this early.

They had left Spencer to be observed overnight in hospital. He had briefly regained consciousness and was confused, but the doctors reassured them that all his preliminary checks were fine. After his ordeal, a little confusion was the very least they could expect. Not long after he had woken, he was sleeping again. Jasmine had insisted on staying at his bedside and the nurses had fetched her blankets while Rich was taken back to Honeybourne by taxi, now sobering up and promising to go straight to the Dog and Hare to let the kids know all was well. All five of them were soaked and caked in mud and there had been a few raised eyebrows when they had tried to give an edited version of the night's events. Dylan and Millie had gone home in a separate taxi, an hour or so after Rich, leaving Jasmine sleeping in a chair by Spencer's bed.

And when the taxi dropped them off outside the bakery, Dylan had watched it drive away in silence before kissing Millie again. From that moment on she had been lost. They didn't care that they were soaked to the bone, shivering, muddy and exhausted. Dylan had swept her into his arms and carried her up to the bedroom. He had laid her on the bed and made love to her with such tenderness that she could scarcely believe this was the same man she had met when she first arrived in Honeybourne. She gave herself completely, in a way that she had never done before, not even with Michael. Afterwards, as they lay in each other's arms, lost in their own thoughts, she wondered whether it was all some sort of weird reaction to the night's events. Perhaps, in the cold light of morning, everything would look as bleak and hopeless as it had done before.

But as she gazed at him now, she knew that a new name had been indelibly inked onto her heart. She had no idea what that meant, whether she had to leave as she had planned in order to protect him or stay to be with him, she just hoped he would feel the same.

He stirred, and then he was looking at her. 'Hey, you,' he smiled.

'Hey yourself. How are you feeling?'

'Amazing. How about you?'

'Pretty amazing too.' She rolled over and he opened his arms for her to snuggle in. 'I suppose you're hungry?'

'Depends what's on the menu…' His mouth met hers, hands plunging into her hair as he stiffened against her. Rocked by a wave of desire undiminished from the previous night, Millie gave herself to him again.

It was a quarter past three when Millie woke and looked at the bedside clock again. Her stomach was growling so loudly she wondered how the racket hadn't woken Dylan. As she tried to extricate herself from his embrace without waking him, his grip around her waist tightened and he grinned. 'Don't think you're getting away that easily.'

'I thought you were still asleep,' Millie said, kissing him lightly. He opened his eyes and gave her an impish smile.

'That's what I wanted you to think. Aren't blokes supposed to look cuter when they're asleep?'

'That depends on the amount of drool they're producing at the time.'

'Harsh but fair.' He propped himself up on one elbow. 'You want breakfast?'

'As we're in my house, aren't I supposed to ask you that?'

'I like to bend the rules.'

Millie raised her eyebrows. 'I already guessed that much.'

There was a knock on the front door that echoed through the house and Millie shot up.

'Are you ok?' Dylan put a hand protectively on her arm.

'It's Rowena. I know it.'

'No. I don't think so. Not after yesterday.' He vaulted off the bed, hauling the sheet off Millie and wrapping it around his midriff as he went to the window. Millie hugged her knees to her chest, feeling exposed and vulnerable in her nakedness. He craned his neck to get a look at the street below, and then turned with a slow grin.

'It's Ruth.'

Millie heaved a sigh of relief.

'Want me to get the door?' he asked.

'No! Imagine what she'd say!'

'Exactly…' He let the sheet fall to the floor and snatched up a sock which he proceeded to arrange around his penis. 'Will I do?'

'Dylan!' Millie squealed.

He bolted from the room laughing as he ran down the stairs. Millie leapt from the bed and hurriedly threw on his abandoned shirt to give chase.

'Don't you dare!' she cried.

She raced through to the front shop but it was too late. The door to the street was wide open, Dylan standing before an open-mouthed Ruth.

'Morning...' he said amiably. 'Or should I say good afternoon? I'm not entirely sure how long we've been in bed.'

For the first time since Millie had known her, Ruth appeared to be dumbstruck. She simply stared at Dylan, her eyes trained on one area of his body as if held there by hooks and string.

'I'll come back...' she finally managed in a feeble voice.

'Are you sure, Ruth? Because it'd be no trouble to make you a cup of tea. We'd have to get dressed first, of course, and perhaps get something to eat because we haven't had time yet with all the sex, but I'm sure you wouldn't mind that, would you?'

Ruth shook her head silently. And then, without another word, she turned and left.

Dylan let the door slam shut and span round with a wicked grin. 'Did you see her face? She'll be straight down the Dog and Hare to see Colleen!'

'What did you do that for?'

'It was funny.'

'No it wasn't...' Millie folded her arms and glared at him. But then a smile appeared at the corner of her lips and she was unable to stop it growing. 'I suppose it was a bit.'

'She won't come snooping around again in a hurry.'

'That's what you think,' Millie laughed. 'She's got hidden depths, that one. She's probably on her way back right now to get another eyeful.'

'Well, who can blame her with such a prime specimen of manhood on display?'

'And so modest too…'

Dylan grinned. 'Naturally. So, now that we're up why don't we grab some food? I don't know about you but I'm starving. We can go out for a late lunch if you like, my treat.'

'It'll be more like supper by the time we're ready. How about we grab a quick bite here and then call the hospital to see how Spencer is? We can always go out later.'

'Jasmine will phone to update us,' he said airily, 'she's good like that.'

'I wonder how she and Rich and the kids are,' Millie said. 'Whatever happened last night seemed like it was serious. Has anything like it happened before?'

'Not to my knowledge. But if there is one couple on earth who are meant to be together, it's them. I'm sure they'll be just fine.' He planted his hands either side of her face and kissed her forehead. 'I could do with picking up some clean clothes from across the road. I might just grab a shower while I'm there… Care to soap my back for me?'

'No chance. I think you can manage.'

'Ooh…' He clutched a hand to his chest in a melodramatic display. 'You know how to break a man's spirit.'

'Shut up,' she laughed.

With a quick grin, he sprinted through the main room to the stairs. Millie heard the echo of his footsteps above her. It was strange, the evidence of someone else in the bakery, but it was nice. It was something she could get used to.

A moment later he returned, bare-chested, with a dressing gown draped over his arm. 'Swap you?'

'Sorry, I forgot,' Millie said, trying not to blush as she handed the shirt back and pulled the gown on. In the light of day and not in her bedroom, she felt embarrassed to be naked in front of him.

'Will you be ok?' he asked as he buttoned his shirt.

'You're only going across the road,' she smiled.

'You know what I mean.'

She nodded. 'I think so. Thank you.'

'No… thank *you*.' He pulled her close and kissed her tenderly. 'Thank you for coming into my life. Thank you for being such a rock last night and thank you for being generally amazing.'

'Wow!' Millie stepped back and regarded him with raised eyebrows, a wry smile about her lips. 'I should be awesome more often.'

Dylan gave an easy laugh as he kissed her again and then headed for the door. 'Don't you go anywhere, I'll be back shortly.'

'I won't. In fact, I might not bother getting dressed either.'

'Suits me… less for me to rip off when I get back.' With that, he headed out into the sun that had, once again, banished the storm of the previous night. Millie squinted as she stood at the door and watched him cross the street. The irony of the weather was not lost on her. It seemed to be the way in Honeybourne these days, that every silver lining had a big, fat, demon cloud just waiting to swallow everything in darkness. She wondered when it would be back to take Dylan from her.

* * *

Dylan returned two hours later with a bottle of good Shiraz, a large dish of piping-hot lasagne, foil-wrapped garlic bread and a bowl of fresh salad. When Millie asked him delightedly where he had got it from, he merely tapped his nose, ordered her to sit down, and set about rooting in her cupboards for the things he needed to lay the table. Millie suspected that he had got Colleen to make it all for him, but it was a gesture that made her face ache from smiling. For a long time she had not been able to believe that a man would want to treat her with anything but contempt and certainly didn't think she deserved more than that. But Dylan seemed to really care. Even if it didn't last, or turned to shit weeks down the line, she promised herself that she would have this memory and not let anything taint it as she had all the memories of Michael.

Millie had just started her second helping of lasagne when the text message came through. Dylan licked his fingers clean of garlic butter and reached for his phone.

'It's Jas. She says Spencer has been given the all clear. They're taking him home now.'

Millie smiled. 'That's fantastic news.' She had spoken to Jasmine on the phone earlier and now understood a lot more of what had happened last night and why. Her heart went out to Spencer, a man who deserved more than the hand life was dealing him right now. Spencer was a good man – beautiful, kind, funny and sweet, the truest friend a woman could hope to have. He would find his princess one day, of that she was sure. Maybe he just needed to run around with that glass slipper a little while longer.

Millie's smile faltered a little as she wondered how much Dylan knew about what Spencer had said and done the night before.

'I'm not going to set on him again if that's what you're thinking,' Dylan said, breaking in on her thoughts.

'How did you…?'

'Jasmine told me a bit. She phoned me just after she'd finished talking to you and gave me a very stern warning.'

'You're ok with him? What he said to Jasmine?'

'I don't know… I can only say that up until now I didn't know what it meant to be crazy about someone and what it could do to you. I despised him; I thought it was somehow a weakness, a failing, something a good slap would knock out of him. But now I just feel sad for him. It must be so hard to love someone and know that you'll never be able to have them… harder still to live in their shadow every day and still be a decent person. He went out after Rich last night, to save his marriage to Jas. I'd say that's an alright bloke.'

'High praise indeed,' Millie smiled. 'I'm glad you see it like that. I think he's had enough pain for one lifetime.'

'As have you…' Dylan reached across the table and squeezed her hand. 'If you'll let me, I'd like to at least try to make you happy.'

'You already have.' She leaned across and kissed him.

'Hmm,' he said as he broke away. 'You taste garlicky… just the way I like you.'

'Cheeky!' Millie laughed.

'I could be…'

He got up from his chair and in seconds had raced around the table and scooped her up into his arms. 'The bedroom, milady?'

'What if Jasmine and Rich come to see us when they've taken Spencer home?'

'Then they'll have to knock extra loud…'

'You're terrible!' Millie giggled. 'What about this dinner?'

'Great idea, we could get kinky and eat it off each other!'

'You're such an idiot!' Millie cried, her giggling saucier still.

Swinging her around, he began to march towards the doorway that led to the stairs. He had barely got halfway across the room when there was a knock at the door.

'You have got to get a doorbell!' Dylan said with a mock frown. 'And some kind of camera system so we know who it is and when to ignore it.'

'I bet it's Jasmine and Rich.'

'It could be Ruth. Shall I strip for her again?'

'No! I'll just peep out of the window and if it's Ruth I won't open the door… Promise.'

With a theatrical sigh, he set Millie down and she went to the window. Her expression when she turned back to face Dylan told him everything he needed to know. His jaw tightened.

'Let me get the door,' he growled.

'No! You'll only make it worse,' Millie whispered.

'I'm going to end this once and for all. You can't live in fear like this, not any more. Whatever debt she thought you owed you've paid it ten thousand times over.'

'It's not that simple… She'll do something. She's clever and she can turn the whole village against me with a click of her fingers. If you stand with me that puts you in danger too.'

He strode over to her and took her by the shoulders to face him. 'After what you did last night? You saved Spencer's life and you probably saved Rich and Jasmine's marriage too just by doing that. Nobody in this village is going to be turned against you, no matter what she says.'

'How can you be sure?'

'Because I'll make it so if it's the last thing I do.'

'Dylan… No!'

But he opened the door and Rowena looked him up and down with a sly smile.

'What do you want?' Dylan asked.

'Aren't you going to let me in?' Rowena sidled past him. 'Well, well…' She looked theatrically between Dylan and Millie. 'I had heard rumours but I had no idea how voracious your appetite was. Two of us in the space of two days… I thought Millie was a little pickier than that but… I don't mind sharing if she doesn't.'

'You know that wasn't his doing!' Millie cried. 'He would never have gone with you in a million years in his right mind!'

'And how do you know he wasn't in his right mind? He let me in, didn't he? There was no wine involved at that point, and a couple of drinks isn't really enough to make anyone do something they don't want to…'

'Bollocks!' Dylan spat. 'There's an empty wine bottle in my house and I intend to find out what else was in it. I don't believe for a minute that it was just alcohol; more like some kind of sedative or acid and when the police help me find out what it is, I'm going to have you prosecuted.'

'For what? Giving you a good time?'

'For GBH. Forcing me to do something against my will… Take your pick, I'm sure the police can come up with plenty more names for it.'

'It didn't seem as though it was against your will to me. As I recall you were rather… what's the word I want? … Energetic.'

Millie glanced at Dylan, and in that instant she could see into his soul as clearly as if he had laid it open for her. Rowena wanted to wear him down until he became, once again, the hollow man she had met when she first arrived at Honeybourne. He had come so far since then that Millie couldn't let that happen. She had saved one life already; it was time to save another.

'I don't care!' she shouted.

Rowena stared at her, momentarily thrown off guard.

'I don't care,' Millie repeated. 'I don't care how many women he slept with because they were before me. I only care about what happens from this moment on.'

Rowena folded her arms, her cockiness back. 'And what makes you think he can be faithful from now on? A leopard doesn't change its spots.'

'Maybe this leopard could have a say in that?' Dylan cut in. 'I am actually in the room.'

'Oh, I know that, big boy…' Rowena grinned. 'My, you're feisty today, aren't you?'

'Stop it!' Dylan advanced on her, his jaw set and his expression stony. 'This is your last chance to get out and stay out.'

'I could… but I don't know what good it would do. Can't you see I'm trying to save your life? You know what she did to my brother?'

'Your brother did that to himself. She couldn't force him to kill himself any more than you could ever make me come near you again.'

'She broke his heart and she tore out his soul!' Rowena screeched.

'No, she didn't!' Dylan yelled back. 'I really don't give a shit if you think differently because I know her. You're leaving now and you're not coming back. And if you're thinking of trying to poison any other villagers – minds, bodies, or otherwise – you can forget it because nobody is interested.'

Rowena scowled at him, and then at Millie. 'We'll see about that,' she hissed. And then she was gone.

Millie stared at Dylan miserably. 'I told you she wouldn't give in.'

'There are ways of making her. Do you have a contact address for her?'

'Not where she's staying at the moment, only her home address back in Millrise. Why?'

'Because I'm going to call in one or two favours that should put the wind up her. Don't worry,' he added quickly, 'I'm not going to get her beaten up or anything, just put some plans in place that should spook her into leaving us alone.'

Millie was quiet for a moment as she stared into space. 'Do you really think that she could have spiked your wine?'

He nodded. 'Hallucinogens could have fooled me into thinking I'd done what she says I did that night. Bits and pieces are starting to fall into place the more I think about it, and what I thought happened, what I thought I did… it doesn't make sense anymore.'

'You don't have to say that to make me feel better, you know,' Millie replied with a pained expression. 'I understand and I've already forgiven you.'

'But what if there was nothing to forgive? Wouldn't that be so much better? If I can figure out what was in that bottle, then I might have the answer.'

'But what if the answer is not what we hoped for?'

'Then…' He paused, running a hand through his hair. 'Then I suppose we'll have to hope we're strong enough to deal with it.'

Millie nodded. 'Alright. So what's the plan?'

He gave her a lopsided grin. 'Well, that all depends on Spencer really. But I think he'll be more than happy to help.'

'You know you can ask me anything at all.' Spencer handed Millie a glass of cola. He looked exhausted, the gash in his forehead now an angry red line tacked together with thin strips of tape, the bruises around his face ripening nicely. But he had given Millie and Dylan a warm smile as he opened the front door and had not stopped smiling since. Millie couldn't help but feel that it might be the smile of a heartbroken clown, but despite this, he was obviously glad to be back home and pleased to see them.

'Your mate who was on the chemistry course when you were at uni…'

'Darren? Who shared digs with me?'

'Him, yeah. Does he have access to a lab?'

'I should think so. He's a leading drug researcher for a big German company. Why?'

'I need something analysing; do you think he can do that?'

'As long as you don't want him cooking up crystal meth, I can ask.'

'Not today, no!' Dylan laughed before producing the wine bottle Rowena had given him. Spencer leaned forwards and peered at it.

'That's weird,' he said. 'Is that the legendary bottle? I forgot to mention, in all the excitement, that I had a bottle just like that left on my doorstep a few nights ago. It was probably around the same time this was left with you.'

Millie exchanged a look of alarm with Dylan.

'You didn't drink it, did you?'

Spencer shook his head. 'I'm not that stupid. Why would I drink a bottle of wine that just appears on my step?'

'I was that stupid,' Dylan said.

Spencer gave him a sympathetic smile. 'Put it down to experience, mate. What do you think was in it?'

'I don't know. Acid maybe?'

Spencer took the bottle from him. 'I'll ask. And I'll give him the other bottle while I'm at it so he can check that for anything weird too. What do we do if we find something illegal? Do we report her to the police?'

Dylan glanced at Millie. 'Not unless we have to. Life has been difficult enough for Millie without new complications. But I've got a mate who's drawing up a fake injunction and with a bit of luck, that's all we'll need to get her off our backs for good.'

'Wow… cool. So what do you need the wine analysis for?'

Dylan grabbed Millie's free hand and gave it a squeeze. 'For peace of mind,' he said. 'So we can finally leave all our ghosts in the past where they belong.'

The shadows on the bedroom walls told Jasmine that it was late morning. It was unusual for the kids to sleep in this late, but the silence of the house meant that they must be. She frowned, and turned over to see that the other half of the bed was empty. A note lay on the pillow.

I've taken the kids out on a bear hunt over the fields. We'll be back for lunch. Wear something nice when you get dressed, because I'm taking you out and you'd better not argue that we're skint.

Rich x

Jasmine smiled as she nuzzled into the pillow again. Rich had been trying so hard since the night at the rope swing. He had taken more responsibility for the kids, he had taken more interest in her business and he had been friendly and gracious towards Millie. She wanted to give him the recognition he deserved for all that, but she couldn't help but wonder if any of it was real. How long would it take for him to forget that he was supposed to be a better dad, husband and neighbour and fall back into his old ways? He had told her, over and over, that he loved her and didn't want to lose her, but how could she really believe that, how could she feel safe and secure in her marriage after all he had said and done only a few short days before?

Spencer had been in her thoughts daily too, and often in a context that just wasn't right. Increasingly, she had found herself dwelling on what he'd said that night – words of passion that had become inked onto her memory. They were worming their way into her heart, taking root, making her doubt her feelings for Rich and wonder about what could have been. When Spencer had declared his feelings for her all those years before, she had laughed it off, convinced that it was a silly crush on the part of her brother's nerdy friend. But if he had harboured that love for her all this time… what did that mean? Jasmine believed in destiny, and right now, all the signs seemed to be telling her that maybe her destiny lay with Spencer and not Rich. But she loved Rich, didn't she? Rich was the father of her children; she had always believed him to be her soulmate, someone who had been through her lows and highs with her, a constant in her life. How could this be right? She had tried to shake off thoughts of Spencer, but they just wouldn't budge. With a deep sigh, she flipped herself out of bed. There was something she needed to do.

Jasmine glanced up and down the quiet row of cottages as she waited for Spencer to answer the door. She wasn't doing anything wrong… at least, she didn't think she was… but somehow the feeling of guilt stuck in her throat.

When at last he opened it with a tired smile, she couldn't get inside quick enough.

'How are you?' she asked as he led her into the conservatory where he had a makeshift daybed set up, exercise books and pens strewn over the duvet.

'I've been marking. I may be on sick leave but this stuff won't red-pen itself,' he smiled.

'That's good,' Jasmine said vaguely. 'At least you feel well enough to do that.'

'I'm fine, honestly. I'm taking advantage of the fact that I can pretend to be an invalid for a while and have a legitimate excuse to lounge around in my pyjamas all day.'

'At least the weather's cooled down a little now.'

Spencer raised his eyebrows slightly as he shoved a pile of books off a seat and gestured for her to sit. 'Yes. Although something tells me that you haven't called round to discuss the weather.'

'That obvious, eh?'

He nodded. 'You're not usually that dull.'

Jasmine perched on the edge of the seat as he made himself comfy on the duvet. 'We need to talk about the other night. About the night of your accident when…'

Spencer gave her a wry smile. 'When I made a dick of myself?'

'No. When you said things that I didn't know. I mean, I knew, I suppose, a little, but the strength of your—'

'Love?' he cut in. 'You might as well say it, because it doesn't hurt so much now.'

'It doesn't?'

'I saw you and Rich together and something clicked, I suppose. I knew that you were devoted, of course, but the fear in your eyes when you thought you'd lost him… I can't imagine any other man making you feel like that.'

'I was scared for you too.'

'It wasn't the same, you know it wasn't.'

'That's just it...' Jasmine took a deep breath. 'I don't know what I feel anymore. I'm so confused.'

'Don't...' Spencer grimaced. 'Please don't do this to me.'

Jasmine gave a jerky nod. 'I know. I'm sorry. And I wouldn't have come today if I wasn't serious about this.'

'Don't you see you're making this worse? You have to stop it. It doesn't matter now and you have to get it out of your head.' He paused. 'I might as well tell you that I'm leaving Honeybourne.'

'What!'

'I've filled in an application to take part in an exchange programme. A teacher from Colorado will come over here and I'll teach in their school for a year.'

'But why? Why this suddenly?'

He frowned. 'You really have to ask?'

'You can't leave because of that. You belong in Honeybourne; it's your home.'

'Yes, and it always will be. But I need to be away from it right now, clear my head and mend my heart. I left before but I don't think I went far enough. This time, thousands of miles away, I'll have no choice but to throw myself into a new life. It'll be good for me.'

'You really think so?'

He nodded.

'The kids will miss you terribly.'

'I'll miss them. But we have Skype. I'll check in for regular updates.'

Jasmine was silent as she gazed out of the window.

'It's for the best,' Spencer said gently.

'I know. But I will miss you.'

'I'll miss you too.'

They lapsed into a brief silence again.

'How about a sandwich?' Spencer said with forced brightness. 'It's nearly lunchtime and I'm a bit peckish.'

Jasmine glanced at her watch. She had an hour to kill before Rich got back but somehow, there didn't seem anything left to say. 'I should get back. Rich has taken the kids out but they'll be in and wanting their lunch soon.'

'Of course.'

Jasmine stood up. 'Don't worry about seeing me out.' Then, at the doorway, she turned back. 'There's no way you'll change your mind about this?'

'No. Just be happy for me about it.'

'I'll try, I promise.'

As Millie opened the front door, Dylan waved a piece of paper at her like an over-excited schoolboy with a good report. 'It came!'

'Your gas bill?' Millie asked with a wry smile as she moved aside to let him in.

Dylan closed the door behind him and grabbed her, pulling her into a passionate kiss.

'Wow!' Millie said as he let go. 'You should get your gas bill more often.' She looked a little dazed as Dylan laughed and kissed her again for good measure. 'So, what is this mystical letter with aphrodisiac properties?'

'The lab result!' Dylan said, waving it again with a flourish.

'And?'

Two weeks had passed since the fateful night of the storm when the full extent of Rowena's plotting had become apparent. Dylan had persuaded his friend to draft the fake injunction and, not knowing where Rowena was, they had sent it to a mutual friend, one who Millie knew would not be able to resist opening it and phoning Rowena immediately to warn her. Whatever she had thought about the validity of the injunction, Rowena had not shown her face in Honeybourne since. And, true to his word, Dylan had made sure that if she did come back the villagers would side with Millie before they listened to a stranger. That had been the most satisfying outcome of all for Millie – that she was no longer an outsider in Honeybourne, but now, most definitely, accepted as one of them.

But the incident that she and Dylan carefully avoided mentioning when they were together, for fear that it would somehow sully their moments of intimacy, still hung over them. The answer he gave now would change all that. She already knew what it was; she just needed to hear it to make it real.

'I was right. Some magic mushroom derivative. There's no way I could even have got the old fella up in that state, let alone do what she said I did…'

'So you didn't have sex at all?'

Dylan gave a sheepish grin. 'I've picked enough mushrooms in the fields around here as a teenager and I've been slipped enough acid in clubs to know that me and LSD don't work well together when it comes to getting the old private to stand to attention.'

'But she could have made you believe that you did?' Millie asked doubtfully.

'No question about it. That's the funny thing about acid – you can be convinced of pretty much anything with very little suggestion, even though the evidence is right there in front of you. Once, I was in a graveyard with some mates. There was a hedgehog on the path and they all told me it was a skull from one of the graves. I could see it was a hedgehog but that didn't matter, I started freaking out about the skull. The same here. All Rowena had to do was jiggle about on top of me and make the appropriate noises…' Millie's shudder stopped him in his tracks. 'Hey… are you alright?' He folded her in his arms. 'Don't cry.'

'It's just… How can you be ok with all this? She messed with your brain and you're talking about it as if it's nothing. And it's all my fault; I brought her here because of what I did.'

'We've talked about this,' he replied softly. 'Whatever you did, Michael's death wasn't your fault. If you're ever going to move on… if *we're* ever going to move forward together, you need to accept that. Michael took his own life and nobody, in the end, could have made that decision but Michael.' He pulled away and held her in a steady gaze. 'Deep down, you must know that?'

Millie sniffed and nodded. 'I suppose a bit of me does. I spent so long beating myself up over it, with Rowena reinforcing my guilt, that it's almost impossible to shake it now.'

'But you must. Because I'm so happy about this result that, aside from the obvious, it must mean something very important.'

'What's that?'

'It must mean that I love you, Millicent Hopkin.'

Chapter Twenty

A crowd of familiar and some not so familiar faces was gathered outside the Old Bakery. After much discussion of names, in the end, the Old Bakery was how she had always thought of her home, and it seemed like as good a name as any to christen it. Not so old anymore, though, Millie reflected as she gazed up at its beautifully restored façade. Things had been tough since she had arrived here last summer with big dreams and a rather smaller bank balance, and there'd been times when she thought she would never see this day. Now, with the generous spring sun warming her back, she felt her heart would burst with pride. She had built this, along with Dylan, a testament to the love that grew stronger with every passing day. She had always had a good feeling about the bakery and about Honeybourne, right from the moment she had seen it for sale online, she just hadn't realised that she was destined to get more than a business out of it.

The buzz of conversation and laughter lifted Millie's spirits even further. There had been a great deal of interest and anticipation when they finally announced the opening date, but Millie had assumed that people were just being polite. Judging by the excellent turn out for their opening event, however, people were genuinely excited after all.

That, or they had come for the free wine, she mused with a slight smile.

'Is that level?' Dylan called from the ladder where he was erecting the last stretch of coloured bunting.

Millie shaded her eyes and squinted up at him. 'Looks great. Now come down before you break your neck.'

'Funny…' Dylan said as he began his descent, 'you didn't seem to mind so much when I was fixing your roof in the snow.'

'You weren't on your own then, idiot. You had Bony with you. And there was no grand opening either. Nothing puts people off buying cakes quite like a mangled body at the front door of the shop.'

'Oh, I see…' Dylan said, wiping his hands down his jeans. 'That's where the priorities are. I'm a poor second to your precious bakery.'

Millie reached up to kiss him. 'As if. You could never be second to anything.'

'I'll remind you of that when Brad Pitt comes calling for you.'

Millie grinned. 'Did you hear from Spencer? What time did he say his flight was landing?'

'Don't panic, he'll be here. He said we could start without him.'

'I don't want to.'

Dylan nodded towards Ruth, who was sitting on a deckchair next to Rich, the pair of them sniggering like naughty children. They both already looked the worse for wear. 'You might have to. Frank Stephenson's famous scrumpy is a particularly potent brew this year. There'll be nobody left standing in half an hour.'

Millie frowned. 'Can't you ask him to hide it for a bit? Just give everyone some nice safe wine for the time being until we can at least do the ribbon cutting?'

'I think it might be a bit late for that. We'll have a riot on our hands if we stop the supply of scrumpy now.'

'Bloody hell. Can you text Spencer, find out where he is?'

'No, I can't. He said he'd be here and he will. Stop stressing; everything will be just fine.'

'It's just…'

'I know, you've said it about a million times this morning. But it was my choice to sell the cottage and partner up with you. I made that decision because I have faith in you and, no matter what you say, I know you won't let me down or cost me my inheritance.' He gave her an impish grin. 'Besides, how else was I going to persuade you to let me move in with you?'

Millie laughed and nudged him in the ribs with her elbow. 'You're so transparent.'

'Like a sheet of Happy Shopper's own-brand Cling Film.'

Millie felt a touch on her arm and turned to find Jasmine. 'I wondered where you'd got to.'

'I was trying to stop World War Three breaking out over at the hook-a-duck stall,' Jasmine said with an exasperated sigh. 'I just wondered if there was anything I could do to help now the kids have entered a brief truce.'

'I don't think so…' Millie glanced at Dylan, who nodded agreement.

'I think we've got it covered, sis.'

Jasmine blew a stray ringlet from her forehead. 'As long as you're sure. Any news from Spencer?'

'Not yet, and we're running out of time,' Millie replied. 'Dylan won't text him.'

'You text him if you want to sound like a nag,' Dylan replied carelessly. 'I'm just off to have a word with Frank Stephenson.'

'Don't you dare drink any of that scrumpy!' Millie called after him. As Dylan left, Rich pushed himself up from his deckchair and ambled over, hands in pockets, swaying slightly.

'Great party,' he said with a wink at Millie.

'I'm sure you'd think the Christmas Lectures were an illegal rave with that much high-octane cider inside you,' Jasmine said.

At that moment, the vicar made his way over, also clutching a glass of radioactive liquid. 'Frank's outdone himself with this year's brew,' he commented cheerily.

'That's just what I was saying,' Rich agreed.

'This really is a wonderful event,' the vicar continued to Millie. 'I know we haven't really had much opportunity to get to know each other, but I'd like to formally welcome you to Honeybourne. If you ever need me, my door is always open.'

'Especially if you're bringing pies,' Rich cut in with a chuckle.

'Yes, quite.' The vicar beamed at them all. Then he turned to Rich. 'While I've got you, I wanted to ask you about some help with the organ on Sunday. Mrs Potts is poorly and we have nobody to stand in…'

As they began to arrange Rich's assistance, Jasmine took Millie to one side, watching her husband as she spoke. 'He still thinks that little success potion you made for him is real. Do you think we should tell him?'

'He's been a regular Mozart over the last few months, hasn't he?'

Jasmine nodded. 'Like a new man.'

'Then let him think it's real. He's happy and productive and you're happy, the kids are happy…' She winked. 'What he doesn't know won't hurt him.'

A slow smile spread over Jasmine's face. 'I suppose so. God help me if he ever finds out, though.'

'Well, he won't find out from me.'

'As long as that brother of mine doesn't blab.'

'What makes you think he knows? A girl has to have her secrets.'

'What are you two whispering about?' Dylan wandered over, hands deep in his pockets.

'We were just remarking on how handsome you look today,' Millie said with a sly smile.

'You might have been but my sister certainly wasn't.'

Jasmine didn't react; instead, her gaze was drawn to a spot over his shoulder.

'Spencer's here!' she squeaked.

Millie and Dylan span round to see him making his way through the crowd towards them. His progress was hindered by the sheer volume of people stopping to express their delight at his return, to ask him how life was in America, wanting to know when he was coming back for good. As politely as he could he gave them the shortest answers and promised to catch them later for a proper chat. Millie and Dylan exchanged huge grins as they watched him fight his way through.

'He's like a celebrity. You'll have to remember to curtsey,' Dylan said.

'I will,' Millie laughed.

'Who's that behind him?' Jasmine asked. 'Wait a minute… Is he holding her hand?'

They looked again and now noticed the petite redhead following in his wake. She wasn't local and he did seem to be leading her through the crowd by her hand.

'Bloody hell…' Spencer grinned as he finally made it. 'You should have employed some bouncers.'

'Some people are never happy, are they?' Dylan said to Millie with a frown. 'You invite him to the party of the century and he's still moaning... Ungrateful bastard.'

'I see you're still ugly too,' Spencer said.

And both men launched at each other in a tight embrace. Dylan clapped Spencer on the back and laughed. 'It's so good to see you, man. It's been weird without you.'

Spencer's grin widened as he pulled away. 'You mean you've actually missed me?'

'Obviously I've been far too busy having sex to miss you. I just had nobody to take the piss out of in the rare moments my girlfriend was able to put me down.'

'Ignore him,' Millie smiled as he turned to hug her next. 'He's still an idiot.'

Spencer then turned to Jasmine, a shy smile suddenly replacing the gawky grin.

'I've missed you,' Jasmine said as they hugged too. 'So have the kids. They ask every day whether a year has gone by yet.'

As they parted, Spencer turned to the girl who had followed him over. 'Dylan... Millie... Jasmine... I'd like you to meet Tori.'

'I've heard so much about you,' Tori said as she stepped forward to shake hands.

'Oh God,' Dylan said, 'and you still came to see us. You must be really brave.'

Tori let out an adorable giggle. She was petite, not much more than five feet tall, and her hair was a fiery red, long with a full fringe accentuating the deep blue of her eyes, a tiny diamond stud in her nose. She seemed like a lot of fun.

'So...' Jasmine said, 'you and Spencer—'

'Yes, we're an item,' Spencer cut in. 'No, she doesn't need a guide dog and she is quite sane, thank you. Any more jokes you want to trot out about my suitability as a boyfriend... Dylan?'

'I was going to ask where you met,' Jasmine replied. 'I guessed the dating bit as you've clearly persuaded her to fly thousands of miles with you to attend a bakery opening in Britain's tiniest village.'

'Britain's drunkest village,' Dylan added. 'Frank's scrumpy is doing the rounds; you should get Tori a glass. That'd be some introduction to British life.'

'Maybe that's one she doesn't need,' Spencer smiled. 'Tori teaches at Riversmeet Elementary, where I'm posted now.'

'As soon as this cute guy with the gorgeous accent arrived I just knew I had to get to know him a little better,' Tori said.

'But then he left and you had to make do with Spencer instead?' Dylan asked.

'Very funny, Dylan.' Spencer flipped a two-finger salute and Dylan roared with laughter.

'Mr Johns! You'd better not let the kids see you do that!'

Ruth appeared, teleported to the scene of new gossip like a magnet drawn to an iron girder. 'Spencer!' she slurred. 'How lovely to see you! And who is this?' She pointed a wandering finger at Tori, who looked vaguely alarmed at the new arrival.

'What time do you make it?' Millie asked Dylan as Rich now joined the group. Spencer and Tori were dragged off to be interrogated and plied with cider.

'We've got ten minutes yet,' Dylan said, glancing at his watch. 'Everything is set up, relax.'

'I've got butterflies,' Millie said.

'Me too, as it happens,' Dylan replied. 'It's good to see him looking so well,' he added, angling his head to where Spencer was being manhandled into a hug by Ruth. For such an old woman, she seemed to be causing him surprising difficulty. Tori was looking on with a bemused expression.

'I knew Spencer would be ok,' Millie said. 'The cards told me so.'

'Oh yes…' Dylan said with a grin. 'Have you done them on our behalf, psychic Sally? I'd like to know what sort of mess this bakery is going to get me in.'

'You said only a moment ago that getting involved with the bakery was the best thing you ever did,' Millie said.

'A boy can change his mind, can't he?'

Millie smiled. 'I have done them, as a matter of fact… only last night while you were snoring in the armchair.'

'And what did you see for us?'

'I saw a lot of sleepless nights, a serious lack of money, some minor stressful situations… and a whole lot of poo and sick.'

'What the hell are you planning to put in the pies?'

Jasmine let out a guffaw. 'I don't think I need cards to see what's going on here.'

'Let me in on the secret then,' Dylan grinned. 'What's this thing that apparently only girls can know about?'

A slow smile spread over Millie's face.

Jasmine smiled too, though she kept her hunch to herself, realising it probably wasn't her place to break news that, judging by Dylan's face, clearly hadn't been broken yet. 'Maybe I'd better leave you two to have a chat,' she said, slipping away.

Millie looked up at Dylan. 'I'm pregnant.'

'Bloody hell! Are you sure?' Dylan looked dazed. His hand was shaking now as he ran it through his hair.

Millie nodded.

'How long have you known?'

'About two days.'

'And you didn't think to tell me before now?'

'I wanted to… but we were so busy organising today and I didn't want to give you anything else to worry about… Please don't be angry.'

He stared at her. 'I'm not angry, I'm just…'

'We should go somewhere a little quieter,' Millie said. She took him by the hand and led him to the secluded yard at the back of the bakery. Once she closed the gate behind them they were swallowed by the shade of the high walls. 'I'm sorry. I should have told you earlier and this was a stupid time to make jokes about the cards. It was just with all the excitement… Well, it felt like another exciting thing to add to it.'

'It's ok,' Dylan said.

'You don't look as though you think it's ok.'

'I'm fine. How about you? Are you sick? Do you need anything? Will you be able to work? What about…'

Millie held up a hand to stop him. 'I feel fine. I don't think I'm far enough gone yet to get morning sickness. As for the baking, I might have to get some help for a while but we'll work something out. I might be pregnant, but you and the bakery are still important. That will never change.'

Dylan sat on a stone bench and stared up at her.

'What are you thinking?' Millie said, taking a seat beside him and smoothing his hair away from his forehead. 'Whatever it is you can tell me.'

'I'm going to be a dad,' he said quietly.

'Yes.'

'Me… a dad?'

'Yes.'

'An actual dad that does dad stuff…'

'Yes,' Millie said. 'Are you scared?'

'I'm bloody terrified.'

Millie took his hand in hers. 'Me too. But we'll be ok, won't we?'

'I suppose so…' He gazed at her. 'What if I let you down?'

'You won't.'

'How do you know?'

'I know *you*. It'll be brilliant.'

'I suppose Jasmine does ok so it can't be that hard.'

'And she's got three.'

'Oh God!' Dylan cried in a strangled voice. 'You don't think triplets run in the family?'

'I hope not,' Millie replied. 'It's pretty rare.'

'Is it?'

She nodded. 'Have you ever met another set of triplets?'

'I don't suppose so.'

'Maybe we'll get twins.'

'That's almost as bad.'

Millie kissed him. 'If they're like you I don't mind if we have twenty.'

'Twenty of me would be awful. Talk sense, woman.'

She laughed and kissed him again. 'You're coming around to the idea then?'

'It'd shut Rich up, I suppose. He's always got top trumps when it comes to the biggest balls in Honeybourne competition.'

'It would. You're going to make an amazing dad. I've seen you with Jasmine's kids.'

'You think?'

'I know.'

He took a deep breath. 'Right then. This gives me an excuse now to get plastered on Frank's home brew?'

'It does.'

'Can we tell people?'

'I think Jasmine has already worked it out.'

'I guess she has. What about everyone else?'

Millie shrugged. 'Maybe just close friends for now?'

'Yeah, ok.'

Jasmine called through the gate. 'Time for the big unveiling. Have you sorted everything?'

'I'm not sure,' Millie said as she got up to let Jasmine in.

'It's cool,' Dylan said, a little of his old confidence creeping back in. 'We've decided that we're having triplets too so we can finally shut Rich up.'

Jasmine threw her arms around him. 'You'll be fantastic.' She pulled away and grabbed Millie for a hug too. 'Both of you. But now you have a bakery to open, so you need to come and face your public.' She left them, hurrying around to the front of the building to take her place in the crowd.

'We'd better do as we're told,' Dylan said, looking at Millie. He paused. 'You know those little potions you make for everyone?'

Millie raised her eyebrows. 'You want one of those? What on earth for?'

'I was going to ask whether you can mix one to make me a good dad.'

'We don't need a potion for that. I have faith in you.'

'You do?' Dylan asked as they made their way, hand in hand, to the front of the bakery where everyone was waiting.

'I do. And you know what else? I love you.'

'That's sad. I'm certain there's a cure for it. That's another potion you'll have to make.'

'I don't want a cure. I'm deliriously happy with things just as they are.'

As they rounded the corner, everyone began to cheer. In the crowd, Jasmine was wiping a secret tear from her eye as she hugged her three children close. Rich was at her side and slid an arm around her.

'Spencer has just proposed to Tori,' he whispered.

Jasmine turned to stare at him. 'The bloody hell he did!'

'And she said yes.'

'The bloody hell she did!'

Rich burst out laughing. 'I thought you'd say that.'

'I'm glad though,' Jasmine said. 'She seems lovely… And I might have a secret of my own,' she added.

'Oh yeah, what's that?'

'I think it's something Dylan and Millie need to tell you.'

Their conversation was cut short by the beginning of the ribbon cutting. Dylan made a few quips about eating all the pies, Millie gave words of heartfelt thanks that seemed too little to truly express just how thankful she was for her new life, but then she was sure the words strong enough to express that feeling didn't exist. The speeches came to an end, and a roar went up from the onlookers as the ribbon gave way to the open door of the bakery.

'We've baked a whole load of stuff today; help yourselves to as much as you can eat!' Millie shouted, standing aside to let people through. Dylan grabbed her in a passionate embrace and kissed her, Ruth watching them, goggle-eyed and weak-kneed.

Jasmine leaned into Rich as she watched her children race off towards the promised cake. 'You know,' she said with a contented sigh, 'I really don't think there's a happier place to live on Earth than here.'

Letter From Tilly

I'd like to come and hug you all personally for picking up *The Little Village Bakery*, but right now I'm sitting in my pyjamas, my hair needs a brush and I desperately need some blusher, so I think it might scare you to death. Instead, I'll send my thanks via this letter – it's safer for all of us.

I hope you've enjoyed reading *The Little Village Bakery* as much as I enjoyed writing it. And I hope that you've managed to fall a little bit in love with the characters, because I'm head over heels with them all, and I'm worried it might be a bit weird. If you liked *The Little Village Bakery*, the best and most amazing thing you can do to show your appreciation is to tell your friends. Or tell the world with a few words on a social media site, or a review on Amazon. That would make me smile for at least a week. In fact, hearing that someone loved my story is the main reason I write at all. And if you wanted to, I do have other books that you could check out, along with plans to revisit Millie, Dylan, Jasmine and Rich, and all the other residents of Honeybourne just in time for Christmas. I hope you'll come along, because you are most definitely invited.

If you ever want to catch up with me on social media, you can find me on Twitter @TillyTenWriter or Facebook, but if you don't fancy

Mel Sherratt and Holly Martin, fellow writers and amazing friends who have both been incredibly supportive over the years and have been my shoulders to cry on in the darker moments. Victoria Stone, my litmus test and my cheerleader, who will cheerfully tell me exactly what she thinks! Thanks to Jack Croxall, Dan Thompson and Jaimie Admans: brilliant authors who have shared the journey with me right from the start and are so supportive.

I have to thank all the bloggers, readers and anyone else who has championed my work, reviewed it, shared it, or simply told me that they liked it. Every one of those actions is priceless and you are all very special people.

Last but never, ever least, is my agent, Peta Nightingale. Where do I begin? She is more than an agent, she is a friend, and she has never lost faith in me, even when I lost faith myself. She is incredibly hardworking, endlessly patient, warm and fuzzy, and great fun to share a glass of prosecco with! I wouldn't be writing this now if it wasn't for her and the team at LAW literary agency, and *The Little Village Bakery* would very probably be nothing more than a dusty manuscript lying on a shelf.

Acknowledgements

The list of people who have offered help and encouragement on my writing journey so far must be truly endless, and it would take a novel in itself to mention them all. However, my thanks goes out to each and every one of you, whose involvement, whether small or large, has been invaluable and appreciated more than I can say.

There are a few people that I absolutely must mention. Obviously, my family, who bear the brunt of every plot-fail tantrum and yet still allow me to live with them. The staff at the Royal Stoke University Hospital, who have let me lead a double life for far longer than is acceptable. The lecturers at Staffordshire University English and Creative Writing Department, who saw a talent worth nurturing in me and continue to support me still, long after they finished getting paid for it. They are not only tutors but friends as well.

I have to thank the team at Bookouture for taking a chance on me, particularly Kim Nash and Lydia Vassar-Smith. Their belief and encouragement means the world to me.

My friend Louise Coquio merits a special mention, never too busy to read a first draft no matter how awful it is, always ready with an endless supply of tea and sympathy. Also Kath Hickton, who's just always there and has been for over thirty years. I have to thank that, you can sign up to my mailing list and will get all the latest news that way. I promise never to hassle you about anything but my books. The link is below:

www.bookouture.com/tilly-tennant

So, thank you for reading my little book, and I hope to see you for the next instalment!

Love Tilly x

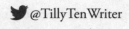

@TillyTenWriter

TillyTennant